as JAN 2015

Excellent

read again
in Oct. 2015 AS

and again April 2016
AS

Love Finds You

IN

PENDLETON

OREGON

Love Finds You

IN

PENDLETON

OREGON

BY MELODY CARLSON

summerside
PRESS

Summerside Press™
Minneapolis 55438
Love Finds You in Pendleton, Oregon
© 2010 by Melody Carlson

ISBN 978-1-61129-598-6

Cover design by Kirk DouPonce.

Interior design by Müllerhaus Publishing Group.

Back cover and interior photos of Pendleton provided by
Melisa McDonald and Melody Carlson.

*Summerside Press™ is an inspirational publisher offering fresh,
irresistible books to uplift the heart and engage the mind.*

Printed in USA.

Dedicated to Melisa and Joe McDonald
(real Pendletonians)

....

I want to express special appreciation to my sister,
Melisa McDonald, for her equine expertise and Pendleton
input during the writing and editing stages. And thanks to
Tammy Knight (Yellow Hawk) for sharing her knowledge and
insights in regard to the Umatilla Indian Reservation. Also,
I want to acknowledge the Pendleton Round-Up and Happy
Canyon Hall of Fame and the Tamástslikt Cultural Institute.

Jackson Sundown

Pendleton, Oregon

LIVING ON A SMALL WHEAT RANCH THAT'S ACTUALLY LOCATED on the Umatilla Indian Reservation, my sister, Melisa McDonald, and her family embrace an agricultural lifestyle that many urbanites can only dream about. I've been fortunate to enjoy many memorable visits there over the years and have always felt that, with real cowboys and horses and Native Americans, it's the perfect setting for an interesting story. A true "western" town in every sense of the word, Pendleton has been home to one of the world's premiere rodeos since 1910: the Pendleton Round-Up. For one incredible week in mid-September, the schools close, a tipi village arises, and this small town suddenly plays host to around fifty thousand visitors. My husband and I have been to several Pendleton Round-Up celebrations over the years—"camping" in our motor home out by the horse pasture, putting on our cowboy boots and hats, and attending the various events. Besides the world-class cowboys and exciting rodeo events, some of our favorite unexpected Round-Up-week moments include the heart-stopping Blue Angels fly-by, the Happy Canyon Night Show, and the Hall of Fame Museum. We also love visiting the Pendleton downtown area, including Hamley & Co., the mysterious underground tours, and all the other delights to be found along Main Street. Pendleton, Oregon, really is one of our favorite places to visit!

Melody Carlson

Chapter One

....

If anyone had told Sunny Westcott that she'd end up modeling for a clothing catalog in her mid-thirties, she'd have told them they were certifiably nuts. But sometimes, like when you're not really looking, life pulls some strange tricks. And Sunny had not really been looking—or if she had, she just hadn't been paying close enough attention.

Only six months ago, Sunny had assumed her life was right on track. About to be tenured in the anthropology department in the small private northwest college where she'd been quietly teaching the past eight years, Sunny had felt confident about her future—both professionally and personally. Of course, she'd been wrong on both counts. Now it was the end of summer, and instead of looking forward to returning to a dignified campus and attentive students, she was modeling warm woolen outerwear for the Pendleton Woolen Mills clothing line. To make matters worse, it was a humid 95 degrees, and barely noon, in the historic park someone had chosen for the setting of the upcoming winter catalog.

"Lean into the tree," Tyrone, the primary photographer, yelled at her. He didn't seem to enjoy the heat any more than she did.

She took a deep breath. Maintaining a pleasant expression, because she knew anything else would simply prolong her agony, Sunny leaned her shoulder into the trunk of the Douglas fir, pulling the fur collar closer to her chin as if she were cold.

"Good. Now look up into the tree," he yelled after a few shots, "like you love the winter, like you think it's about to snow."

"Or like you're a real Oregon tree hugger," her friend Aubrey teased from the sidelines.

Sunny controlled herself from responding as she would've liked and instead looked longingly up at the green branches above her, trying to picture winter. But all she could imagine was ripping off the full-length fleece coat, throwing it at the photographer, and storming off of the shoot like some kind of overworked fashion diva. Unfortunately, she couldn't afford a hissy fit right now. Finances were tight these days—and until she secured a real job, she needed this one.

"Loosen up," Tyrone yelled. "And look back at me *now*."

She slowly turned her head back toward him, wishing that this day would end.

"Look *happy*!" he commanded in an irate voice.

She already knew that he wasn't supposed to "give direction" and that models were supposed to "know how to model," but then she seemed to be that unfortunate exception for everyone today.

She attempted a smile, but apparently it wasn't believable because the director of the shoot came over, shaking her head with a frown. "That's enough," Marsha told her. "*Next* model!"

"I'm so sorry…." Sunny opened the coat to let some cooler air rush inside. "But it's so hot, and I'm just—"

"It's okay," Marsha interrupted. "Go get some water and cool off—take a break."

The wardrobe girl removed the heavy coat from Sunny's shoulders. Feeling strangely free in her perspiration-dampened T-shirt and shorts, which looked strangely incongruous with the tall, shiny leather boots, Sunny walked over to the refreshment table and stuck both hands into the ice chest. After a few chilly seconds, she extracted a bottle of water, which she slipped beneath the back of her long dark hair and pressed into her neck. After a bit, she ran it down her bare arms, holding it for a few seconds at each wrist—a trick she'd learned while doing thesis research in the Arizona desert during grad school. Cooling the pulse points helps to cool the entire body.

"I'll bet you'd like to kill me for getting you into this," Aubrey said as she joined her.

Sunny opened the water bottle, took a long swig, and forced a smile. "You can't exactly take the blame for the weather."

Aubrey smiled sheepishly. "Unfortunately, this kind of thing happens all the time. I guess I should've warned you about it."

"Oh?"

"We're always shooting off season. You end up freezing your rear off in summer clothes during the middle of winter and then, well, you get days like today."

Sunny nodded, then took another swig. Maybe this had been a mistake.

"But, if it's any consolation, I heard Marsha talking to Tyrone just now. She said she wanted him to cut you some slack."

Sunny blinked. "Really? That was generous of her. Is it because this is my first modeling stint?"

"No. Marsha would toss you out of here like last year's stilettos if she wanted. She's being nice to you because she *likes* your looks." Aubrey's eyebrows lifted with a knowing smile.

Sunny pressed her lips together as she considered the meaning here.

"Yeah, yeah, I know what you're thinking, Sunny. And you're right. Marsha likes that you *look* Indian. That you look stunning in those Indian-patterned coats. And she likes that the camera likes you too." Aubrey made a face now. "And if I didn't like you so much, I'd be totally jealous. I wish I were an Indian too."

Sunny flipped a long strand of hair back over her shoulder and squared her shoulders. She knew that Aubrey meant no offense, but because of Sunny's background in anthropology, her reaction to being called an "Indian" was not positive. Although to be fair, her grandmother, who'd been full-blooded Native American, had never thought twice about the *I* word—whether using it or hearing it. Not that she did either much.

"And"—Aubrey grinned—"it sounds like she wants to use you in future shoots."

Sunny frowned now. "But I'm not sure I want to do future shoots."

"I know and you know." Aubrey lowered her voice and nodded over to where the fashion minds were at work. "But you don't have to let them know."

"Right."

"Aubrey Lowenstein," an assistant called, "you're on deck."

"Break a leg," Sunny said as Aubrey dropped her unfinished water bottle into the trash.

Aubrey waved a finger. "That's theater talk—not fashion."

"Okay, then break a nose."

Aubrey laughed, then turned away, striding with confidence over to the tent where the wardrobe area was set up. Aubrey and Sunny had been friends for only a few months—a somewhat unlikely alliance that began at the fitness club back before Sunny lost her job. With more leisure time on her hands now, the casual relationship had slowly evolved into coffee after workouts, and thanks to Aubrey's unrelenting charismatic pursuit, the friendship had grown from there. Sunny knew that Aubrey had been modeling since her late teens and that, to her, this sweltering photoshoot with blaring music and hyper fashion people running about was normal. But for Sunny, accustomed to quiet collegiate structure and academic restraint, she felt she needed a passport. Nothing in life had prepared her for anything like this. It was bad enough having strangers attending to your makeup and hair, not to mention undressing and dressing in front of total strangers. But to take direction from a cranky photographer, striking pose after ridiculous pose while his camera snaps…well, it was way beyond Sunny's comfort zone.

"It's easy money," Aubrey had promised a couple of weeks ago when she'd first told Sunny about this great opportunity. "You should at least give it a try."

"But I'm too old," Sunny had protested.

"No, you're perfect. You're only a year older than me, and we're both right in the center of their demographic. A lot of the models are even older than we are." Then Aubrey handed her a printed page. "Look, this is what the agency gave me. Come on, it'll be fun."

And so, despite strong doubts and serious insecurities, Sunny had gone and done what Aubrey called a "go see." After a brief interview and some quick photos, Sunny was offered the chance to participate in today's shoot, which had started at eight in the morning, when the temperature was still in the seventies. But Sunny hadn't realized her opportunity was related to her Native American roots. In fact, most of the time she forgot that she even had Native American roots. A sad truth that probably would've disappointed Sunny's mother…if she were alive to know.

Sunny's mother, who hadn't looked anything like a Native American, had been one-quarter Cayuse and one-quarter Nez Percé—and proud of it. And Sunny's dad, with no native blood to brag of, had been proud of his wife and daughter. But her parents had both died in a plane crash over the Andes when Sunny was ten. Like Sunny, who'd followed in her parents' steps, they'd been professors and had happily gone off for an archaeological dig during spring break. Meanwhile, Sunny had remained in the care of her grandmother—and there she'd remained into adulthood and beyond after her parents never returned from their expedition.

Sunny did not want to think about how her education-driven parents would feel about what she was doing here in the park today. But this, Sunny reminded herself, was about survival. Surely they would respect that. Besides, she had been doing everything possible to find another teaching position. Unfortunately, cutbacks and reductions still seemed to be the general rule, and as a result, no schools appeared to be hiring. Or else, and this was something Sunny had recently started to suspect, her references from her old job were letting her down.

Sunny gathered some fruit and a fresh bottle of water, then went over to a shady bench, where she sat down to watch the continuing photoshoot—determined to put her mind to it and to learn how this was done. But it was too late to focus on models and cameras. Her mind was already stuck on Reuben Hollister. Was it possible that Reuben had somehow poisoned everyone in his department against her, and that no one was willing to give a good reference when asked now? But wasn't that childish—not to mention unethical and maybe even illegal?

"You should not be with him," her grandmother had advised Sunny more than five years ago when Sunny had first revealed an interest in Reuben. Grandmother had known that Reuben was Sunny's superior and had adamantly, almost knowingly, warned that this man might use his power against her granddaughter. At first, Sunny had heeded this prudent counsel, but it seemed the more she resisted Reuben's advances, the more persistent he'd become. Then her grandmother had died in her sleep one night, and lonelier than ever, Sunny had warmed to Reuben's attentions. She couldn't deny she was attracted to him—or that she admired and looked up to him.

Intelligent, charming, and a confirmed bachelor, Reuben had been about forty when they'd first started dating—secretly, because they both knew and respected how it would rock the department's boat. But the secrecy had only added to the allure. And for some reason, Sunny had believed she was the one who would hook this elusive guy. She actually had thought their relationship was special— and that if she played it all just right, they would be engaged after a year or so, then be married and possibly even having children by her mid-thirties.

Of course, she'd been wrong. Wrong on all counts. When she'd discovered Reuben with one of his academic assistants in a very compromising position, she had lost it. And, as a result, she had lost everything. Oh, everyone said it was because of budget reductions, department cutbacks, the lack of a recovering economy—all the usual excuses—but she had known exactly why and how she'd lost her job last spring. And, despite a suspicion that she could fight this thing, she had chosen to quietly go her way. Really, what good would come of putting the whole thing out in the open anyway? She had been naïve to believe in him…and foolish to disregard her grandmother's counsel.

"Sunny Westcott," the assistant called out. "You're on deck."

Sunny stood and, relieved to exit her unexpected and unwanted sentimental journey, mentally prepared herself for her next photography session as she walked toward the tent. *Really,* she told herself as she was helped into yet another thick woolen coat, *I should be able to handle a challenge like this.* After all, she came from a long line of strong and resilient people. One afternoon of being roasted alive shouldn't get the best of her.

Of course, she wasn't feeling quite as enthusiastic by four o'clock when someone finally had the sense to shut the shoot down before anyone succumbed to heatstroke. "I want everyone to be sure and check their e-mail tonight," Marsha called out. "We're setting up a new location for tomorrow's shoot. Hopefully someplace on the coast, where the temperatures are better suited for winter wear."

A cheer rose up amongst the group, but Sunny remained quiet, wondering if it might be wise to bow out now. Her last session with Tyrone had not gone well. The more impatient he grew, the more uncoordinated she became, until it seemed their vicious cycle was rolling like a freight train. And as his language got more colorful, she honestly feared he was about to pick up his camera and hurl it at her head.

"Are you okay?" Marsha asked Sunny.

Sunny blinked and stood straighter. "Well, I was thinking I'm probably out of my league here. Perhaps it would be best for everyone if I just—"

"No, no, no." Marsha held up both hands. "Today was a bit hard on everyone. And, really, you didn't do too badly."

"But I'm driving Tyrone to despair."

Marsha chuckled. "Oh, don't worry about Tyrone. He hates the heat more than anyone. And it's his nature to throw a fit at every shoot. He'd be sad if he didn't have at least one model to snarl at."

"It's true," Aubrey told her. "Tyrone is a real drama king."

"So you'll come again tomorrow," Marsha said firmly. "I don't need to remind you that you signed a contract."

"I'll come if you want me," Sunny promised.

"Check your e-mail." Then Marsha was off, snapping directions at the rest of her crew.

"See," Aubrey said as they walked back to Sunny's car, "I told you she likes you."

"*I told you she likes you,*" Sunny imitated her back, like they were both in fourth grade.

Aubrey laughed. "Hey, this is just the nature of the modeling game. Forgive me for being jealous of the newbie."

"That's nuts, Aubrey. I watched your shoot. You actually know how to model." Sunny unlocked her Prius, opening the door up to let the hot air escape.

"Even so, if Marsha had to choose between you and me, I'd be out of there in a heartbeat."

"Well, don't worry. I have no aspirations to make a full-time career out of modeling."

"Good, because at our age, that would be a challenge at best. Without my transcribing work, I'd never make it."

They both got into the car and Sunny hurried to roll the windows down. "I just wish I could find a teaching job."

"No luck yet?"

Sunny shook her head as she started the engine. She was tempted to confess her concerns that Reuben was the reason, but saying it out loud sounded so paranoid.

"I heard Marsha mention that she's setting up another photoshoot in Pendleton in a couple of weeks," Aubrey said as Sunny pulled out into the traffic.

"Pendleton? You mean the company?"

"I mean the town. Pendleton, Oregon. I think the shoot's in connection to Round-Up."

"Round-Up?"

"That's the *rodeo*—a really huge event that happens every September." Aubrey sounded astonished at Sunny's lack of knowledge. "Are you saying you've *never* heard of Pendleton the town or the Round-Up?"

"Of course I've heard of Pendleton the town. In fact, my grandmother came from around there."

"Really?" Aubrey sounded skeptical now.

"My grandmother didn't like to talk about her past, but I know it was near Pendleton. I think maybe my parents mentioned it to me before they died."

"Well, as a matter of fact, I happen to be from Pendleton too."

"Really?" Sunny glanced at Aubrey as she stopped for a light.

"Oh, yeah." Aubrey nodded with what seemed an almost smug smile. "My family goes way back there. If I get the chance to be part of the Pendleton photoshoot, I'm absolutely going. How about you?"

Sunny considered this as she pulled into the intersection. "Oh, I don't know, Aubrey. Probably not."

"Why not?" Now Aubrey sounded slightly defensive. "What's wrong with Pendleton?"

Sunny smiled weakly. "Well, hopefully I'll secure a teaching job before then."

"Oh." Aubrey nodded. "Okay, I get that. But if you were dissing Pendleton, I'd have to take you on. Sure, it's not everyone's cup of tea, but it's an interesting place—especially during Round-Up."

But as Sunny continued to drive, she knew her resistance to Pendleton was more than her unrealistic hopes of finding a teaching job this late in the game. It was almost like a foreboding instinct, buried deep beneath her skin or maybe even tucked inside her DNA. Perhaps it was something her grandmother had said or that she'd overheard as a child. Or maybe it was an innate sense that she wouldn't belong in Pendleton, wouldn't be welcome there—that she would be much smarter, much safer, to stay put. Besides, wasn't that how she lived her life? Always staying put or taking the path of least resistance? Why stop now?

Chapter Two

· · · · · · · · · · · · · · · · · · · ·

After a long, cool shower and a bite to eat, Sunny went upstairs to open the windows and let some of the heat out of the house. This second-floor bedroom had been Grandmother's for as long as Sunny could remember. Even now, in its unchanged state, it still felt like it belonged to her grandmother. Sunny had never known her grandfather, but she was aware that he'd purchased this small Craftsman bungalow with his veteran's loan after serving in World War II. He had lived the rest of his days here, as had her grandmother. And Sunny had lived here for nearly twenty-five years too.

With the windows open, a bit of air in the stuffy room, Sunny paused to scrutinize the space. For years, she'd been promising herself that she'd redecorate up here. At one point she'd even considered some furnishings from Pottery Barn. But the busyness of work and life, as well as a focus on redoing the first floor, had distracted her from it. Now she finally had the time but was no longer bringing in the income. Still, there might be some inexpensive ways to improve it. She'd managed to do a lot of things downstairs on a shoestring. Frugality was a learned behavior in Sunny's life. Despite the allure of stores like Pottery Barn, shopping thrift stores and garage sales for furnishings came quite naturally to her.

Sunny sat down in the old padded rocker and looked at the blond bedroom furniture. Suddenly she found it rather charming, not to mention more collectible now that mid-century modern was in vogue. Perhaps it was worth keeping after all. The pale pink bedspread would definitely need to go, since most of its chenille was nearly worn off, and the dust-coated pink ruffled lampshades were beyond saving too. But the faded rag rug was sweet and the blond bedside tables a nice touch.

This room, with a good cleaning, some new curtains and bedding, and a cheerful coat of paint, maybe apple green, could provide a realistic source of additional income. With fall coming, and the convenient location to campus, this room might help ease her burden if a teaching position failed to surface. Getting this room ready to rent couldn't be any more work than what she'd done in the park today.

Sunny went over to the low bureau that matched the other furnishings. She wondered if her grandmother had picked these pieces herself…or perhaps she and her husband chose them together. They seemed fairly solid and probably had not come cheaply. Yet Sunny knew that money had always been tight with her grandparents—even more so after her grandmother was widowed. Also, her grandmother had always disliked credit and was frugal almost to a fault. The furnishings in the rest of the house, before Sunny had refurbished it, had been a mishmash of things, like worn vinyl recliners, metal TV trays, and old rickety pole lamps, which made her wonder how they'd afforded a full set of bedroom furniture back in the fifties. Perhaps they'd won it on a game show. Or, more likely, they'd used layaway or purchased one piece at a time.

Sunny opened the top drawer and was taken aback by the aroma, as if her grandmother had just walked through the room. It was musty, somewhat spicy, and laced with old lavender. For as long as

Sunny could remember, her grandmother had always grown lavender and other herbs in the small backyard, and now Sunny continued this tradition. This drawer was full of old lady kinds of things: boxy cotton underwear, frayed knit undershirts, and worn flannel nightgowns. Sunny pulled out the drawer, deciding that as long as she was up here, she might as well get started. So she dumped the contents of the drawer onto the bed, continuing with the other drawers, until she had sorted through them all, removing the few items she wanted to save and bagging up the rest for the homeless shelter.

But when she dumped the bottom drawer onto the bed, she discovered a wooden box wrapped in an old gray sweater, almost as if it were meant to be hidden. It had a rustic look, as if handmade, and was about the size of a cigar box. It was tied tightly closed and securely knotted with blue ribbon. Sunny felt fairly sure it wasn't a jewelry box because her grandmother, worried that something precious might be lost, had shown Sunny where she hid her "valuables" several years before her death.

Sunny gave the box a cautious shake, but it seemed solid inside. Then, unable to untie the knotted ribbon, she finally gave it a hard tug, and the old fibers fell apart. Removing the ribbon, she saw a word crudely carved on the lid and peered closely at the letters. They seemed to spell *Polly*.

"Who is Polly?" Sunny said to herself as she sat down in the rocker, lifting the fitted lid from the box to reveal what seemed to be a packet of papers, photos, postcards...memorabilia from a long time ago. Knowing enough about archaeology and museum archives, Sunny knew these items needed to be handled with care. So she took the box downstairs and, after washing her hands and spreading a dishtowel on the dining room table, she very carefully removed the first item in the box. It was a yellowed newspaper clipping with a grainy old photo of what appeared to be a Native American. The man was wearing an impressive cowboy outfit and a rather noble expression. The headline read: JACKSON SUNDOWN WINS BUCKING CONTEST. Sunny peered closely to read the faded print and was surprised to discover that this event occurred at the Pendleton Round-Up in 1916.

One by one, Sunny gingerly removed more newspaper clippings and photos. This memorabilia seemed related to the same man— Jackson Sundown. As she arranged the fragile pieces on her dish-towel, she noted that they all seemed to fall within a short period of time: the earliest date was 1911 and the latest date 1923, an obituary for Jackson Sundown, who died at the age of sixty. But what did it mean?

She closed her eyes and leaned back in the chair. The man's name rang a faint bell in the back of her mind. And then she remembered a conversation that took place in this very room not long before her parents had left on their Andes expedition. Her dad had been picking her up at Grandmother's, where Sunny spent most of her after-school time while her parents taught at the nearby college. Dad had burst into the house, talking very excitedly about his old college buddy who was in town and working on a book of great significance.

"And you're going to love this, Mary," he eagerly told Grand-mother. "The book is about *your* father!"

Grandmother's dark eyes had widened with what seemed to be genuine surprise, but then, just as quickly, her expression turned solemn. Without saying a word, she simply shook her head—her clue that she was not interested in participating in this conversation.

"Come on, Mary, hear me out," her son-in-law had pleaded. "I told my friend you might be willing to talk to him, share some of your memories, and he can share some of his findings with you."

Grandmother had folded her arms across her chest, holding her head high, so high that even Sunny, who was only ten, knew this was not a good sign.

"It's an amazing story," Dad persisted. "A story that needs to be told."

Sunny wanted to beg her dad to tell it right then and there but knew that Grandmother's wrath could be fierce. So she simply stood back, waiting.

"Jackson Sundown was an amazing man," Dad proclaimed. "A man I would be proud to have as my father or grandfather." He grinned at Sunny then. "Or, as in your case, your great-grandfather."

"He was *not* my father," Grandmother had sternly told him. "Do not speak to me of this again. It is a pack of lies."

And, until now, that was the last time Sunny had heard anything about this Jackson Sundown character. Well, other than a few bits and pieces she'd eavesdropped when her parents spoke of it— always in hushed tones because it seemed that Grandmother had forbidden them to mention any of this to her. Even the time Sunny brought it up many years later, Grandmother's response had been to ignore Sunny for the remainder of the day. It was clear that anything connected to: (1) Jackson Sundown, (2) Native American history, or (3) Grandmother's side of the family was clearly off limits.

Sunny picked up the lid of the wooden box and studied it carefully. The wood looked like pine, and the pieces were rustically fit together. It was obviously fairly old, maybe even older than the name carved on it. She still didn't know who Polly was, but she suspected it might be her grandmother's mother. Why else would her grandmother still have this box? Or keep it hidden?

The next item Sunny picked up was a sepia print of a Native American in full native garb. Something about this attractive young woman felt strangely familiar. Wearing a white, fringed dress, a beaded headband, and a cheerful smile, she was captivating. The penciled caption on the back of the photo was difficult to decipher. But Sunny held it close to the light, squinting to read: POLLY WIKIAPI, PENDLETON ROUND-UP, 1911.

Next she found a small newspaper clipping from the vital statistics section. Sunny knew by the name and birthday that it was her grandmother's birth announcement: MARY SUNRISE WIKIAPI, BORN MAY 17TH, 1912, UMATILLA INDIAN RESERVATION. It seemed obvious that Polly Wikiapi was Grandmother's mother, and this box contained her things. Probably given to Sunny's grandmother before she'd left the reservation.

Sunny set the photo of Jackson Sundown next to the photo of Polly Wikiapi and stared at the two very attractive Native Americans. Was it possible that there really was a connection between those two people? A connection that had produced a child? She remembered now that Aubrey had mentioned that Round-Up was always in September. Counting the months on her fingers, she realized that her grandmother's birthday was about nine months after the Round-Up date. Still, if any of this were true, why would her grandmother so adamantly deny it? Like Sunny's dad had said, Jackson Sundown was someone to be proud of. And, based on the articles Sunny had just read, she had to agree.

That's when it hit her: Sunny's grandmother (also Sunny's name-sake) had been named Mary *Sunrise*. Was it a coincidence, or did the words *Sundown* and *Sunrise* have more in common than merely separating the darkness? Just then the phone rang. Still feeling stunned by the possibilities of this information, she answered with a quiet, throaty "hello."

"Sunny?" It was Aubrey.

"Yes." Sunny cleared her throat.

"Are you okay? You sound funny."

Sunny turned away from the photo montage she'd created on the dishtowel. "Uh, yes, I'm fine. Sorry."

"Nothing's wrong? There's not an ax murderer holding you hostage?"

Sunny laughed, weakly. "No, nothing like that. I guess I'm kind of in shock."

"What happened?"

So Sunny, in a way that was out of character, poured out this crazy little story, finally ending it with, "But I'm sure it's not even possible."

"You're kidding!" Aubrey let out a little shriek. "You are Jackson Sundown's great-granddaughter?"

"No, no, probably not. It's just that this box of memorabilia took me by surprise. I vaguely remember my father talking about this when I was a kid, and I was trying to put the pieces together."

"This is so exciting, Sunny. Do you know how exciting this is?"

"Not exactly." Sunny turned back to the photo.

"Jackson Sundown is a legendary cowboy, Sunny. And not just in Pendleton either. He made rodeo history across the country and—"

"But I have no evidence it's even true, Aubrey. Really, I shouldn't have said anything. Please, forget I ever mentioned it. Okay?"

"Oh, yeah, sure. You get to keep something this cool—this big—to yourself. That's real nice, Sunny. I thought we were friends."

Sunny almost reminded Aubrey that they'd only been friends a few months but decided not to go there. "We are friends," she told her. "But this connection to Jackson Sundown is unverified. All speculation on my part. There's no real evidence."

"Yeah, yeah. You're a scientific girl. But can't you simply enjoy the possibility? Hey, if I thought for a minute that Jackson Sundown was my great-grandpa, I'd be doing the happy dance. I'd go out and tell the whole wide world about it." She chuckled. "Although my parents might have a fit."

"A fit?"

"Well, to suggest that my great-grandma had had an affair with Jackson Sundown when she was supposedly married to my great-grandpa might ruffle a few family feathers."

"Oh." Sunny wondered if that was why her grandmother had wanted this kept hush-hush. But what family feathers would've been ruffled by this? As far as Sunny knew, her family on Grandmother's side was all dead or unknown. And the next generation, Sunny's parents, had been proud to imagine they were connected to Jackson Sundown, although Sunny had never understood why that was so special.

"Anyway"—Aubrey interrupted Sunny's thoughts—"did you get Marsha's e-mail?"

"No, I haven't checked."

"Well, the shoot's all set, and I wondered if I could hitch a ride with you tomorrow."

"I don't even know if I've been invited."

Aubrey laughed. "You are a real piece of work, Sunny. If they were giving out awards in false humility, I think you'd clean up and then still act surprised."

"Thanks a lot." Sunny felt fairly sure that was *not* a compliment.

"I'll wager the cost of your gas tomorrow that you *are* invited. The shoot's going to be at Cannon Beach, and we're supposed to be there by nine, which means we need to hit the road by around seven. Are you going or not?"

"Sure, I need the money. That is, if Marsha actually e-mailed me."

"Just to show how positive I am, I'll be at your house by seven. Okay?"

"Okay."

After she hung up, Sunny looked back down at the photos and memorabilia. Seeing it all spread out there on the white linen dishcloth was like looking into a foreign country. What did it all mean? She picked up the beaded band, comparing it to the photo of her great-grandmother. It appeared to be the same headdress she had been wearing that day, nearly a hundred years ago. Sunny studied the cheerful smile, the hopeful glint in her big dark eyes. What was true? What was not? Early in life, Sunny had been influenced by her scientific parents and later on by her own academia—and she knew that most questions had answers. But some answers could only be uncovered by thorough research.

She opened her laptop, determined to begin her research journey tonight. But first she checked her e-mail to discover that Aubrey was right. Marsha did want her for the photoshoot tomorrow. She also found out that yet another university, not even an impressive one, had rejected her application for a last-minute opening on their staff. With only one school left to hear from, Sunny was more than a bit concerned. To distract herself, she got lost in the story of Jackson Sundown. By the time she fell into bed, a bit concerned that six hours' beauty sleep might not be enough for tomorrow's shoot, all she could think about was the surviving Nez Percé tribe members making their way through the Rockies, cold and wounded and starving, heading north to the Canadian border—and Jackson Sundown among them.

Chapter Three

Posing for photos in the foggy pine forest not far from the beach was a great improvement over yesterday's fiasco, which was now being referred to as the Shake and Bake Shoot. With coastal temperatures barely reaching sixty, the warm outer clothing, coats, and jackets were welcome.

"This is a beautiful setting," Sunny told Marsha during a short lunch break. "Besides being more comfortable, I'm sure it's very photogenic."

"And you're doing much better today," Marsha said quietly. She had come over to where Sunny was standing off by herself, hoping to regroup her thoughts and get herself into a model-mindset for the rest of the afternoon.

"Thank you." Sunny smiled. "I have to admit that modeling isn't as easy as I thought."

Marsha laughed. "Yes, it's funny how people see those photos and assume it's no big deal to get them. Just point and shoot, right?"

Sunny shook her head. "Yeah, right."

"So, Sunny, I'm taking a few models to Pendleton in a couple of weeks. Any chance you'd be interested?"

"I…uh…I don't know." Just hearing the word *Pendleton* sent a strange rush through Sunny. Whether it was excitement, fear, or something else, she couldn't be sure.

"The plan is to spend a few days there right before Round-Up, utilizing some of the local color and activities for the backdrop while we shoot. And, of course, we'll take some shots at the woolen mill and possibly the Cunningham Sheep Ranch, where Pendleton Woolen Mills gets their wool."

Aubrey headed over to join them, and Sunny wasn't sure what to say...or do.

"I'd like to know by the end of the day," Marsha told Sunny. "I'm trying to set it all up, and I only plan to take about eight models."

Aubrey looked both interested and disappointed now. "Are you inviting Sunny to the Pendleton shoot?" she asked Marsha.

Marsha looked surprised but simply nodded.

"Man, I'd give anything to be part of that." She smiled at Marsha. "Did you know I'm from Pendleton? My family has a big wheat ranch, and my sister was a Round-Up princess back in the eighties."

Marsha looked slightly impressed. "Interesting."

Aubrey glanced at Sunny, who wasn't saying anything. "But you probably already heard about her Pendleton heritage?"

Marsha turned to look at Sunny now. "You have Pendleton heritage too?"

"Well, not really. My grandmother was born on the Umatilla Indian Reservation, but she left that area back in the thirties."

"Sunny is Jackson Sundown's great-granddaughter!" Aubrey blurt out.

Sunny clenched her fists and mentally counted to ten. Afraid to speak, lest she lash into Aubrey for bringing this up, she wondered if this was how Grandmother felt when her dad had tried to bring it into the open. Still, this was different.

Marsha actually grabbed Sunny by the arm now, peering intently into her face. "*You are Jackson Sundown's great-granddaughter?*" she said slowly with a look of both disbelief and curiosity.

Sunny let out a slow breath. "This is pure speculation."

"Pure speculation?" Aubrey rolled her eyes. "Sunny found a box of memorabilia from her grandmother. It was full of photos of Jackson Sundown and Sunny's great-grandmother, who was there at Round-Up the same year as Sundown. She must've collected all these things about him and her and put them in this box. She even put a birth announcement in there—nine months after that 1911 Round-Up, Sunny's grandmother was born, and her mother named her Mary *Sunrise*."

"And your name is Sunny," Marsha stated with far too much interest.

"She was named after her grandmother," Aubrey supplied, as if Sunny wasn't even there.

"I'm sorry," Sunny interrupted. "It all makes for a very interesting story, but I have no real facts. No birth certificate, no family records, and this particular subject was always completely taboo with my grandmother. I only found this box last night and, while I've started to do some research, I've barely begun."

"She's a scientific girl," Aubrey said quietly, as if this were something to be embarrassed by.

"Well, you're right," Marsha told Sunny. "It *is* an interesting story. And if I were you, I'd want to get to the bottom of it. But, really, what better place to research your family roots than in Pendleton? And here I am, offering to pay your way—all expenses, as well as wages."

"Why don't you go, Sunny?" Aubrey urged. "You'd be crazy to pass on this."

Sunny glanced at Aubrey now. Part of her wanted to strangle her outspoken friend. But another part of her couldn't help but admire Aubrey's enthusiasm. Sunny turned back to Marsha. "I might be willing to go if my bigmouthed friend here could go with me."

Marsha shrugged. "Sure, why not."

"Seriously?" Aubrey's eyes lit up.

"Very seriously." Marsha smiled. "And didn't you say your family has a ranch?"

Aubrey nodded.

"Any chance we could use that setting as a backdrop for some photos?"

"Absolutely!" Aubrey nodded eagerly. "My mom would love that. She'd probably cook everyone lunch."

Marsha shook hands with both of them, as if it was a done deal. Then she turned back toward the rest of the group and announced it was time to get back to work.

"Thank you, Sunny!" Aubrey hugged her. "This means a lot to me."

"You're welcome," Sunny told her. "I'm curious as to why you're so anxious to do this. I mean, it's just a photoshoot in Pendleton. What's the big deal?"

"It's a long story," Aubrey said as they walked back to the changing area.

"Well, we have a long drive home. I'll hold you to telling it to me then."

As Sunny changed outfits, posed for shots, and did her best to take direction—in addition to "showing some creativity," as Tyrone kept reminding her—she thought she might be getting a little better. Still, and despite the cooler conditions today, modeling was hard work.

Sunny would've much rather been in a classroom talking about the courtship rituals amongst the indigenous tribes in the Sepik River region of Papua New Guinea.

"Well, that was a good day's work," Aubrey said as they headed for the car. "Want to stop and get a bite to eat? My treat, since I didn't give you any money for gas, although I did bet you that you'd be included today."

Sunny's first response was to say no to dinner, that she'd rather just drive and make it back into Portland before dark. But that sounded like such an old lady thing to say—almost as if her grandmother was speaking through her. "I guess that would be okay," she agreed. "Do you know of any place?" And so they drove through town until a small restaurant caught their eye. Snagging a parking spot right in front, they went inside.

"This looks like a popular spot," Sunny said as they waited in the busy foyer. But before long they were seated and browsing the menu.

"How about if I get us a bottle of wine?" Aubrey offered. "To thank you for including me in the Pendleton shoot."

So far, drinking hadn't really come up in their friendship. Not specifically anyway. Usually Sunny just ordered iced tea when Aubrey ordered a glass of wine. Or else she claimed she was driving, which was tempting to do right now. On the other hand, maybe it was time to be honest. "I, uh, don't really drink."

"You don't *really* drink? Or you just plain don't drink?"

Sunny nodded. "I just plain don't drink."

"Oh?" Aubrey's eyebrows lifted. "Is it a religious thing? I mean, I know you go to church…sometimes anyway. I know you don't go every Sunday."

"No. It's more of a personal thing." Sunny sighed. "I grew up hearing a few bits and pieces about my great-grandmother. She was an alcoholic. A rather bad alcoholic, in fact. And my grandmother always made me promise that I'd never drink."

"Wow, so you *never* drank at all?"

Sunny sighed. "Actually, I did start to drink a few years ago. Just casually, socially. Remember the guy I told you about—Reuben?"

Aubrey nodded eagerly. "The jerk."

"Yes. The jerk. Well, when we started going out, he encouraged me to drink. And since my grandmother had passed on, I figured it wouldn't matter if I had a drink or two. It's not like she would know."

"And?"

"Well, one drink led to another and another. Before long I had what I'd call 'a drinking problem.'"

"Oh." Aubrey nodded. "Like maybe you've got that gene thing going on? Like you shouldn't touch alcohol at all?"

"Yes." Sunny smiled. "And so I quit."

"Was it hard to quit?"

Sunny thought about it. "To be honest, it wasn't that hard. Maybe because I hadn't let it get that far along. And, if you haven't noticed, I tend to be a serious person. I took my job very seriously...well, except for getting involved with Reuben. That wasn't my smartest move. In fact, that might have had something to do with our breakup, because Reuben didn't like the fact that I no longer wanted to drink with him."

"Oh, that breaks up a lot of relationships."

"So, I suppose I was lucky."

"I'll say."

Sunny pointed to the wine menu. "But, really, it doesn't bother me at all to be around others who drink. Well, as long as they don't overdo it."

"And it doesn't bother me that you don't imbibe." Aubrey grinned. "In fact, it's kind of nice knowing there's a designated driver."

Now the waiter came and they scrambled to make up their minds, finally both agreeing to the special: lamb and risotto.

"So now it's your turn to talk," Sunny told Aubrey. "I'm curious as to why you were so determined to do the Pendleton photoshoot. Is it mostly so you can see your family?"

"Sure, that's part of it." Aubrey paused as the waiter set their drinks—red wine for Aubrey and iced tea for Sunny—on the table. "But the truth is, I'm still trying to impress my family."

Sunny frowned. "Why wouldn't they already be impressed with you?"

Aubrey laughed. "You obviously don't know my family."

"I thought you said they were ranchers. Are they that hard to please?"

"In some ways, not really. In other ways, yeah." Aubrey took a sip of wine. "I grew up in my sister Lorena's shadow. And, of course, she was perfect."

Sunny nodded, thinking how she'd always longed for a sister.

"Anyway, Lorena was a real cowgirl. She could rope and ride and barrel race and everything." Aubrey wrinkled her nose. "Whereas I didn't like the smell of manure—at all. Plus, I was skittish around horses. But, to be fair, I got kicked hard as a kid, and not long after that I got thrown. I figured the horses liked me about as much as I liked them."

"That's understandable."

"But I tried to pretend I liked that whole horse scene, putting on this big act for my dad's sake. But when Lorena made Round-Up princess…well, that was an act I couldn't follow."

"But you're so beautiful," Sunny said. "You'd make a pretty princess."

Aubrey chuckled. "A pretty ugly princess when I fell off my horse facedown in manure. You see, to be in the Round-Up court you have to be an excellent horsewoman. And I was not."

"Yes, but that was so long ago," Sunny pointed out. "Why would anyone even think about it now?"

Aubrey shook her head. "When you go to Round-Up, you'll see why. Tradition is the name of the game. Ranchers have a lot of pride. They take pride in their ranches and their land, their livestock and their kids. I always felt like I let my dad down." She sighed. "It doesn't help that I never finished college, or that I'm divorced, or that I haven't given them any grandkids. Overall, I'm a fairly big disappointment. A twisted limb in the proud Westcott family tree."

"Yet you want to go back there?"

Aubrey nodded eagerly. "I know it would impress them to see me modeling in a Pendleton catalog. I called my mom when I got the job in Portland, and she was so excited. If I get to be in that Pendleton shoot, at Round-Up nonetheless, and if they possibly use our ranch in the shoot…well, that might just untwist that limb a bit."

"Then all you need to do is get married and have a couple of kids, right?"

Aubrey laughed loudly. "You get the picture."

"I'm still not sure I want to go on the Pendleton shoot," Sunny admitted.

"But you won't back out, will you? Please, promise me you won't."

"I gave Marsha my word," Sunny remembered. "We shook on it. I'm going."

"Oh, good, because I plan to call my mom tomorrow morning. I can't wait to hear how excited she'll be. I can just imagine her bragging to all her friends. You know, it's the one hundredth anniversary this year. It's going to be packed out."

"But I want you to make a deal with me, Aubrey."

"Sure. What kind of deal?"

"No more talking about my family, okay? Specifically, no mentioning to anyone about my possible but unlikely connection to Jackson Sundown."

Aubrey looked truly disappointed. "But it's so exciting."

"I don't know if it's even true. And until I have real evidence, I'd rather no one else know about it."

Aubrey frowned. "We wouldn't have to tell anyone it's for sure, Sunny—only that the possibility exists. Don't you get how people would love to hear the story?"

Sunny shook her head. "No. I don't get it. But I do know that my grandmother would turn over in her grave if she thought I was going around telling everyone that I was Jackson Sundown's great-granddaughter. I can't do that to her. The woman raised me after my parents died. She sacrificed to give me everything, and I loved her more than anyone. For some reason she didn't believe she was related to Jackson Sundown. And without having some positive proof, I don't really believe it either."

"Okay. I understand. Unless you get solid evidence, these lips are sealed. Does that work for you?"

"Thanks."

"But you will do some research while we're there, won't you?"

"Sure. I'm already doing research. But I honestly think it's going to be hard to prove this thing—one way or the other."

"You never know."

For the next few minutes Sunny told Aubrey what she'd learned about Jackson Sundown from her research so far. "He was really an amazing person," she said with enthusiasm. "He was related to Chief Joseph. When Jackson was fourteen, he participated in the Nez Percé war, mostly caring for the horses. When the tribe was defeated, he and a few others escaped to Canada."

"Yeah, that sounds familiar." Aubrey buttered a piece of bread.

"You mean you know all this?"

"Sure. I grew up in Pendleton, Sunny. Almost everyone knows about Jackson Sundown there. He's a legend."

Sunny was still trying to get her mind around all this. The possibility that her great-grandfather was someone legendary seemed too much to absorb. Was that the reason her grandmother had refused to believe it? Or was it because her grandmother had a reason not to believe—something she'd never disclosed but had convinced her it wasn't true? If only she'd spoken of it with Sunny. It wasn't like Sunny hadn't tried to get her grandmother to talk about her roots or her upbringing. But her grandmother's reaction was always one of two things: she would clam up and take offense, or else she would share a bit of sadness and tear up. About all Sunny really knew of her grandmother's past was that, like Sunny, her mother had died when she was young. Also, like Sunny, her grandmother had helped to raise her. But, for some unknown reason, she couldn't wait to get off the reservation—and she never wanted to go back.

Chapter Four
. . . .

Labor Day came and went, along with another rejection letter. As far as Sunny could see, this was it. She would not be teaching this year. To distract herself from this grim reality, she thrust herself completely into researching Jackson Sundown. Becoming so immersed in his life and times—what she could find of it—she began to feel a real sense of kinship with him. And as her notes piled higher, she realized why this man had become a legend.

Jackson Sundown had an amazing gift with horses—riding, training, and breeding. Nez Percé were known for being horsemen, but Jackson Sundown had raised the bar for his tribesmen. He could do anything on his horse—without reins or saddle. His skills didn't stop with horses, either. A great bull rider, he'd ridden one of the wildest rodeo bulls until the bull wore out. As for being a cowboy, he was renowned throughout the rodeo circuit. Sunny had to chuckle when she read that if other cowboys discovered they were competing against Jackson Sundown in a particular event at a rodeo, they would often back down. She could imagine those "tough" cowboys slinking away.

Jackson Sundown's Native American history was impressive too. Not only had he been in the company of Chief Joseph, but Sitting Bull as well. Some sources said that Jackson Sundown actually hid out with Sitting Bull after the Battle of Little Big Horn. Both were considered war criminals at the time, though they'd been considered heroes among their own people.

Jackson Sundown was also a handsome man. Not only had he been frequently photographed, he'd modeled for bronze statues. Sunny smiled to read how he'd grown impatient after long hours of posing until he nearly ran down the artist with his horse. She could definitely relate to that. But who would've known this legendary cowboy had been a model, as well? He was also clever and charming, with a sharp sense of humor. Sunny could imagine how many a female heart might've beat a little faster when a man like Jackson entered the room…or the tipi.

Sunny had been a bit surprised to learn that he enjoyed the finer things in life—whether clothing or automobiles—and was good at both making and spending money. She also learned he was between wives that September in 1911. He seemed to enjoy his own fame, as well as the adoration of fans—and he did have fans. He also liked pretty women and partook in the occasional drinking binge, so it wasn't unreasonable to think he'd been attracted to Polly Wikiapi— a pretty woman not opposed to alcohol. Yet, though the theory was believable, it still wasn't solid evidence.

Jackson was close to fifty the year her great-grandmother's path may have crossed his—and it seemed more than likely their paths had crossed, even if nothing more than a tip of the head had occurred. Although he'd been more than thirty years older than Sunny's grandmother, judging by his photos, he could've easily passed for thirty at the time.

As Sunny compiled pages and pages of notes on her laptop, she couldn't believe that no one had written a book about this interesting man. Sure, there was the late Ken Kesey's *Last Go Round*, but that was a fictional retelling of three cowboys. As far as she could tell, no one had written Jackson Sundown's story. But perhaps it was being retold in the native oral tradition. If so, maybe she'd get the chance to hear it for herself in Pendleton. The one solid thing her research had accomplished was that she now wanted to go to Pendleton. In fact, wild horses couldn't keep her away!

* * * * *

On the day before the scheduled Pendleton trip, Sunny took her morning coffee out to the small backyard and sat in the old metal rocker beneath the covered patio. This used to be her grandmother's favorite spot. No matter the time of year or the weather, if Grandmother wasn't in the house, she could almost always be found out here. Usually she was poking around in her garden, but if it was unbearably hot, she would bring a glass of water or lemonade and just sit and look. If it was cold, and the garden was "sleeping," as she used to say, she would simply bundle up in a woolly blanket with her mug of herb tea to warm her hands. And here she would sit just looking…gazing at things Sunny couldn't see.

For as far back as Sunny could remember, Grandmother's garden had grown back here. Tomatoes, cucumbers, squash, garlic, peppers, and pumpkins had always grown in the raised beds, and herbs like lavender, mint, and parsley had filled the beds around the house. Flowers were reserved for the front yard—for *show*. But during the years following Grandmother's death, this space had been neglected. Busy with work and life, Sunny had turned her back on the yard until it was so forlorn that she could barely stand to see it outside the kitchen window.

But last spring, after losing her job, she had thrown her energies into restoring the garden and herb beds, and now the yard looked better than ever. She knew Grandmother would be pleased. While this was a comfort, Sunny knew Grandmother would not be pleased to know Sunny was returning to Pendleton. And, as weird as that sounded, since Sunny had never been in Pendleton, it did feel as if she were returning.

"Please, forgive me, Grandmother," she said quietly. "But I need to do this. Not only for me, but for you...and for my mother. I need to see where I came from, what made me who I am."

Then she closed her eyes and committed her way to God, just as her grandmother had taught Sunny to do long ago. Grandmother had been firm in her faith, believing that God, the good Creator, had given them life and that the way they thanked Him was to let Him direct their paths. Sunny believed that God was directing her path now—leading her to the roots of her people.

She finished her coffee, picked up Grandmother's old harvest basket and shears, and headed for the garden. After cutting a few cucumbers, tomatoes, banana squash, peppers, and a couple of zucchinis, she walked to Mrs. Purdy's house next door and knocked.

"Oh, hello, Sunny." Mrs. Purdy, still in her robe, smiled as she stepped back, waving Sunny into the house. "Come in, come in. It's been awhile since I've seen you."

Sunny followed her in. "The garden is coming on really well now." She unloaded the produce onto the counter. "I hope you can use these...or give them away."

"Oh, thank you." Mrs. Purdy picked up a ripe red tomato. "Just beautiful, Sunny. As good as Mary ever grew."

"Thank you." Then Sunny explained she was going to be gone for a while. "I wondered if you would mind watering for me if it gets real hot again."

"Oh, not at all."

"The system is set up. All you need to do is turn on the spigot by the backdoor and let it run about thirty minutes. I meant to get a timer on it, but—"

"Never you mind about that. You know I love that little garden. It's so nice that you got it back to its old self again. Your grandmother would be so happy."

"Thank you. And, of course, help yourself to any of the produce. It's all coming on right now. Share some with the neighbors if you like."

"Yes, I'm sure that Misty and her little boys would enjoy some of this."

Sunny handed Mrs. Purdy a small card. "Here's my cell phone number if you need to reach me about anything." She smiled. "Not that I expect the house to burn down while I'm gone. It's just that I've never really left the house alone for more than a day or two."

"How long will you be in Pendleton?"

"I'm not sure exactly. But more than a week, anyway."

"Well, don't worry about a single thing, dear. I'll have my eye on your little house for as long as you need me."

Sunny hugged her and thanked her, then went back home to finish her preparations for the trip. Oh, she felt a bit silly for making such a big deal about what someone else (like Aubrey) would consider a short three-hour car trip, but the truth was, except for her big trip to Arizona during college, she'd never really gone anywhere. And she'd rarely spent more than a night away from this little house. Grandmother always fretted over the idea of Sunny being gone or traveling far from home, and most of all, she worried about a plane going down. Consequently, Sunny had never been on a plane. And at this stage of the game, she had no intention of getting on one. Reuben had teased her about her phobias, saying there was a paranoid old woman trapped inside her. He'd always been certain he could exorcise that old woman. For a while, she had believed him. But now she knew better.

Sunny stood at her closet, not sure how she should pack for this trip. As she looked at her usual teaching clothes, she wondered how suitable they'd be for a cowboy town like Pendleton. What would the weather be like? And what did one wear to a rodeo? Aubrey had made it clear that Sunny *had* to go to the rodeo, even if only for one day. Her parents always had a row of reserved seats, and Aubrey had already told them to save two tickets for her.

Sunny picked up the phone, deciding that since Aubrey got her into this, she better help her out. "I'm sorry to seem like such a dummy," she began after Aubrey answered, "but I have no idea how to pack for Pendleton."

"That doesn't mean you're a dummy. I'm going through my own closet right now, and I don't even have all the right things."

"Oh, what *are* the right things?"

"Well, jeans, of course, and according to my family, that would be Wranglers. I have plenty of those. I could loan you a couple pairs since we're the same size. But you really need a good pair of boots and a good hat—even a western belt would be nice."

Sunny opened the wooden box sitting on her dresser and stared at the photo of Jackson Sundown, so resplendent in his cowboy regalia. "Sounds like this could get expensive."

"We can probably borrow some of those things from my folks. My dad's got lots of belts and prize buckles, not to mention a cool collection of old western shirts. I used to tease him that he never threw anything away, but now I can't wait to get my hands on those retro cowboy shirts that used to be my grandpa's."

That all sounded nice for Aubrey, but it didn't really help Sunny much. "So, seriously, Aubrey, what should I pack?"

"Tell you what—I'll zip on over and look at your wardrobe. Then we'll take it from there."

Thirty minutes later, Aubrey was standing in front of Sunny's tiny closet and shaking her head. "This is everything?" she asked for the second time. "You really don't have stuff in another closet somewhere?"

"This is it," Sunny admitted. "I've always been practical when it came to clothes. I stick to the classics and buy quality, but I've always felt less is more."

Aubrey pulled out a gray blazer and nodded. "I can see how this is good for work, but what about the rest of your life? Don't you have any fun clothes?"

Sunny just shrugged.

"Or jewelry?"

Sunny took Aubrey over to her dresser and opened her grandmother's old jewelry box to reveal a few pieces of fine jewelry and pearls. "This is it."

"Okay, you're coming with me." Aubrey grabbed Sunny by the arm.

Before long they were at Aubrey's condo, where Aubrey took Sunny into her bedroom and started pulling all kinds of things out of her walk-in closet, which was stuffed with clothes.

"Start trying on these jeans," Aubrey commanded.

Sunny realized it was futile to resist. After a couple of hours, she thanked Aubrey and loaded her pile of secondhand clothes into the back of her car.

"We're not done yet," Aubrey informed her as she got into the passenger side of Sunny's car.

"What next?" Sunny asked.

Aubrey directed Sunny to a western wear store, and before long, Sunny was trying on boots.

"We could do this in Pendleton," Aubrey explained, "but I want us to arrive in style."

Sunny was impressed by how much Aubrey knew about western clothes. She knew the makers' names—what was good and what was not. After another long hour, she had helped Sunny find several "necessities," including a beautiful pair of boots. Unfortunately, the boots were quite pricey.

"But they're gorgeous," Aubrey said persuasively. "Old Gringo is the best."

Sunny looked down at the boots and nodded. "I'm not saying they're not gorgeous. I'm just saying I'm *unemployed*."

"And that is why God invented plastic."

Sunny frowned. "First of all, God did *not* invent plastic. Second of all, I do *not* use credit."

"Are you joking?" Aubrey looked so stunned that Sunny wished she hadn't said that.

"No." She smiled awkwardly. "My grandmother taught me that credit was wrong…so I don't even go there."

"Seriously?" Sunny looked skeptical now. "But how about your house? Don't tell me you didn't take out a loan—"

"I inherited it from my grandmother."

"Okay, then, what about your Prius? There's no way you paid cash for—"

"Actually, I did."

"Wow. And you *never* use credit cards?"

Sunny shook her head.

"That is really amazing." Aubrey glanced at the small pile of clothes they'd collected with a concerned expression. "So how do you plan to pay for all this?"

Sunny held her head high. "I'm not broke, Aubrey. But I don't really want to tap into my savings either."

Aubrey blinked. "So, let me get this right, Sunny. Not only do you have no debt and own your car and your house is free and clear, but you have a savings account as well?"

Sunny nodded, wishing this conversation would end.

Aubrey stretched out a finger to touch Sunny's shoulder. "I just want to make sure you're real."

"Very funny." Even so Sunny smiled.

"You are one odd girl, Sunny Westcott."

"Thanks."

"And you *are* getting these boots," Aubrey commanded.

Sunny sat down to pull off the boots. She held one of them to examine it more closely. The stitching, the leather, the colors, the tooling—it was all exquisite. Deep inside, she really did want them. Yet, she could imagine her grandmother's shock at the price tag.

"Listen, Sunny, you *deserve* these boots. The whole no debt thing aside…you're a descendant of *Jackson Sundown* and—"

"We don't know that for sure, Aubrey."

"Let's pretend, okay? What if you *were* Jackson Sundown's great-granddaughter? Wouldn't you want to honor his memory by arriving in Pendleton looking like someone he'd be proud of?"

Sunny knew this reasoning was flawed—that she could easily argue Aubrey down and walk out of this store without buying a single item. The problem was, she didn't want to. As crazy as it was to splurge on clothes—especially western wear she might never wear again—she just couldn't resist. And so she didn't.

Chapter Five

....

As Sunny packed her bags, marveling at the western wardrobe she'd accumulated so quickly, something kept gnawing—blurry, yet persistent—at the back of her memory until finally she went upstairs to her grandmother's room. The closet was tucked into the eaves of the roof and lined with cedar. Though bigger than the closet in Sunny's room, the contents inside were even more sparse.

Sunny slid her grandmother's few dresses and jackets aside until she came to a brown craft-paper-covered item pushed far to the end of the rod, clear against the wall. It was heavy enough to make her think it was exactly what she thought it was—although she only recalled seeing it once and then only briefly as her grandmother had quickly returned it to the depths of her closet, as if it were a skeleton or a shameful piece of her past.

As Sunny peeled the paper away, recycled grocery bags taped together with what was now very brittle masking tape, she saw the golden leather beneath and knew she was right. The paper shroud fell to the floor and she held up the fringed leather jacket—even more beautiful than she recalled. She fingered the intricate beadwork of red roses and small white flowers and green vines across the fringed yoke in wonder. The buttons appeared to be slices of antler. The garment was obviously handcrafted—and extraordinarily beautiful.

The smell of the garment was a mixture of musty lavender, from the sachets tied to the hanger, as well as cedar and wood smoke. As

Sunny unbuttoned the soft hide, she wondered whose jacket it had been. Why had her grandmother kept something this incredible hidden away? The lining in the jacket was light brown satin, well worn, with a few tears here and there. But thanks to her grandmother's training, Sunny could use needle and thread and knew it was repairable. Now, if only it would fit.

She almost reverently carried the jacket down the stairs, feeling like she'd uncovered a great treasure. A piece of her past—but whose had it been? Most likely, it was her grandmother's…unless it had been her great-grandmother's. That would explain Grandmother's need to hide it away. In her room now, Sunny removed the jacket from the hanger and slipped it on before turning to look in the mirror. Not only did it fit, it looked like it had been made for her. That alone told Sunny it probably hadn't belonged to her grandmother, because she was shorter than Sunny.

Sunny opened the box of memorabilia again, taking out the only photo of her great-grandmother and studying it closely. It was hard to estimate height based on a photograph, but judging by the graceful lengths of the fringed native dress or even her head-to-body proportion, Sunny suspected that Polly Wikiapi was taller than average—probably much taller than average for her generation and ethnicity. Sunny's best guess was that her great-grandmother might've been close to Sunny's height of five feet, ten inches.

Still holding the photo, Sunny stood in front of the mirror again—this time, comparing her features to her great-grandmother's. She took in the high brow, large dark eyes, straight nose, high cheekbones, full lips. Sunny set aside the photo to pick up the beaded headband, tying it across her forehead. Now she picked up the photo and looked into the mirror once more. She wasn't even surprised at what she saw. It all made sense. The resemblance was striking—she and Polly Wikiapi could've been sisters.

* * * * *

If Sunny had been boarding a ship bound for China, she couldn't have been more nervous or excited than she was as she backed her car from the driveway the next morning. She knew her apprehension was unfounded, and she had no intention of revealing her true anxieties to Aubrey, but as she drove over the Burnside Bridge, she hoped this wasn't all a big mistake. It wasn't too late to change her mind, but she'd given her word, and Marsha was expecting both Sunny and Aubrey to meet her at the shoot location at one. *No,* she decided as she parked in front of Aubrey's condo, *there's no turning back now.*

Sunny was barely out of her car when she spotted Aubrey coming out of her unit loaded down with bags and luggage. "Do you need help?" Sunny called as she got out of her car and went over to the stairs.

"No, I got it." Soon Aubrey's bags were in the back of the car. Then she turned to Sunny and let out a low whistle. "Well, look at you, cowgirl."

Sunny held up her hand as she looked down at her western attire of Wrangler jeans, retro shirt, and gorgeous boots. "I figured I might as well put my best foot forward." She grinned at Aubrey. "You look like a cowgirl too."

Before long, they were zipping down the road.

"Let 'er buck!" Aubrey yelled just as Sunny entered the freeway.

"What?" Startled, Sunny glanced at Aubrey.

"*Let 'er buck!*" she cried again. "It's the official Round-Up cheer."

"Oh." Sunny turned her attention back to the traffic moving east on I-84.

"Come on then, cowgirl-friend, let's hear you say it."

"Say it?"

"Let 'er buck!"

"Okay. Let 'er buck."

"Come on, you can do better than that. Let 'er buck!"

Sunny took in a deep breath, then yelled, "Let 'er buck!"

"Woo-hoo!" Aubrey threw back her head and laughed loudly. "All righty then, you might be ready for Pendleton."

"So people walk around town yelling let 'er buck?"

"During Round-Up, some people do. And this is a big year—the hundredth anniversary. I'm guessing enthusiasm is going to abound."

"But it's five days until Round-Up officially begins," Sunny pointed out. She'd done her research and knew that Saturday's Dress-Up Parade was the official kickoff.

"And it might take you that long to loosen up and get into a Round-Up state of mind."

Sunny couldn't really disagree with her on that account. Even under normal circumstances, loosening up didn't come naturally to her.

"Hey, I took the liberty of changing our hotel accommodations with Marsha," Aubrey informed her. "I hope you don't mind."

"You changed our hotel?"

Aubrey chuckled. "I changed our hotel to Lowenstein Ranch."

Sunny's brows lifted. "We're staying at your parents' house?"

"Sure. And Marsha's going to reimburse us for the hotel expense." She chuckled. "That might almost buy another pair of boots."

Or at least it might make up for what she'd paid for the last pair, Sunny thought. "So your parents don't mind having me too?"

"My mom can't wait to meet you."

"Really?" Sunny frowned. "Why is that?"

Aubrey didn't answer.

"Did you tell—"

"It's because you're a model, Sunny. I told you my mom was nuts about that kind of thing."

"I'm not really a model, Aubrey. I mean, you're a model. I'm just trying to make some extra money until—"

"You're modeling for the Pendleton catalog and that makes you a model, okay?"

"Okay."

"Why are you so hard on yourself, Sunny?"

Sunny glanced over at Aubrey, who was leaned back in the seat, flipping through a thick, glossy magazine. "What do you mean?"

"I mean, it's like you're afraid to have fun. Like you think something bad is around every corner. Like if you don't keep everything under your control, well, it might all fall apart. You know?"

Sunny frowned. Unfortunately, she did know. She just didn't know it was that obvious.

"Why?"

"Do you really want to know?"

"That's why I asked." Aubrey flipped another page.

"It looks like you're reading your magazine to me."

"I'm mostly ogling the jewelry." Aubrey laughed, then closed the magazine. "It's just Cowboys and Indians."

"What?"

"The magazine." Aubrey held it up. "It's called *Cowboys and Indians.*"

"Seriously?"

"You've never seen it?"

"No. It's really called that?"

"Uh-huh. Does that offend you?"

"What?"

"The word *Indians.* I mean, you always refer to it as *Native Americans.* And it's not that I don't want to be PC. But where I'm from, most people just call them *Indians.*"

"Them?"

"You know, Native Americans."

"But you think of Native Americans as *them*?

"No, I don't think of Native Americans as *them*." Aubrey sounded slightly offended.

"But you do see them as different from you, right?"

"Well, they are different."

"Really?" Sunny took in a deep breath. "And you think I'm different too."

"I don't mean you, Sunny. I mean *some* of the Indians—the ones on the reservation. They're not like you."

"So you know a lot of…uh, Indians?" It wasn't easy using the *I* word. But Sunny reminded herself of how her grandmother had always used it with no concerns.

"I know a few Indians. And, just like white people, there are all kinds. Some Indians are good for nothing. And some are great."

Sunny just nodded.

"So you didn't answer my question, Sunny. Why are you so hard on yourself and afraid to have fun? Is it because you're part India—I mean, *Native American*?"

Sunny thought about this. "Maybe. Although I've never really given my ethnicity much thought."

"Really?"

"I know it sounds incongruous, considering my anthropology background. But after my parents died, my grandmother raised me. I think, looking back, that she was ashamed of her heritage."

"So she made you ashamed too?"

"I don't know that I'd go that far. Mostly she made me feel like I had no heritage—she raised me like an average American Caucasian. To be fair, I'm only one-quarter Native American." She shook her head. "Ironically, I look more Native than my mother did, and she was half. But she got my grandfather's genes."

"And you got the other side?"

Now Sunny told Aubrey about her great-grandmother's fringed jacket and the photo. "I couldn't believe how much I looked like her. And I'm sure she was nearly as tall as me because the coat fits."

"Where is it?" Aubrey asked eagerly. "I want to see it."

"In a garment bag back there." Sunny nodded toward the backseat. "I'll show it to you later. It's really gorgeous."

"It sounds gorgeous."

"I can't believe my grandmother hid it away all these years. Thankfully she didn't get rid of it altogether. It's like she wanted to keep anything connected to her Native past pushed far, far away from her...and even further away from me."

"That's not so surprising."

"Really?"

"Oh, yeah. I've heard stories of people in Pendleton who pass for white, keeping their roots a secret. Then someone will need a bone marrow transplant, or an inheritance will be in question, and suddenly you find out your next-door neighbor is a half-breed."

Sunny grimaced. "*Half-breed*?"

"Sorry. Blame it on my upbringing. My dad comes from a long line of redneck ranchers and cowboys. Sometimes I forget myself."

"So if you find out your neighbor is, well, of mixed ethnicity, do you look at that person differently?"

"Not if they were a good neighbor."

"But a bad neighbor?"

Aubrey didn't answer.

"So you chalk it up to being Native American then."

"No, that's not what I meant. I guess people just are what they are, and it doesn't matter what their bloodlines are. Do you get what I mean?" Aubrey sounded worried.

"Sorry." Sunny reached for her sunglasses. "I didn't mean to sound so touchy. This whole thing is foreign to me, and I'm trying to figure it out as I go. You know what's really ironic?"

"What?"

"My parents were both fairly liberal college professors and never shirked from our Native heritage. If they'd lived, I'm sure I would've learned all about my ancestors, and we'd probably have visited Pendleton. I'd have been totally comfortable with all this. But being raised by my grandmother, well, sometimes I wonder what my parents would think."

"Because she did things differently from your parents?"

Sunny nodded. "And it's not that I blame her. She was in her sixties when she got guardianship of me. Her life hadn't been exactly easy."

"So she was born on the reservation?"

"Yes, and she couldn't wait to get off of it. She married the first white man who came along and promised to take her away to a better life. Unfortunately, her first husband was not a good man."

"So she was married more than once?"

"Yes. Ironically, despite her aversion to alcohol, her first husband turned out to be an abusive alcoholic who treated her like his slave—he even called her his 'squaw.'" Sunny shuddered. "I remember being so shocked when I overheard a conversation between her and my mother when I was little."

"So she divorced him?"

"No. He died in an accident. I'm not sure how exactly, but I think it was related to some kind of construction. Then she met my grandfather several years later. I think she was thirty by then. Although he wasn't Native American, I know he really loved her. Even so, she was very wounded by then."

"Poor thing."

"As a result, she always led a very cautious life—and taught me to do the same." Sunny sighed.

"Okay, I'm starting to get it. Hey, do you think your grandmother noticed that you looked like her mother?"

"Probably so." Sunny considered this. "And that might explain the overprotection or her heightened concern about me making bad choices—or why she had such a fear of me drinking. She might've thought I was going to turn out like her mom. Who knows? Maybe I would've."

"Wow. That's a heavy load to grow up with, Sunny."

"But I know she did that because she loved me. And she sacrificed a lot to get me through college, always putting my academics over everything else. Without her pushing me, I might've given up a couple of times. So don't get me wrong. I really do love her."

"I know you do."

"But her influence? I suppose it might've had a negative impact on my life as well." Although this was true, it was still hard to admit.

"Not in regard to money." Aubrey chuckled. "I'm still in shock over the fact you've never used a credit card. Do you even have a debit card?"

"Of course."

"I think your grandmother sounds like a cool lady. I grew up in exactly the opposite way. My parents gave me way too much freedom, never taught me much about finances, and acted like being on the Round-Up court was more important than anything."

"And you're still compensating for that," Sunny observed. "Do you think we'll spend our whole lives trying to overcome our upbringing?"

Aubrey laughed. "I sure hope not."

Still, as Sunny drove east, admiring the constantly changing scenery that moved from rain forest to a dryer climate, she wondered. She knew from years of study that the influence from environmental factors was nearly as strong as the predestined influence of genetics. But what if the environmental influence was at war with genetics? What then?

Chapter Six

....

The Columbia Gorge was spectacular, with the Columbia River slicing through an enormous, rolling hill canyon, the blue sky with white clouds, and all the light and shadows. At first she'd been a little overwhelmed at the hugeness of it—the vast barrenness. But before long, she realized that a part of her resonated with it. Those rolling, grassy hills were strangely familiar, as if she'd been here before.

"Bighorn sheep!" Aubrey cried, pointing to the right.

Sunny's gaze darted over to several animals grazing rather close to the freeway—they were bighorn sheep! "Wow!" she exclaimed, cautiously turning her attention back to the road.

"When I was a girl, my dad would offer a prize to whoever spotted a bighorn on our way to Portland. He probably just wanted to keep us kids busy and quiet."

"How many siblings do you have?"

"There were three of us then. Jeremy, my older brother, Lorena, and me."

"Then?"

"Lorena died."

Sunny glanced at Aubrey. "I'm sorry."

Aubrey nodded. "Yeah, me too."

"Were you two close?"

"Not really. As a kid, I could never match up to her. I guess I was jealous too. Then we went our separate ways." She sighed. "It's not that I didn't like her, or love her. I did. But we were so different. I still feel guilty about it."

"How did she die?"

"Breast cancer."

"Oh."

"She found out too late. She did surgery and chemo and everything, but it had already spread too far. She fought it for a couple of years, then died about four years ago."

"I'm sorry." The car grew quiet. Sunny couldn't think of anything to say in response to that. She felt guilty for having been jealous before, when she'd heard that Aubrey had a sister.

"Lorena's daughter is twelve now. Mom says my dad is already grooming her for the Round-Up court."

"To follow in her mom's footsteps?"

"I guess. I just hope Echo wants it as much as my dad does."

Sunny checked her rearview mirror.

"Echo is a good kid, though. I know that losing her mom was hard on her, but she's been a little trooper."

"You mentioned a brother?"

"Jeremy. He's seven years older than me and has always been into the ranch. He and his wife, Holly, and their three boys live down the road from my parents. Someday the ranch will be theirs."

"Nice that he has three sons. Are they all into ranching too?"

"So far, they seem to be. I guess time will tell."

Sunny wanted to ask if that was normal in Aubrey's family—handing down valuable property only to the son—but at the same time didn't want to stir anything up. So she was quiet. Aubrey grew quiet too, and before long, Sunny realized that her friend was asleep, which was just as well. Sunny wasn't used to this much conversation. Although it was somewhat therapeutic, it was also exhausting. The silence was welcome. And since Sunny had printed out a yahoo map, she knew that I-84 was a straight shot from Portland to Pendleton, and there was no need for Aubrey to give her directions.

It was a little before noon when Aubrey stirred. Sitting up and stretching, she looked around. "Hey, looks like we're almost there," she announced.

"This is beautiful country," Sunny said. "So wide and open—like you can see forever."

"My dad calls it 'his ocean.' He wouldn't even let my mom plant rows of trees like a lot of ranchers do, because he was worried it would obstruct his views."

"Is that Pendleton?" Sunny asked as they came up onto a slight hill that led down to a valley below.

"There she is." Aubrey let out a hoot. "Let 'er buck!"

Sunny felt a surprising rush as she drove down toward the town— almost a sense of having been here before. So much so that she wondered if her parents might've made a trip here when she was very young. It would make sense. Still, she didn't have a conscious memory of that.

"What do you think?" Aubrey asked after they had exited the freeway and were driving through the town.

"I think I like it. It feels like an old-fashioned sort of place, like what you'd see in an old TV sitcom."

"You mean like Mayberry," Aubrey teased.

"I'm sure it's bigger than Mayberry."

Aubrey directed Sunny toward the downtown section, explaining that the town hadn't changed too much since she was a kid. "Actually,

I don't think it's changed a whole lot in the last hundred years. We kind of went into a slight decline during the eighties, but it started coming back to life. And wait until you see Hamley's."

"Hamley's?" Sunny wondered why that sounded familiar. "Are they the saddle makers, the ones who made the prize saddles like the one Jackson Sundown won?"

"Yep. And they've totally redone their business these past several years. I haven't been here for a couple of years, but I hear it's really undergone some improvements. I thought we could have lunch there."

"We're going to eat in a saddle store?"

Aubrey laughed as she told Sunny where to park. "Something like that."

As they got out of the car, the air was cool. "I thought it was going to be hot here," Sunny said as she reached for her bag. "I didn't bring much in the way of warmer clothes."

"Mom said they'd been overcast and damp the past couple of days, but it's supposed to get hot again before Round-Up. Don't worry. Hey, where's that cool jacket you were telling me about?"

Sunny grinned. "Okay, don't look." She quickly got into the backseat, removed it from the garment bag, and slipped it on. "Tah-dah!"

"Holy guacamole, Sunny, that is a beautiful coat." Aubrey was walking around her on the sidewalk now, really checking it out. "Wowzers, girlfriend, you better not take that off and lay it down anywhere."

"Why not?"

"Because it would probably walk away." She touched the beadwork. "Seriously, that's probably a valuable piece. Keep an eye on it. You never know during Round-Up. People get crazy." She pointed to an old brick building with display windows filled with western wear, saddles, blankets, hats, and jewelry. "And this is Hamley's. Let's check it out." Aubrey led the way and was barely in the door when someone greeted her.

"Aubrey Lowenstein," a dark-haired woman said, "how long has it been?"

"About three years, I think." Aubrey glanced around the well-stocked store. "Wow, this place looks better than ever."

"Well, we're just trying to be ready for Round-Up. It's a big—" The woman stopped herself to stare at Sunny, or, rather, Sunny's jacket. "Where did you get that buckskin coat?" she asked with wide eyes.

Aubrey gave Sunny a quick introduction to her old friend Jeanette, then Sunny explained how the jacket had been in her family for quite a long time.

"It's obviously an heirloom and handmade." Jeanette actually put on her glasses to examine it more closely. "That beadwork looks old."

"It was her great-grandmother's," Aubrey offered. "Probably about a hundred years old and—"

"Yes," Sunny said quickly, worried that Aubrey was about to spill the Sundown beans. "My grandmother managed to save it all these years. She grew up on the Umatilla Reservation, then later moved to Portland."

"It's a beautiful garment. You're lucky to still have it."

"And you'll never guess why we're here," Aubrey told Jeanette.

"For Round-Up?"

"Well, yes, but more than that." Aubrey grinned proudly. "Sunny and I are modeling for the Pendleton catalog, and they're going to shoot some of it in town."

"That's right. I heard they're going to do some of it right here tomorrow morning, before we open up."

Aubrey nodded. "Anyway, I wanted to show Sunny around. Then we're going to get some lunch. My mom said you guys have a full restaurant now."

"We do." Jeanette pointed toward some doors. "And a coffee shop too." She nodded to Sunny. "Nice to meet you." And then Aubrey led Sunny on a tour of a store that was much, much more than just a saddle shop.

"What a beautiful store," Sunny said when the tour ended. "I feel like I barely even saw it. Clothing, jewelry, boots, hats, belts, blankets…and those saddles. They were so beautiful they made me want a horse."

Aubrey laughed. "Have you ever been on a horse?"

Sunny sadly shook her head. "No. I never even had a dog."

"Well, I'm sure we can find you a nice docile horse if you want to give it a try. Not that I'd recommend it, mind you. But it's a free country. And my mom's got a sweet mare that never hurt a fly."

Next, Aubrey led them over to what appeared to be a restaurant, just past a coffee shop—all of which seemed to be connected to the Hamley's building. Aubrey explained this was the new addition, although it all appeared to have been built to match the style of the older building. Inside the restaurant, Sunny admired the impressive woodwork, high embossed-tin ceilings, western artwork and accents, taxidermy animal heads…all giving the impression of a prosperous nineteenth-century western building.

"Is the rest of Pendleton's architecture this well done?" Sunny asked as they were seated.

Aubrey laughed. "It's kind of random."

After lunch, they went over to the Pendleton Woolen Mill where, Aubrey explained, the actual Pendleton fabric was woven. Their first shoot was scheduled for here, and the tent was all set up outside. They were barely through the door, and Marsha was already giving orders. "Glad to see you could make it," she said when she spotted them.

"Are we late?" Sunny looked at her watch with concern.

"You're right on time," someone said. "Marsha is just antsy."

"What's that you're wearing?" Marsha came over to Sunny now, closely investigating the buckskin jacket.

Sunny quickly explained, wondering if this was going to happen everywhere she went, or whether she simply was crossing paths with the fashion-conscious people today.

"It's exquisite." Marsha made her turn around now. "Very, very nice. In fact, maybe you'd want to wear it for one or two of the shots."

"But it's not a Pendleton design." Sunny was confused.

"That can be explained. It might be a fun touch for the catalog. Perhaps we pair it with a native print skirt and boots. Yes, that would be attractive. We won't do it today in the woolen mill, but when we do an outdoor shoot. If you don't mind."

Sunny wasn't sure. "I guess not."

"Oh, good. Now you girls start getting changed." She eyed the jacket again. "But you better put the jacket with our purses and things. It's too valuable to leave lying around."

The Pendleton Woolen Mill was both a retail store and a working mill. Most of the shots were taken in the mill area, near looms and machinery or huge bolts of fabric. Sunny wanted to check everything out but knew her job was to stay focused and model.

"I wish we had more time to actually see the mill and how it works," she said as they were changing into what were supposed to be the final outfits.

"They have tours all the time," Aubrey explained. "You can come back and see the whole thing if you want."

"Oh, good." Sunny slipped into a plaid 49-ers jacket, then waited as one of the fashion assistants added accessories and another one made adjustments to her hair. Tyrone was the main cameraman again, but either she was improving or his patience had increased, because he hadn't snarled at her once today.

Finally, Marsha seemed satisfied, and everyone was free to go. "But I'll see you all at Hamley's tomorrow at seven o'clock sharp. We only have two hours, so don't be late."

"And now we go home," Aubrey said as they got back into Sunny's car. "Hey, thanks for driving. My Beemer's been so temperamental lately I wouldn't trust it outside the Portland city limits. Maybe I should trade it in for something like this."

"I actually traded my grandmother's '58 Chevy Bel Air in for this. I felt a little guilty at the time, because I know how she loved that old car—although she hardly ever drove it. She hated to drive. But the Chevy's gas mileage was ridiculous. I figured in about ten years what I saved on gas would pay for the Prius."

"Such a practical girl."

Sunny tried not to bristle. It wasn't as if she'd never heard that comment before. Reuben used to drive her nuts with his "playful" little jabs. He did it so much that he finally had the entire staff giving her grief for simply being sensible. In some ways, she wouldn't miss that job.

They drove about five minutes out of town, down an asphalt road, through a tall log archway with LOWENSTEIN LAZY L written in metal letters above it, then down a long driveway. "Wow, this looks like a big place," Sunny observed as she drove toward a group of buildings, including a long, low ranch-style house, a smaller building, several barn-like structures, and some other outbuildings.

"It's not the biggest ranch around—five thousand acres—but it's enough to keep my dad and brother busy, as well as some hands. We raise cattle, hay and alfalfa, and grain." She pointed over to the smaller building not too far from the main house. "Park over by the bunkhouse."

"That's a bunkhouse?"

"That's what we call it. It's actually a little bit nicer than that. But Mom is putting us out there because she already promised the guest rooms to other relatives for Round-Up. That way we won't have to move. Plus, we get more privacy in the bunkhouse anyway."

That sounded good to Sunny. She pulled up in front of what looked like a hitching post. "Is it okay to park here?"

"Perfect. We'll dump our stuff inside, then go see if my mom's home. I'm sure the guys are out in the field. Mom said they're just finishing up harvest."

As they unloaded the car, Sunny started feeling nervous. This was all so outside her comfort zone. Being away from home was one thing. But being a guest in a place where she was virtually a stranger filled her with real anxiety. *Just breathe,* she silently told herself as they went into the rustic bunkhouse. *Just breathe.*

Chapter Seven

The bunkhouse turned out to be less rustic and bigger than she expected. With three bedrooms, a compact kitchen, a bath and a powder room, it was about the same size as Sunny's bungalow in Portland. And everything was done in western décor. With pine floors, open-beamed ceilings and log posts, rough-hewn wooden furnishings, leather sofa and chairs, and numerous Pendleton blankets, the house had a cozy cowboy sort of feel.

"This place is great," Sunny said after Aubrey had showed her around. "I really like it."

"We can have private rooms until the Tuesday before Round-Up," Aubrey informed her. "Then we have to bunk together. But I asked Mom for the big room."

"I hope we're not putting her out."

Aubrey laughed. "Hey, I'm the daughter. Don't you think I should get a room when I come home to visit?"

Sunny wasn't so sure about these arrangements. It was one thing for Aubrey to crash in on her parents like this, but that didn't necessarily mean Sunny was welcome.

Aubrey made a sly grin. "Mom actually had to cancel on her cousin Glenda. She told her that she and her family would have to stay in a tent if they still wanted to come next week."

"So we really did put someone out of a bed?"

Aubrey chuckled. "Glenda is not my mom's favorite cousin." She pointed to the oversized couch now. "And that thing makes into a queen-sized bed. So during Round-Up, this place will be packed with eight adults sharing a bath and a half. But, if you don't tell anyone, you and I can sneak into the big house and use my mom's shower if we want. And my dad rigs up outdoor solar showers for the guys to use."

"Outdoor solar showers?" Sunny blinked. "Isn't that kind of risqué?"

Aubrey laughed. "My dad makes them private with plastic tarps."

"Oh, right. So how many people will be staying here at your parents' ranch during Round-Up?"

"Good question. I'm guessing about fifty, but since this is the hundredth anniversary, it could be more. It's like everyone and their great-aunt Betty want to be here next week."

"Wow. Your parents' house must be really big to hold that many people."

"They'll put up about twelve people in the house. Everyone else will be camping."

"Oh." Sunny tried to imagine this.

"Okay, do you want to flip for the big bedroom or—"

"No," Sunny said quickly, "I'm happy in a smaller room. And, if it would help, maybe I can get a hotel room once this place starts filling up."

"Good luck with that." Aubrey chuckled as she tossed her suitcase onto a king-sized bed. "There won't be an available hotel room for a hundred miles."

"Really?" Suddenly Sunny was feeling uneasy, not to mention slightly trapped. Maybe it wasn't such a good idea to stick around for all of Round-Up week. Once the photoshoot was finished, there was no reason Sunny couldn't go home.

"Oh yeah, every room has been booked for months. Do you realize that close to a hundred thousand people are predicted to pass through this town next week?"

"And what's the town's population normally?"

"Around sixteen thousand, I think."

"How can a town that small possibly accommodate so many people?"

Aubrey laughed. "Oh, it'll get interesting. Trust me, it'll get real interesting."

Sunny took her things to one of the smaller bedrooms, setting them neatly in a corner and wondering if she should start unpacking yet. But before she could decide, Aubrey popped in. "Come on," she urged. "Let's go see what Mom's got cooking."

As they walked over to the house, a pair of large black dogs ran up to Aubrey, barking and jumping happily as if they were glad to see her. "Meet Jasper and Jake," Aubrey said as she stopped to stroke their sleek coats. "How you boys doing?"

"Labrador Retrievers?" Sunny asked as she bent down to pet a smooth head.

"My dad's babies. Bird dogs."

"Hey, Aubrey!" a woman's voice called happily from the house. "Get yourself over here!"

"That's Momma. We better get moving." Aubrey started jogging toward the house with the dogs right on her heels. Sunny could almost imagine a younger Aubrey just then, running into the house to help her mom. What would it have been like to grow up in a place like this? It was so far outside of Sunny's imagination that it almost made her head hurt just to think of it.

"And that must be Sunny," a tan-faced woman with platinum hair called out. "Come on over here, and let me get a look at you, girl. A pair of fancy Pendleton models staying right here at my house. I've been bragging up you girls to all my friends. Crystal Sparks is pea green with envy, Aubrey. Remember how her daughter, Chelsea, tried to get into modeling for years?"

Sunny was on the back deck now, face-to-face with Aubrey's mother.

"This is my good friend Sunny Westcott," Aubrey said.

"Pleasure to meet you." Her mother reached out for Sunny's hand, warmly squeezing it. "Such a pretty girl. No wonder you and Aubrey got picked to model."

"Thank you. And it's a pleasure to meet you too. You have a beautiful ranch here, Mrs. Lowenstein, and I—"

"No, no, don't call me Mrs. Lowenstein. That just makes me feel old. Call me Cindy." Now she looked at Sunny's buckskin coat and smiled. "That is quite a jacket, young lady. Where on earth did you find that?"

To Sunny's relief, Aubrey gave a quick explanation.

"Thank you," Sunny said, "and thank you for your hospitality too. The bunkhouse is really nice."

"I told her you had to throw Glenda out to accommodate us," Aubrey said in a teasing tone.

"Now, don't you go around saying things like that, Aubrey Louise. I told Glenda that we'd let them use our good camp tent and our camping things if they still want to come." She slowly shook her head. "Do you know we'll have about seventy people here? Your dad just cut the west hayfield for the big circle."

"The big circle?" Sunny asked.

Cindy nodded. "That's what we call the place where they circle the wagons."

"They bring wagons here?"

Cindy laughed loudly. "Haven't you told Sunny about any of this?"

"Circling the wagons is where they park their camp trailers and RVs," Aubrey explained. "We usually have about eight or so."

"This year we'll have about twenty," Cindy announced.

"Wow!" Aubrey looked impressed.

"And there'll be tents as well."

"This is going to be like a three-ringed circus." Aubrey shook her head.

"Tell me about it. I've been cooking for a week already." Cindy was leading them into the house now.

"You mean you plan to feed all those people?" Sunny was stunned.

"No. Not all of them. But the ones who stay in the house. And not for all the meals. I just cook a bunch of stuff up, put it in the freezer, and pull it out as needed. I like to have things on hand. But a lot of people will eat at town or at the rodeo grounds or the levy."

"The levy?"

"Well, it's not actually on the levy anymore." Cindy went over to the stove to check on an oversized pot. "We old-timers just call it that. It's in the park now, where the Indians set up their wares—you know, food and jewelry and whatnot." She stopped talking now, turning back to consider Sunny with a slightly curious expression.

"Sunny's grandmother was born on the reservation," Aubrey said quietly. "Sunny grew up in Portland, and she's never been here."

"I'm one-quarter Cayuse," Sunny told Cindy, waiting for her reaction.

Cindy put the lid back on the pot. "That's not so unusual around here, Sunny. I'm sure you'll find you're in good company."

Sunny wasn't sure how to respond to that "good company" comment, so she scanned the spacious room. "What a beautiful kitchen," she said with real admiration.

"Thank you. I had it redone a few years ago. It used to be about a third this size. I just love it now. Especially at Round-Up."

"I've been thinking about redoing my kitchen," Sunny said. "But now I'm in between jobs, so it might be awhile."

"Sunny owns her own home," Aubrey bragged. "And she doesn't have any debt."

Cindy looked impressed. "Good for you. I hope you rub off on Aubrey."

Aubrey made a face at her mom as she snatched a big sugar cookie from a cooling rack. "Help yourself," she told Sunny.

Sunny hesitated.

"Does that mean you're not a full-time model?" Cindy asked Sunny as she rinsed the wooden spoon off.

"I thought I already told you she used to be a college professor," Aubrey said to her mom.

"Oh, I must've forgot."

"The college I worked for did some downsizing," Sunny explained.

"Then I guess you were lucky to get involved in modeling."

"And I can thank your daughter for that."

Cindy went over to Aubrey, slipping an arm around her waist. "Well, good for you, sweetie. Now you girls just make yourselves at home for the next few days. But get ready for the onslaught on Tuesday and Wednesday next week."

"Do you need help in here, Mom?"

"I don't think so. I've got a roast in the oven, and we'll probably eat dinner around seven or so since your dad's trying to get that hay turned over." She reached over and ran her hand through Aubrey's long blond hair. "It's so good to see you, darling. And you look so pretty. Maybe you'll catch yourself a husband this year."

"Oh, Mom!" Aubrey stuck out her tongue.

"I'm just jerking your chain." She looked at Sunny now. "Does your mother do that to you too? Nag about getting married and having—"

"Her mom died when she was a girl," Aubrey filled in.

"Oh, I'm sorry." Cindy's eyes grew really sad. "Well, we know all about that around here, Sunny." She sighed. "By the way, Echo is out there, Aubrey. She's been riding almost every day this summer. You should go say hello to your niece."

"For sure." Aubrey patted her mom's cheek now, glancing at Sunny with hopeful eyes. "Can we just tell her?"

"Tell me what?" Cindy glanced curiously from Aubrey to Sunny.

"Do you mind, Sunny?"

It took Sunny a moment to realize what Aubrey was talking about. "Oh, I don't know. I mean, it's—"

"Tell me what?" Cindy looked worried now. "What's going on with you girls?"

"Please," Aubrey begged. "Mom won't tell anyone else. We'll swear her to secrecy."

"Of course," Cindy said quickly. "You can trust me."

Sunny was caught now. She could tell by Cindy's expression that she was worried about Aubrey's sudden announcement. She was probably thinking the worst. And Sunny knew the comment about understanding losing a mother was related to the loss of her other daughter. "Okay," Sunny said solemnly. "You can tell her. But do you mind if I use your restroom?"

"Down that hallway to your right," Cindy said.

Sunny could hear their voices as she went down the hallway. She didn't like that Aubrey had already broken her word. But she sort of understood. Aubrey had probably been trying to distract her mother from focusing on the loss of her other daughter. But hopefully Cindy would keep her promise and not mention this to anyone.

The restroom had a cowboy theme too. The mirror was framed in tooled leather, horseshoes served as robe hooks and towel bars, and several pairs of spurs hung decoratively on the plaid wallpaper. As Sunny dried her hands on towels embossed with bucking broncos, she wondered if the whole house was western décor—or if the Lowenstein family ever grew weary of cowboy chic. Probably not. It was their way of life.

When she returned to the kitchen, Cindy eagerly awaited her. "That is so exciting, Sunny. But I honestly don't see why you want to keep it a secret. Jackson Sundown is a Round-Up legend. Everyone would be happy for you to have such an exciting heritage."

"Except that I don't know if it's really true."

"Sunny needs some solid scientific proof." Aubrey frowned like this was a bad thing.

"Scientific proof?" Cindy studied Sunny closely. "Like DNA tests? Because that might be a little hard to come by at this stage of the game."

"Yes, I know," Sunny said, "but I plan to do a little research while I'm here. Native Americans have a strong oral tradition—a heritage of storytelling. I hope to find someone, perhaps even a relative, who might have some recollection of my family history."

"Doesn't she sound like a college professor?" Aubrey teased.

"Sorry." Sunny shrugged. "I taught anthropology classes and tend to think along those lines."

"That makes a lot of sense," Cindy said as she rinsed a dishrag out. "And, unlike my impulsive daughter, I respect that you want to go carefully about this. Making false assumptions about family roots could get a girl in trouble. Your secret is safe with me, Sunny."

"Thanks." Sunny ran her hand over the wrought-iron back of the barstool. "If I find out anything that makes me certain of my ancestry, I'll be sure to let you know."

"You know"—Cindy wiped down the granite countertop with a thoughtful expression—"I'll bet Cody could be of some help to you."

"Cody?"

"He's my son-in-law—he was married to Lorena. Anyway, he works as a drug and alcohol counselor on the reservation. He might be able to introduce you to someone who knows about your family."

Sunny knew Cindy was only trying to be helpful. But hearing that she wanted to introduce Sunny to someone who worked with drug addicts and alcoholics rubbed her the wrong way. Did she really think that Sunny wanted to talk to people with dependency issues? Or did she suspect that Sunny came from people like that? How much had Aubrey told her mother anyway?

"Thank you." Sunny forced a smile. "But I think I can make connections on my own. I've already collected some information from my online research." She glanced outside the wide window over the sink. "Do you mind if I look around your property? I've never been on a ranch like this. It's very interesting."

"No, not at all." Cindy opened a bag of tortilla chips, pouring them into a colorful ceramic bowl, which she placed on the island counter. "I hope you'll make yourself at home, Sunny. Feel free to look around wherever you like."

"Just steer clear of the bulls," Aubrey warned. "They can be mean."

"I've got some homemade salsa here," Cindy said as she set a small bowl next to the chips. "Help yourself."

"Thanks," Sunny said as she made her way to the back. "Maybe later."

She just wanted some time to herself. She didn't realize how unaccustomed she was to so much social interaction. After all, she used to stand in front of a large class, talking for hours of the day. But that had been different. She'd been talking about what she knew, and everything in the classroom had been subject to her control. Not a whole lot like real life, now that she thought about it. Perhaps her grandmother hadn't been the only one to overprotect Sunny. Perhaps Sunny had done some self-insulation as well.

Chapter Eight

Sunny liked the smell of the farm—a wholesome, earthy mix of soil, animals, and growing things. She heard what sounded like the nickering of horses and, curious to see more, went around the side of one of the barns to find a pasture, corral, and large riding arena. About a dozen horses or more, mostly shades of brown, grazed contentedly in the pasture, and another horse, a shiny black one, was trotting around the arena with a young girl in the saddle.

Sunny knew this must be Cindy's granddaughter, Echo. So far the girl seemed unaware that she was being watched as she rode with a straight back and fixed concentration, skillfully directing the horse to the right and then to the left. She wore a purple sweatshirt and a red helmet; her long, thick, brown ponytail bounced behind her. Her boots were practical looking and covered with dust; her jeans, Wranglers, looked well worn. Standing in the shadows close to the barn, Sunny watched, mesmerized. The girl's grace in the saddle and control over the horse were quite impressive. Sunny assumed that she'd inherited her mother's skills as a horsewoman. It seemed understandable that her grandfather would have high hopes for her to be a Round-Up queen someday.

"Who are you?" the girl called out suddenly when she finally observed her audience of one.

"I'm Sunny Westcott," she replied. "A friend of your aunt Aubrey."

The girl's eyes lit up as she walked her horse closer. "Aunt Aubrey is here?"

"She's in the house with your grandmother."

"How do you know who I am?" The girl leaned over slightly to peer down at Sunny.

Sunny smiled. "I just assumed you're Echo. Your grandmother said you were out here riding."

Echo nodded and sat straighter, patting the horse on the side of the neck. "And this is Sylvester. He's mine."

"He's beautiful." Aubrey nodded. "What kind of horse?"

"Quarter horse." Echo nodded toward the grazing horses. "The only kind of horse my grandpa owns."

"Oh."

"You don't know much about horses, do you?"

Sunny chuckled. "No. Not much."

"Have you ever ridden?"

She shook her head. "I always wanted to ride, as a child. But, well, I was pretty much raised by my grandmother, and she had a phobia of horses. She was certain I'd get hurt or killed if I ever got on one."

"Are you part Indian?"

Sunny tried not to look offended by the blunt question. After all, Echo was only a child. "Yes, as a matter of fact, I am."

"I thought so." Echo nodded.

"I don't know much about horses," Sunny said, "but it looks to me like you're a very good rider."

Echo smiled. "Thanks."

"And I don't want to interrupt your ride."

Echo's eyes lit up. "Hey, do you want to ride too?"

Sunny didn't know what to say. "I, uh, I don't know."

"I can get a horse saddled up for you if you want. I'd pick a real gentle one."

Sunny couldn't even imagine herself on a horse—and yet she wondered.

"We could stay in the corral if you like. It's small."

"Okay," Sunny said suddenly. "Why not?"

"All right." Echo pointed to the barn-like building attached to the corral. "You go through over there, and I'll meet you inside the stables, okay?"

Sunny nodded and walked over to where there was an opening, then walked into the shadowy corridor of what did turn out to be stables.

"Down here," Echo called. "We'll saddle up Brownie Anne for you. She's twenty-two years old and a real sweetheart."

And, just like that, Sunny found herself in a stall with Echo and Brownie Anne, watching as Echo went to work. "This is a halter," she said as the horse lowered its head into the leather nose band. Echo slipped leather straps behind the horse's ears and fastened it. "And this is the lead rope," she explained as she snapped a rope onto the halter. "If you want, I could use a longe line, but Brownie Anne is so gentle, I don't think we need to."

"I trust your judgment."

Now Echo slid open the stall door and led the horse out to the alleyway, where she loosely looped the lead rope on a hook. Now she opened the door to what looked like another stall, but instead of a horse inside, it was full of saddles and horse equipment. "This is the tack room," Echo said as she turned on the light.

Before long, Sunny was learning how to use a curry comb to get the horse's back ready. Then how to arrange a saddle blanket, and how to place the saddle on top of that. Finally, how to tighten a cinch—and how to tighten it again when the horse let the air out of her belly. After that, Echo held up another set of leather straps trimmed in silver. "This is a bridle," she informed Sunny. "This is what you use when you actually ride." Now she exchanged the halter for the bridle, finally placing the reins in Sunny's hands.

"This is very educational," Sunny told Echo. "You're a good teacher."

"Thanks." Echo smiled. "Okay, then, let's go out to the corral."

Sunny felt a flutter of nerves and excitement as she stood next to the saddled horse out in the corral.

"You always get on a horse from the left side," Echo told her. "Watch, I'll show you how." Then, with her left hand on the saddle horn, Echo lifted her left leg, planted her foot in the stirrup and gracefully swung her right leg over the saddle and sat.

"You make it look so easy," Sunny said.

"Because it is." With equal grace, Echo got off the horse. "And you're taller than me, so it should be even easier for you."

"Okay." Sunny nodded as she grasped the saddle horn and tried to imitate Echo. Next thing she knew, she was on top of the horse. "Wow." She looked down at Echo. "I did it."

Echo grinned. "You did." Now she helped her loop the reins around the horse's head. "It's simple—steer right and left. You don't have to pull hard. Just the touch of the rein on the opposite side of her neck and she'll turn. She's a good horse." Then Echo was on top of her horse and next to Sunny. "Give her a gentle squeeze with your knees—or simply click your tongue and she'll start moving."

Sunny did as Echo instructed, and the big animal began to slowly move. "Hey, it works," she said happily. She was surprised at how unafraid she was as the horse walked around the corral. Really, it was a good feeling, swaying in the saddle, being up high. Sunny thought maybe she could get used to this.

"You look like a natural," Echo told Sunny. Then she continued to coach Sunny, helping her to steer the horse, stop the horse, and even to make her back up.

"This is really fun," Sunny told her. "You're a great teacher, Echo."

"Thanks."

"Do you think I'm ready to try anything faster than walking?"

"It's up to you."

And so, with a little help from Echo, they moved the horses into the arena and soon Sunny had the horse trotting.

"Try to follow the moves of the horse," Echo told her. "Move your body up and down as she moves hers."

While trotting felt less secure than walking, it was a fun challenge to try to match the horse's movements. After a few times around the arena, she was getting it. "This is good exercise," she told Echo when they stopped to walk for a bit.

"I guess so."

"Do you think I should try to gallop on her?"

"It's up to you," Echo said again.

Then with Echo's help, Sunny soon had the horse going from a trot into a gallop. She couldn't believe how much smoother that gallop was, compared to the trot. In a way it felt like she was flying—and she loved it.

"Hey, cowgirls!" Aubrey waved from the other side of the arena. "Let 'er buck!"

"Hopefully not," Sunny said as she slowed the horse to a trot and then a walk, going over to where Aubrey was standing.

"I didn't know you rode." Aubrey looked up at Sunny.

"I didn't either."

"Hi, Aunt Aubrey," Echo said as she came over to join them.

Aubrey climbed up and sat on the top rail of the arena fence. "Hey there, gorgeous," she said to Echo. "You get prettier every time I see you."

Echo rolled her eyes. "Yeah, right."

"Seriously, Sunny, when did you take up riding?"

"Just now. Echo is an excellent teacher."

"Maybe for you," Aubrey said, "but I am hopeless. Horses can smell the fear on me as soon as my hind end hits the saddle. Then they usually try to get rid of me about that fast too."

"Brownie Anne wouldn't do that," Echo told her.

Aubrey shook her head. "She would, and she has."

"But that was probably when she was younger," Echo tried.

"I was younger then too. And now I'm old enough to know that horses and I don't mix. End of story. But at least I supplied a friend for you to ride with."

"Sunny's a natural." Echo patted Brownie Anne's neck.

"Thanks to your help." Sunny smiled happily. "I can't believe how much fun it is to ride. Do you think I could get good enough to ride outside of the arena?"

"Sure—you're good enough now."

"Really?"

Echo nodded, then glanced at her watch. "I'd offer to go with you now, but Dad's going to be here any minute. And we still need to put the horses away."

"Hey, I'll take care of your dad," Aubrey offered. "I'll tell him that you guys have to stay for dinner. Mom already mentioned that anyway. You cowgirls go have yourself a ride, and I'll take the blame."

Echo's eyes lit up. "Okay."

The next thing Sunny knew, she and Echo were riding their horses out alongside the freshly cut hayfield.

"We'll ride down to the creek," Echo explained. "Grandpa likes us to stay along the fence line here, so I'll take the lead. Watch out for gopher holes. Usually the horses avoid them, but you need to be ready in case they don't."

"Okay." Sunny watched Echo riding ahead of her, trying to mimic her ways with the horse and totally enjoying the entire experience. She couldn't believe she'd waited until her mid-thirties before ever getting on a horse. But at least she'd done it.

They made it to the creek, then dismounted, giving the horses a chance to drink.

"Looks like the sky is clearing up," Sunny told Echo.

"Yeah, it's supposed to start getting hot again."

"So do you live around here?" Sunny asked.

"We live on the reservation."

"Really?"

"My dad runs my grandpa's ranch."

"Your grandfather has *another* ranch?"

"It's my other grandpa. My dad's dad. He lives on the ranch too, but he's too old to do much. So Dad and I take care of most of the chores. We only have eighty acres and some livestock. Nothing like this place." She waved her arm toward the golden wheat fields west of them.

"But it's on the reservation?" Sunny queried. "Does that mean you're Native American?"

"You don't have to be an Indian to live on the reservation," Echo said as she led her horse away from the creek, pausing to check the cinch on her horse's saddle, explaining that it could loosen after a short ride.

"So white people can own reservation land?" Following Echo's lead, Sunny moved her horse away from the creek and checked her cinch too.

"They can. But the Indians don't really like it."

"I can understand that." Now Sunny focused her attention on getting safely back onto the horse. Echo might think she was a natural, but the truth was, Sunny was really concentrating and trying hard. She didn't want to end up with any broken bones.

"Want to try galloping back to the horse barn?"

"Sure, if you think I can handle it."

"I think you can, but you need to be comfortable with it. And I didn't notice any gopher holes, so I think we should be okay. But hang onto the saddle horn as much as you need to."

"Right."

"And if you want to slow down, feel free." Then, just like that, Echo and Sylvester took off in a fast gallop. Sunny had barely clicked her tongue when Brownie Anne took off after them. Sunny gave her full concentration to riding now, feeling the thrill and the rush of the horse beneath her, enjoying every second…and at the same time hoping she'd remain seated on the horse. A part of her was in shock that she was actually doing this, while another part could almost believe she'd been riding horses her whole life. Then, too soon, they were back at the horse barn.

"I don't see Dad around," Echo said as they walked the horses into the alleyway by the stalls. "Hopefully he's not mad at me."

"Well, if he is, let Aubrey and me take the blame."

Echo laughed as she snapped a lead rope on and looped it over the hook. "Right. Maybe Dad will ground you."

"Your dad would ground you for being late like this?"

"No, I was kidding." She grinned as she snapped a lead rope onto Brownie Anne, hooking it about a horse's length away from Sylvester. "My dad's actually a real softie. Most of my friends think he spoils me. I think it's just his way."

Sunny wondered briefly how different her life might've been if she'd lost only one parent and been raised by the other. Then Echo, working on her own horse, was instructing Sunny how to remove the saddle, slide it down, and carry it back to the tack room, where she set them over some big blue barrels. Then they removed the blankets, brushed the horses down, checked their hooves, gave them a squirt of fly spray, then returned them to their stalls, removed the halters, and gave them hay, grain, and water.

"I always feed and water the other horses when I'm here too," Echo explained as she went into another stall. "This is Hero, but he's not real friendly, so you better wait out there." Sunny helped by bringing "flakes" of hay and refilling the grain can, and before long, they were done.

"I feel like I just went to horse school," Sunny told Echo as they walked back to the house.

"I'd give you an *A* today."

Sunny laughed. "Thanks."

"If you're around, I'll be out here every day after school until Round-Up if you want to ride some more."

"I'd love to. But I'll have to check my schedule."

"Oh, that's right. Grandma said you and Aubrey are modeling for the Pendleton catalog. Is that fun?"

Sunny shook her head. "Fun? No, I wouldn't exactly describe it as fun. I'm not really a model, you know, not like your aunt is. I'm just trying to make a few extra bucks until I find a new job."

"And there's my little renegade now," a male voice called from the shadows of the back deck.

Echo broke into a big smile as they went up the steps to the deck. "Hey, Dad," she sang out sweetly, "you're not mad at me, are you?"

Sunny spotted a guy wearing a cowboy hat coming toward them now. Dressed in western wear, he was of medium build and looked about six feet tall.

"Sunny, this is my dad, Cody Barrett," Echo said politely. "Dad, this is Aunt Aubrey's friend Sunny."

He stuck out a weathered-looking hand and smiled. "Pleasure to meet you, Sunny." His sandy-colored hair, tinged with gray, fringed out from beneath his hat.

"You too." She looked into his eyes as they shook hands. Golden brown, they were exact replicas of his daughter's…or vice versa. His face was lined and tanned; his smile seemed warm and genuine.

"I hear Echo's giving you riding lessons."

Sunny nodded. "Your daughter's an excellent teacher."

"I just gave Sunny an *A* for her first riding class," Echo told him.

He studied Sunny closely. "Your *first* riding class? Does that mean you'd never been on a horse before?"

"Never," she admitted.

"But Sunny's a natural," Echo told him. "Probably because she's part Indian."

"You mean Native American," he said gently.

"Yeah, whatever."

Her dad looked at his daughter's hands now. "Hey, you better go wash up. Grandma could probably use a hand setting the table since we're crashing her dinner party."

Sunny glanced over to the bunkhouse. "I should go wash up too." She smiled at him. "It was a pleasure to meet you—and your daughter too." But as she turned to walk toward the bunkhouse, he came with her.

"Cindy mentioned you want to do some research on the reservation," he said casually.

"That's right. I do."

"I thought maybe I could introduce you to some friends," he offered. "You see, I work and live on the reservation, and I know a few people."

"So I heard." She turned to look more closely at him. "I'm curious, Cody. Do you find it awkward—being a white man living on the reservation?"

He grinned. "Probably not any more awkward than the reverse situation."

"You mean me?" She paused, wondering why she was making an issue of this...except that she was curious. "You mean being a Native

American living in the white man's world?" She could hear the cynicism in her voice and didn't much care for it.

He shrugged. "Things aren't always as they seem, Sunny."

"No," she told him, "they're not."

He gave her what seemed like a nod of appreciation. "Nice jacket."

"Thank you. I think it belonged to my great-grandmother."

"And she lived on the reservation?"

"Yes. My grandmother did too—at least until she was old enough to leave. Then she left and never looked back."

"Some do that."

She nodded. "I better get cleaned up."

He tipped his hat. "Keep my offer in mind. Sometimes it's hard being an outsider, trying to break into a new culture."

"Thanks, I'll remember that."

As she went into the bunkhouse, she was unexplainably irritated, as much at herself as she was at him. But as she cleaned up and unpacked her things, she convinced herself that she was probably blowing their conversation all out of proportion, reading things into it that hadn't even been there.

When she walked back to the house, she told herself to stop taking everything so personally, so seriously. Aubrey's family was simply being friendly and interested and helpful. Why should she fault them for that?

Chapter Nine

. . . .

"That was a delicious dinner," Sunny said as she helped Cindy and Echo clear the dining room table. Aubrey had gone with the others down to the basement with the guys, and Sunny felt like the best way to say thanks was to help out. "Everything was just perfect."

"Thank you." Cindy set some dishes in the sink. "But you run on downstairs with the others, Sunny. Echo and I can take care of this, can't we, Echo?"

"I'm happy to help," Sunny insisted. "And this gives me a chance to have a closer look at this gorgeous kitchen." Truth was, Sunny wasn't that comfortable around the others. Aubrey's father, Doug, was polite enough, but a little hard to read. And maybe she was mistaking his quietness for something it wasn't, but Sunny couldn't help but feel slightly in the way.

It didn't help that she already felt awkward around Cody. Why she had locked horns with him over the Native American issue was confusing. He'd only been trying to help. Why couldn't she have just politely declined his offer to introduce her to his "friends" and gone on her way? Her plan from here on out was to keep a low profile and to stay only as long as necessary to complete the photography sessions. Whatever research she could manage to squeeze into her spare time would have to suffice.

"These are beautiful dishes," she told Cindy as she rinsed a dinner plate. "I see that they're made by Pendleton Woolen Mills. I didn't realize they made dishes too."

"They make all sorts of things," Cindy told her. "The dishes are Lakota. I got them last Christmas."

Sunny studied the bold design on the plate. "Do you think this is an authentic Lakota Sioux motif?"

"I don't know that for sure. But Pendleton does use a lot of Indian names and designs. I have an early Chief Joseph blanket." Cindy's eyes lit up. "Did you know that your great-grandpa was related to Chief Joseph?"

Echo looked curiously at Sunny now. "Who's your great-grandpa?"

"I don't really know," Sunny said quickly.

"Uh, that's right," Cindy said even more quickly. "I was thinking of someone else." She laughed. "Maybe it's my Alzheimer's starting to kick in."

"Oh, *Grandma*." As Echo bent down to push in the full bottom rack of the dishwasher, Cindy mouthed "I'm sorry" with sincere-looking eyes.

Sunny made a stiff smile. Hopefully that wouldn't happen again.

"Looks like our work here is done for now," Cindy announced. "Why don't you run downstairs and see what the others are up to?"

"Or I might just turn in." Sunny set the damp dishrag down and dried her hands.

"Did you see the whole house yet?" Echo asked hopefully.

"I think so." Sunny glanced at Cindy. "And it's really beautiful."

"Did you see the Cowgirl Room?" Echo asked.

"Uh, no. I think I just saw the main parts of the house."

"Can I show Sunny the Cowgirl Room?" Echo asked her grand-mother.

"Of course. Go ahead. I think I'll go put my feet up."

"Come on," Echo urged her. "It's really cool."

Sunny followed Echo down a hallway and into a bedroom, which was painted a bright pink and decorated with yet more western-looking pieces. Except the things in here, unlike the rest of the house, were more glitzy, sparkly, and feminine. Echo pointed to a large portrait of a pretty blond woman wearing a white cowboy hat. "That's my mom when she was Round-Up queen back in the eighties."

"She was beautiful, Echo."

Echo showed Sunny more photos and memorabilia from her mother's cowgirl days and during her reign of the Pendleton Round-Up. She handled each item with reverence, carefully replacing them in the exact same spots. The room seemed almost like a museum, or a shrine. Not having known Lenora, Sunny felt slightly intrusive just being there.

Echo held a small framed photo of her mother on a horse in her hand. "Grandpa says my mom had dreamed of being Round-Up queen her whole life."

"Aubrey told me that your grandpa wants you to be a rodeo queen someday too." Sunny studied the smiling blond girl in the photo. She appeared so comfortable on her horse, in her own skin, like she literally sparkled with life and light. Yet now she was gone.

Echo set down the photo and picked up the white cowgirl hat. Running her finger over the ornate silver hatband, she sadly shook her head. "I know."

Sunny sensed that Echo wasn't quite comfortable with her grandfather's expectation. "But that's probably still a few years away," she said offhandedly. "I'm sure you have to be quite a bit older to be a Round-Up princess or queen."

Echo gazed at Sunny with troubled eyes. "Can I tell you a secret?"

Sunny was taken aback slightly but didn't show it. "Do you mean, can you trust me?"

Echo nodded.

"Absolutely. I'm very good at keeping secrets."

"I haven't told anyone—not even Dad—but I don't want to be in the Round-Up court."

"Oh." Sunny studied Echo's smooth, even features. Such a pretty girl, but in a calmer, quieter way than her mother. At least that was Sunny's impression.

"But I think I have to do it to make everyone happy. My grandparents would be so disappointed if I didn't. Even my dad expects me to do it."

"Is there a reason you don't want to be in the Round-Up court?"

She shrugged. "I love riding, but I don't like being the center of attention."

Sunny could relate to this. "But do you think you might feel differently about that someday—you know, a few years down the line?"

"I don't think so. When I see the Round-Up queen riding into the rodeo grounds with both hands in the air as she jumps the fence— she always looks so happy. I don't think I could do that—I couldn't be that happy with so many people staring at me. Do you know what I mean?"

Sunny smiled. "I do. I've never been comfortable in the limelight, either. Even doing this modeling thing with your aunt has been hard. But I needed the money."

"I thought you'd understand." Echo gave a meek smile. "And you won't tell anyone, right?"

"No, I won't. The good news is, you don't have to make up your mind about any of this today. And who knows? Maybe in a few years you'll feel differently. If you don't, I'm sure everyone will understand."

Echo set the hat down. "I hope so. But sometimes—especially at Round-Up time—it worries me. I don't want to let my family down."

"Just don't let yourself down," Sunny said as they left the room.

"Hey, there you are," Aubrey called out as Sunny and Echo entered the great room. "We were getting ready to watch a DVD. Want to join us?"

"Thanks anyway, but I think I'll call it a night," Sunny told her.

"But it's a movie about Jackson Sundown," Aubrey said emphatically. "I thought you'd want to see it. It's a documentary made by a local couple. It's even won some awards. Come on, Sunny, don't be a party pooper."

"Speaking of party poopers"—Cody took his daughter's hand—"it's a school night, and I'll bet you have homework."

Echo groaned.

"Besides," Cody added, "we've already seen that movie several times." He looked at Sunny now. "But I highly recommend it. I think you'd enjoy it."

"Yes," Echo agreed as she pulled on her jacket. "You really should watch it, Sunny."

"Thanks," Sunny told her. "And thanks again for the riding lesson."

Echo's eyes lit up. "Don't forget I'll be out there every day after school if you want to ride again. It was nice having someone to ride with."

"Don't worry, I won't forget. I'll probably be dreaming about horses tonight too."

Echo laughed as she and her dad told everyone good-bye.

Once they were gone, Aubrey put the DVD in, turned on the big screen TV, and the room grew quiet.

Sunny was mesmerized by the documentary…so much so she could hardly speak when it ended. Seeing the historical footage and photos, nearly a hundred years old, and hearing the stories about Jackson Sundown, told from a number of perspectives, left her feeling so emotionally overwhelmed that the only thing she could do was thank her hosts for their hospitality and for sharing the film with her and excuse herself.

It was dark outside, but she paused to let her eyes adjust, breathing in the chilly night air and the smells of freshly cut hay, animals, and earth before she went over to the bunkhouse. Once in her room, she closed the door. With the light still off, she sat down on the chair by the bed and tried to make sense of the emotions churning inside her. She really needed to process all of this.

"Hey, you," called Aubrey's voice. "Did you go to bed already?"

Sunny was tempted to say "yes" but knew that was not only false, but not good manners, either. "No," Sunny called back, getting up to turn on the light and open the door.

"So what did you think of the movie?" Aubrey came into her room and sat down on the bed, making herself at home. Of course, this was her parents' ranch, so why shouldn't she?

"It was very good—and well done. I liked it a lot."

"Did it make you feel like Jackson Sundown was related to you? Did it make it seem more real? Did you hear when someone mentioned that he was tall?" she asked eagerly. "And so are you."

"But so was my great-grandmother," Sunny reminded her. "At least I think she was."

"Is that her photo there?" Aubrey hopped off the bed and went over to the dresser where Sunny had set out some of the memorabilia.

Now Sunny wished she'd had the good sense to stick it in a drawer. "Yes." She turned away, carefully hanging up her buckskin jacket in the closet.

"Wow, she was really beautiful, Sunny. You look a lot like her."

"Well, we are related."

"And look at that sweet smile. I can imagine how she would've caught the eye of someone like Jackson Sundown."

"That's assuming a lot."

"I don't see why." Aubrey picked up the photo of Jackson Sundown now, holding the two of them together side by side. "Don't they make a handsome couple?"

"A handsome *fictional* couple, you mean."

Aubrey frowned at Sunny. "It's like you keep shoving it away from you. I'd love to have such a glamorous family tree. Seriously, why are you so dead set against this being real?"

"Because I feel it's disrespectful to Jackson Sundown," Sunny said quietly. "Dishonoring to his memory."

"It's dishonoring to claim him as your great-grandfather?" Aubrey looked confused now. "Why? Wouldn't he be just as proud to claim you as you would be to claim him?"

"That's not what I mean."

"What then? What's the big deal?"

Sunny thought hard. She didn't want to offend Aubrey, but she did want her to understand her position. "This is the big deal—to me, anyway. You see, I *know* that my great-grandmother was an alcoholic and, according to my grandmother, not a very respectable woman. I don't know all the sordid details but enough to understand that my grandmother was ashamed of her own mother. So ashamed that she tried to bury all memories of her. And when she ran away from the reservation, she was trying to run away from her own mother's disreputable past."

"Okay, I get that. But, really, what does it have to do with Jackson Sundown?"

"What does it have to do with him?" Sunny couldn't believe Aubrey was this obtuse. Wasn't it obvious?

"Sure, I get that your grandmother was ashamed of her mom," Aubrey went on. "Who isn't embarrassed by their parents sometimes? We all make mistakes. But what if it's true? What if Jackson Sundown had been attracted to your grandmother? What if they'd had a little fling, a romantic interlude, an affair? Those things do happen, Sunny. They happened back then just like they happen now. So what?"

Sunny stared at Aubrey. "So what?"

"Yeah, what's the big deal?"

"The big deal is that, the more I learn about Jackson Sundown, the more respect I have for the man…and his legend. As a result, the less I can believe that he would've gotten involved with someone like my great-grandmother. Can't you understand that?"

Aubrey shook her head, still looking unconvinced.

"Then you'll just have to respect that it's the way I feel. Now, more than ever, I refuse to believe that Jackson Sundown is my ancestor. And I refuse to dishonor his name by mentioning it to anyone. My only connection to Jackson Sundown is one of an admirer."

"So you're not going to research into this now? You don't even want to find out the truth?"

"I do want to find out what I can about my family history," Sunny told her. "But I refuse to go with a single agenda—that of proving I'm related to Jackson Sundown."

"Okay." Aubrey slowly nodded. "I get that. And I think I can respect that."

Sunny sighed. "Thank you."

Aubrey made a face. "Even if it is a little boring."

Sunny gave her a half smile. "Sometimes the facts are boring, Aubrey."

"Okay, then, I won't keep bugging you about this."

"I appreciate it."

"Anyway, I wanted to let you know that it's okay to use a bathroom in the house tomorrow morning, if we both end up trying to get ready at the same time—since it's going to be an early morning."

As Sunny got ready for bed, she was slightly dismayed that she wasn't thinking about Jackson Sundown nearly as much as she was thinking about Cody Barrett.

Chapter Ten

....

The photoshoot at Hamley & Co. finished a little before ten, then Marsha told everyone that the next session wouldn't be until Monday morning. "We'll meet at the rodeo grounds at ten," she told them, "where we'll use the actual stadium, as well as the tipi village as a backdrop."

"What's the tipi village?" one of the other models asked.

"It's where the Native Americans camp by the rodeo grounds," she explained, "and all those tipis make for a very interesting setting."

After changing into their own clothes, Sunny and Aubrey decided to look around the store for a while. While Aubrey was ogling silver jewelry, Sunny went over to check out the price on a pair of boots she'd worn during the shoot. Not as fancy as the ones she'd bought in Portland, the calfskin Lucchese boots looked both practical and beautiful, plus they were comfortable. And, hearing that the Pendleton models were offered a one-time-only discount, Sunny decided to splurge.

"Will these boots be good for riding too?" she asked the clerk as she was putting them back into the box.

"Of course." The girl smiled. "Can I help you with anything else?"

"I guess I might look around the store a little more," Sunny told her. "Since that discount is only for today."

The girl nodded. "Yes, you should definitely look around. I'll put these up front for you."

By the time Aubrey and Sunny left the store, Sunny had managed to collect a couple of western shirts and a fringed leather vest.

"You're turning into a real cowgirl," Aubrey teased as Sunny drove back to the ranch.

Sunny laughed. "Who knew being a cowgirl was so costly? But I figured my fancy boots weren't that practical for riding."

"So you really do like riding?"

Sunny nodded eagerly. "I love riding. It felt like something I was born to do." Okay, so her rear end was a bit saddle-sore today, but she figured that was the price to be paid. Not so much different than working out at the gym after a long break. She'd get over it.

"See"—Aubrey pointed a finger—"just like your great-grandpa."

Sunny tossed her a warning look.

"Hey, I didn't mention any names. I'm just saying…."

"Speaking of my ancestors," Sunny began, "I want to do some investigating today. After I drop you home, I plan to drive over to the reservation and see what I can find out."

"Want any company?"

Sunny didn't want to sound rude or unappreciative, but she really didn't. "I, uh, don't think so."

"Okay, I get it. If it makes you feel any better, I didn't want to go with you anyway." Aubrey chuckled. "I was just trying to be nice. I'll be surprised if you want to stick around there for too long anyway. Besides the casino, there's not that much to see out there."

"So you've spent a lot of time there?"

"Not a lot of time. But don't forget that my sister used to live on the Rez."

"The Rez?"

"Yeah, I used to go out there to visit my sister sometimes. I even stayed with Lenora and Cody one summer, back before Echo was born, and when my parents were driving me nuts."

"Right." Sunny nodded. She was still having a hard time linking the glitzy cowgirl photos of Lenora with the slightly serious Cody. For some reason they seemed so very different. Of course, Sunny knew that opposites attract. "I'm curious—how did Lenora and Cody meet?"

"Meet?" Aubrey frowned as if trying to remember. "It seems like they always knew each other. They'd been sweethearts, off and on, since junior high. And Cody used to be really into rodeo. When Lenora was in the court, they started dating again, and then got engaged in college. Not that my parents were too pleased."

"Really? Why not?"

"Oh, you know, the whole reservation thing. My parents aren't bigots or anything, but they didn't warm up to the idea."

"You mean they didn't like the fact that Cody lived on the reservation?"

"I don't think that bothered them as much as that he was Indian. Not that they admitted it to anyone, but I could tell it bugged them… at first anyway."

Sunny was shocked. "Cody, your brother-in-law, is Native American?"

"Yeah. But just on his dad's side."

Sunny was turning down their driveway now, still trying to take this in. "Cody is half Native American?"

"No. His dad is half. Cody is just a fourth. And, believe me, my parents totally accept him now. But, well, it was a bit of an issue at first. In fact, I used to think that was one of the things that attracted Lenora to Cody. Like it was her own personal rebellion—just to show our parents that they couldn't control everything she did."

"You don't think she married Cody because she loved him?"

"Oh, sure, she loved him. But I always secretly suspected that Lenora liked rocking my parents' boat…just a little. Probably because they were always telling her what to do, how to walk, talk, act—you know—grooming her for the Round-Up court and the rest of her life."

Sunny remembered Echo's secret confession last night and her resistance to being Round-Up royalty. It sounded like, while an honor, it might be a somewhat heavy load for a girl to grow up with.

"Thanks for the ride," Aubrey told Sunny. "And good luck on the Rez. You've got your cell phone, right?"

Sunny winced. "Actually, it's dead. And I forgot to pack the charger."

Aubrey frowned. "I don't want to scare you, but the Rez can be a scary place sometimes. Even though there are a lot of good people, there are a lot of not-so-good ones too. You don't want to get a flat tire somewhere and have a truck full of drunk and crazy guys offer to help you out. Seriously, I can tell you some stories, Sunny."

Sunny didn't want to hear Aubrey's stories about "Indians." Besides, for all anyone knew, Sunny was one of them. Why would one of her own people want to hurt her? "Don't worry," she assured Aubrey. "I'll be fine."

"I can run in the house to see if there's a spare cell phone or a charger cord you can borrow."

"No, that's okay. After all, my ancestors didn't have cell phones, and I'm sure they managed to find their relatives just fine."

Aubrey rolled her eyes. "Well, you could always send up a smoke signal."

Sunny laughed at that, but as she drove down the driveway, she hoped she wouldn't be sorry. Yet, the idea of being disconnected from some of the "comforts" of modern electronic culture was rather appealing. Almost like turning back the clock.

As she turned down one of the roads that was supposed to lead toward the reservation, she was still trying to absorb what Aubrey had just told her—that Cody was part Native American. She replayed some of his comments from last night now, reviewing them from her new perspective. Suddenly it seemed clear that she had overreacted to him. Oh, she could blame it on feeling the need to defend herself, but the truth was, she'd been offensive in doing so. Cody probably thought she was either crazy or plain rude. Hopefully she'd get the chance to apologize to him before she left Pendleton next week.

Sunny knew she was on reservation land now. It was clear that something was different. As she surveyed the landscape and houses, her emotions vacillated between a real sense of disappointment and an unexpected sense of exhilaration. The disappointment was in regard to some of the properties she saw: decrepit cracker-box houses and rundown old trailers, many with broken windows or screen doors hanging off their hinges. Old vehicles and miscellaneous junk strewn about the yards in a way that suggested nobody really cared...or they had given up. Sunny found this deeply troubling. Was it symptomatic of how these people, perhaps even her own relatives, regarded their lives?

On the other hand, she felt an irrational elation at being right there on the same land that her ancestors might've walked upon. This positive emotion, less tangible and harder to comprehend than the disappointment, resonated with the wide open spaces, rolling grass, and wheat fields. She wanted to drink in the big blue sky and white clouds. To think she was actually driving through an independent nation—one governed by the Cayuse, Umatilla, and Walla Walla tribes—was slightly overwhelming.

She drove for some time, not paying much attention to where she was going. Perhaps feeling so much at home that she assumed it was impossible to get lost. But after about an hour, she wished she'd brought a map because, suddenly, she realized it was easy to get turned around on one of these back roads.

Eventually she decided it was time to get some directions. She'd seen the signs along the freeway, as well as the flashing lights up at the crossroads—all for the purpose of directing, or perhaps enticing, travelers to stop at the Wild Horse casino. Feeling a bit like a lemming, she trailed behind an old beater car that seemed to know where it was going. Soon she was on a busier road, and then, like the old car, she turned at the crossroads and followed a couple of other cars to several very large buildings. She was pretty sure she was coming into the casino development.

She wasn't surprised when the cars ahead of her turned into the parking area by the largest of the buildings, which the sign confirmed was the actual casino—Wild Horse. She was slightly relieved to be back in "civilization" but at the same time saddened that the casino and other buildings created such an imposing presence on the otherwise peaceful grasslands. Yet she had to admit that architecture of these structures seemed well planned. She parked her car and slowly walked toward the casino. As she got closer, she could see it was constructed of a combination of natural elements, like stone and wood. Unlike its flamboyant advertisements and flashing lighted signs, the general look of the exterior was pleasant enough. Still, it was a casino.

Although Sunny was well aware that a number of tribes in Oregon had casinos, she also knew there was an untold story about which parties actually lined their pockets with the bulk of casino dollars. While many assumed that the tribes were the only ones to benefit from gamblers' losses, Sunny had read that in some instances the out-of-state casino developers, not the Native American population, most profited from the numerous gambling establishments popping up all over the Northwest. Sure, the casinos provided jobs and some small kickbacks to tribal members, but for the most part, Sunny suspected that, unless the Umatilla Reservation was different from all the others, they too might be the victims of a legalized sort of fraud.

Not that she wanted to dwell on all that as she entered the building. Mostly she wanted to find a map. She was immediately assaulted by electronic clanging, ringing and dinging, loud music playing, lights flashing, and stale cigarette smoke—all of it distasteful to her senses. She'd only been in a casino once before—during an anthropological conference at the coast—and only because Reuben had talked her into it. But she'd only lasted a few minutes, telling him that the lights and noise were going to result in a serious migraine headache. Today felt no different. Except this time, she was slightly more curious.

Bolstering herself against the onslaught, she strolled through the casino, studying the various people sitting in front of the obnoxious machines. She noted their glazed-over stares as they pushed buttons and gazed blankly at screens where colors and noises and lights blasted at them…almost to the point where Sunny feared someone might actually suffer a stroke or a seizure as a result of the cacophony of elements.

As she walked and observed, Sunny's scientific mind began to categorize the gamblers. One group, predominantly Caucasian, although some Native Americans fit the profile, seemed to be older—most likely retired and fairly well off. Perhaps they were bored and enjoyed the excitement of tossing their money at the greedy machines. They probably could afford the losses that seemed inevitable.

The next group had a different kind of intensity. These were the ones Sunny suspected to be serious gamblers, perhaps even gambling addicts. They seemed to be primarily Native Americans and, unless Sunny was wrong, appeared to be the ones who couldn't afford to be here. That reminded her of the discrepancy she'd noticed in the parking lot. More than half of the vehicles were expensive-looking, late-model cars. The rest seemed to be clunkers. Some appeared so dilapidated that it looked like they'd barely made it to the casino in the first place and might actually break down before making it back home.

Sunny was seriously worried as she watched a shabbily dressed Native American woman pulling cash from an envelope in her purse. She seemed to be about Sunny's age. For some reason, Sunny suspected this woman was a mother. Was she gambling with her family's grocery money? Squandering funds meant to purchase her children's winter coats? Sunny frowned down at the woman's feet, shod only in rubber flip-flops. Then she looked up in time to see this woman stuffing bills into the slot machine—enough money to buy a good pair of shoes. Sunny stood there, mesmerized, as she witnessed first twenty, then thirty, and finally forty dollars all being consumed by the machine. Just like that, it was gone. And the woman merely sat there, staring at the machine.

By now Sunny's head had begun to throb. Not only was the scene disturbing, she felt physically ill. Turning away, she hurried over to a nearby counter where two employees were standing. A Native American woman and a white man.

"Is there someplace I might find a map?" she said politely.

"You want a map of the casino?" the woman asked.

"No, a map of the reservation."

"The reservation?" The man looked curiously at her. "You mean, like how to get to the hotel and golf course and restaurant and all that?"

"No, I mean a map of the Umatilla Reservation," Sunny said plainly. "With names of the streets and roads so I can drive around without getting lost."

The man and woman stared blankly at her, then turned to each other and shrugged as if they were clueless.

"Maybe you should try the hotel," the woman suggested. "I think they have things like that." Then she explained where the hotel was located, which seemed fairly obvious since it was next to the casino.

"Enjoy your visit to Wild Horse," the guy said with a bright smile.

"And be sure to sign up for some of our giveaways," the woman added.

Sunny thanked them and headed straight for the exit.

Although she suspected it was a waste of time, she decided to swing by the hotel. Parking her car in front, she went directly into the lobby and asked about a map.

"All the maps and brochures are over there." The woman pointed to a neat wooden rack of tourist information about local sites and activities. But when Sunny browsed through the materials, there was no actual map of the reservation. And, really, why would there be? Why had she even bothered to look here?

She left the hotel with a real sense of disappointment. These things—the casino, hotel, golf course—felt all wrong to her. They were bizarre and incongruous, ironically misplaced. Kind of like a bad joke.

She got into her car and sat there, trying to wrap her head around this strange world. The Umatilla Reservation, a self-governing nation within a nation: this should be a people filled with pride and purpose. Yet, from what she'd observed today—the derelict properties, a glitzy casino—these people seemed slightly lost.

As she drove away from the casino, she wondered if everyone related to the casino and its amenities was oblivious to the fact that they were located on a sovereign land—a place of natural beauty, grace, history, and value. Or perhaps these people were simply in some form of dark denial. Sunny thought about her grandmother. She had lived in her own form of denial, as if she'd never been a part of this reservation and had no real ties to the Native American community or culture. As unsettling as it was to realize, in some ways, her grandmother wasn't a whole lot different than this casino.

Chapter Eleven

....

"Hey, you made it," Echo called out happily to Sunny. She waved as she turned Sylvester, trotting him across the arena. "Aunt Aubrey said you were looking for relatives over on the reservation. Find any?"

Sunny shook her head. "No. I think your dad was right."

"Right about what?" Echo dismounted her horse.

"He thought it would be helpful for him to introduce me to some of his friends—to make some connections within the tribe."

"Yeah, that makes sense." Echo tipped her head toward the horse barn. "So do you want me to help you saddle up Brownie Anne?"

"I'd love to ride. If you have time."

Echo looked at her watch. "It's only four. Dad doesn't usually get here until after five."

"And this time, I want to try to do as much as I can for myself," Sunny said as they met by the tack room. "That way I'll really learn."

"You got it. I'll just coach from the sidelines."

With a few helpful tips and reminders, Sunny soon had Brownie Anne all saddled and cinched and trotting around the arena. Echo continued to coach Sunny as she rode, but mostly only with words of encouragement. After fifteen minutes, they took the horses back out into the field, riding over to the creek again.

"How did you like the movie last night?" Echo asked as they dismounted to give their horses a drink.

"It was really good."

"But it's kind of sad too."

Sunny was surprised at the young girl's sensitivity. "Yes. Did you think that?"

Echo nodded. "It's hard to hear about how hard things used to be for Indians—I mean, *Native Americans*."

"I know your dad uses the term *Native American*," Sunny began, "but you and your grandparents and your aunt say *Indian*. I'm curious how you feel about those words. Do they even matter?"

"I grew up hearing the word *Indian* all the time, so it seems normal to me. And lots of Indians—or Native Americans—call themselves and each other Indians too. It's not like it's offensive to anyone. Not really. Maybe some people don't like that word. I know Dad has to say *Native American* because of his job, but when he lets his guard down, he says *Indian*."

"I get that." Sunny nodded. "But in college, we were taught that it's more culturally correct to say *Native American*. In real life…well, I'm starting to question it myself. I feel a little odd saying *Native American* when everyone else just says *Indian*."

"Yeah, it sounds a little weird to me. Kind of formal—or like you're from someplace else."

Sunny smiled. "I am from someplace else."

"I know. But around here, you can just say *Indian* if you want to."

"I'll try to remember that."

"You know, the name I really don't like is *half-breed*."

"I don't like that one, either."

"I know I'm only part Native American, but some of my full-blooded Indian friends call me *half-breed* sometimes. I act like I don't care, but it hurts my feelings. I don't think they're trying to be mean, but it makes me feel like an outsider. Like I'm not as good as them because I'm not all Indian. It's like they want to remind me that I'm different sometimes...like I don't fit in."

"I know what you mean. Not that I've been called *half-breed*, but the part about not fitting in—I've felt that way most of my life. However, I don't think it has much to do with my...uh, my Indian roots. I think I was just a misfit." Sunny half smiled.

"Me too!" Echo nodded vigorously. "It's weird, though, because my other friends—you know, my white friends—don't really seem to care about it one way or another. None of them have ever put me down for being part Indian. Not really. But maybe it's because I don't really look like it."

"So, are you saying your Indian friends put you down?"

Echo's brow creased thoughtfully. "No, it's not like that. It's more like they set me apart...like they don't totally relate to me. And they're not always like that. I have some great Indian friends too. I'm probably making it sound like a bigger deal than it is. Maybe it's because I feel jealous sometimes."

"Jealous?"

"That I'm not full-blooded Indian like them."

"Oh."

"Anyway, Dad's probably here by now. We better get moving."

And, just like that, they were back on their horses, with the solidity of Brownie Anne beneath her, galloping after Echo and Sylvester, gracefully moving along the fence line of the wheat field. Once again, Sunny felt that sensation—complete freedom, almost like flying.

Cody was waiting for Echo in the stables. But instead of pointing out that she was running late, he simply helped both her and Sunny remove the saddles and feed the horses, casually chatting with them in a friendly way that put Sunny at ease.

"I'm sorry for keeping Echo out late again," Sunny apologized as they stood outside the house while Echo ran in to get her backpack and tell her grandmother good-bye.

"No problem," he said easily. "I'm really glad that Echo likes to ride—and grateful that her grandparents are around to encourage her. The only reason I try to keep her to a schedule is so we can get home in time to have dinner with my dad."

"Your dad lives with you?"

"Not in the same house." He adjusted the brim of his cowboy hat to deflect the late afternoon sunrays. "He has a singlewide parked on the property"—he chuckled—"because he likes his privacy and his pipe. But we try to keep regular mealtimes with him when we can because he has diabetes."

"Oh…"

"And he doesn't always think about his health." Cody smiled. "He's kind of an old-school cowboy…you know, the tough Marlborough man who wants to die in the saddle."

"So does he still ride?"

"Just his John Deere."

"He sounds like a character."

"Oh yeah, he is."

"Hey, I wonder if he'd know anything about my relatives."

"Would you like to talk to him?"

"Sure—if you think he wouldn't mind." She smiled sheepishly. "By the way, you were right. I struck out on gathering information on the reservation today. It was mostly useless."

"Well, maybe you should talk to my dad."

Echo came out of the house now. "Okay, I'm ready."

"Do you think your dad would really be willing to talk to me?" Sunny said to Cody. "Would you ask him?"

"Why don't you ask him yourself?"

Sunny wasn't sure if that was a challenge or an invitation and so she just waited.

"You're going to talk to my grandpa?" Echo asked.

"Maybe," Sunny said with uncertainty.

"Hey, why don't you come over for dinner tonight?" Echo said eagerly.

"Oh, no, I didn't mean—"

"Come on, Sunny," Echo urged. "It's okay, isn't it, Dad?"

"Sure, if Sunny wants to come." He grinned. "That is, if she likes *elk stew.*"

"Elk stew?" Sunny wasn't sure if he was teasing or not.

"Yeah," Echo said, "it's really good."

"Elk stew." She studied them both and decided, whether this was a dare or a joke, she was going to take them up on it. "Okay then, fine. I've never tasted elk anything before. If you really have elk stew, I'm game."

He laughed. "Was that a pun?"

She smiled. "Maybe so."

"Give us about thirty minutes to get our act together," Cody told her as he pulled out a business card and wrote on the back. "Here are the directions. It's pretty simple."

"Cool!" Echo looked pleased. "I'll use the good dishes."

As they got into Cody's pickup and drove away, Sunny stood there wondering what she was getting herself into. She went to the bunkhouse to see if Aubrey was around, but not finding her, decided to check in the house. Plus, she needed to let Cindy know that she wouldn't be here for dinner.

"Hey, there," Cindy called out as Sunny came into the kitchen. "Did you have a good ride with Echo?"

"I did." Sunny nodded. "And I'm falling in love with Brownie Anne."

Cindy smiled. "Brownie Anne's a sweetheart. She used to be my horse."

"Used to be?"

"I hurt my back when the kids were teenagers. I haven't ridden in years."

"Oh."

"Aubrey just called. She's meeting some of her friends at the Rainbow for drinks. She said for you to call her if you want to meet up with them. Otherwise you're welcome to join Doug and me."

"Actually, Echo and Cody invited me for *elk stew* tonight." Sunny's mouth twisted to one side. "I, uh, I've never had elk before."

"Oh, it's really good when it's cooked right. And Cody makes a mean pot of elk stew."

"Cody thought I could talk to his father—to see if he knows or remembers anyone or anything about my family. Maybe point me in a direction for talking to some others."

Cindy nodded. "That's a good idea. Take it from me: Hank Barrett can talk the hind leg off of a mule. I'm sure he has lots of interesting stories to share."

Sunny looked down at her dusty jeans. "I suppose I should go clean up then."

"Have a nice evening," Cindy called.

"Thanks. You too."

As Sunny walked back to the bunkhouse, she suspected that Cindy was relieved not to have company for dinner tonight. So maybe this was a good plan all the way around. Still, she felt nervous as she cleaned up. Social interaction and small talk had never been her strengths. Oh, she had gotten by in the academic world by talking about her studies and subjects of interest to her. But it was always a challenge to engage in a purely social way. She knew this had to do with her upbringing. Grandmother had never engaged socially with anyone. Even though she went to church, taking Sunny along with her, her friendships there were all rather superficial. For the most part, at least as far as Sunny knew, her grandmother had been a hermit. And Sunny was a fair ways down that same road, following in her footsteps.

Sunny decided to wear one of the shirts she'd purchased at Hamley & Co. today. It was a vintage-style shirt, red cotton with ornate black stitching, and the salesgirl had gone on and on about how great it had looked on her. It was a lot flashier than the kind of clothes Sunny was accustomed to, and she hoped the shirt's flamboyance might rub off on her social skills tonight. Also, it looked great with her Old Gringo boots and buckskin jacket. For whatever reason, she wanted to make a favorable impression on Cody's father.

Before she left, she decided to take her box of memorabilia with her, slipping it into her oversized purse and zipping it closed. Not that she planned to mention any connection to Jackson Sundown. But perhaps she might show Cody's father the few bits and pieces she had that were related to her grandmother's family. Just in case. Sunny went over the directions Cody had penned on the back of his card. They did seem straightforward, but as she got into the car, Sunny wished her cell phone wasn't dead. And, not for the first time today, Sunny felt slightly hopeless, like she was on a fool's errand. But this time, she decided to ask for help. So sitting there in her car with the sky starting to glow red with the sunset, Sunny bowed her head to pray.

"Dear God, please help me. If I'm supposed to find my family connections, help me to do so. And if I'm not, help me to be satisfied with how things are. Amen."

Then, feeling as if a bit of her burden had been lifted, Sunny drove east toward the reservation, admiring the pink rays of light on the golden wheat fields, contrasting against the dark blue sky in the distance. This really was amazing country—big, open, vast. A girl could get lost out here.

Fortunately, and thanks to Cody's clear directions, she didn't get lost. And the drive took less than ten minutes. She had barely pulled into the driveway when Echo and a black and white dog came bounding out toward her car.

"You made it," Echo said as Sunny got out of the car.

"Yes." Sunny waited as the dog circled around her. "And who is this?"

"This is Lady. Sit." Echo pointed her finger down and the dog obeyed, sitting with tail wagging.

"Lady"—Sunny reached down to pet the dog's head—"what a good girl you are."

"Grandpa put on a tie," Echo told her as they walked toward a ranch house.

"Oh?"

"Yeah. He only puts on ties for weddings or funerals, so you should feel special."

Sunny laughed.

"Just don't say anything about it."

"No, of course not."

"Welcome," Cody said as they came into the house. He wore a black-and-white checkered apron and a big grin. "Although it looks like the welcoming committee already met you."

"And your directions were perfect," she told him.

Now a white-haired man stepped forward. He was a few inches shorter than Cody and, indeed, was wearing a white western shirt, leather string tie, and silver bolo. "Sunny Westcott, I'd like to introduce you to my father, Hank Barrett."

The old man's brown eyes lit up as he took her hand. "Pleasure to meet you, Miss Westcott."

"Please, call me Sunny," she said as they shook.

"And you call me Hank."

"It's a deal."

"Now you two make yourselves comfortable in here while Echo and I put dinner on the table."

"You don't need any help?" Sunny offered.

"Nope. My assistant and I have everything under control."

"May I take your coat?" Hank offered.

"Yes." Sunny carefully removed the fringed jacket.

"This is a beauty," he said as he hung it in a coat closet by the front door. "It looks like it's been around for a while too."

"It has," she said. "It belonged to my grandmother, and I think it may have originated around here."

"I'm sure that's likely. My guess is, it was a man's coat originally."

"Really?"

He waved to the sofa for her to sit down. "Probably made by an Indian woman…for a man she regarded highly."

As Sunny sat down on the leather sofa, she wondered: Was it possible that her grandmother had made that jacket for a man? But, if so, who would that man have been? Certainly not the first husband—the one she had loathed. And why would Grandmother resort to old Native ways for her second husband, when she had so stringently buried all ties to her people? No, the most sensible answer was that it had belonged to, perhaps even been made by, her great-grandmother, Polly Wikiapi.

Hank sat in a chair adjacent to her, folding his hands in his lap and gazing intently at her. "Do you mind if I say that you are a beautiful woman, Sunny Westcott?"

Her cheeks grew warm. "No, of course not. Thank you."

He smiled. "Thank *you*."

She scanned the room. With its rustic furnishings and western décor, it reminded her of Aubrey's parents' home—only it had a cozier, more natural feeling. And, of course, it was smaller. "This is a nice room," she said, for lack of anything else to say.

"This is the house Cody grew up in," Hank told her. "Oh, it looked a lot different back then. Cody's mom liked colonial style furniture and lots of frills. I sort of let the place go after she died. Never did feel comfortable in here after she was gone. But Lenora and her mom redid everything when she and Cody got married. That's when I moved out to my little trailer." He chuckled. "My bachelor pad."

"Where you smoke your pipe?" she ventured.

His dark eyes twinkled with mischief. "So he told you about all my vices then?"

She smiled back. "No. Just the pipe. Do you have a lot of other ones?"

He cupped his hand by his mouth. "Just sneaking sweets sometimes," he whispered. "But don't you tell."

She shook her finger, but her smile remained. Really, he was quite the charmer.

"Cody tells me you want to find out about your family."

"If it's possible."

He frowned. "Don't recall anyone in these parts named Westcott."

"Oh, that was my grandfather's name. He wasn't from here." She reached for her purse now, removing the tin, as well as her great-grandmother's photo and the birth announcement. "My grandmother was born here." She handed both pieces to him. "Her mother is the one in the photo. Her name was Polly Wikiapi. I think she was around eighteen when it was taken."

He let out a low whistle. "Your grandmother's a beautiful woman too."

"No, that's my *great*-grandmother."

He flipped over the photograph, squinting to read the writing. "Polly Wikiapi, Pendleton Round-Up, 1911." He smiled and turned the photo back over. "That was quite a year for Round-Up history. Not that I was around way back then, but we've all heard the stories."

She nodded.

"I'll bet your great-grandmother, pretty Polly Wikiapi, had some good tales to tell. Chances are, she even met Jackson Sundown that year."

Sunny pressed her lips together and waited.

Hank was still studying the photo. "Yep. Chances are, a woman this pretty would've caught his eye for sure." Now he picked up the birth announcement, pausing to read it, then looking up at Sunny with a curious expression before moving his gaze back to the photo of Polly. "Your great-grandmother had a baby about nine months after this photo was taken, but there's no naming of a father in this newspaper clipping. Do you know the name of your great-grandfather?"

Sunny felt a rush of anxiety then. Why had she shown him these things? Why hadn't she known it would be like a runaway train? "Well, no," she said quickly, "I don't know the name of my great-grandfather. Truth is, my great-grandmother wasn't married when she had her baby. And my grandmother had a rather difficult life... thanks to a number of things."

His eyes softened with compassion. "This isn't a new story, Sunny. Unfortunately, it happens a lot amongst our people."

She forced a smile as she reached for the pieces. "I'm sure it's next to impossible to find out who my great-grandfather is," she said quietly. "But perhaps I can find out if there are other relatives. People by the name Wikiapi."

"I'm guessing Wikiapi was your great-grandmother's first name, Sunny."

"Oh. It's not a family name?"

"I don't know for sure, but I've never heard it."

"So it might not be that easy to trace my roots here after—"

"Dinner is served," Echo announced.

"We'll talk more later." Hank pulled himself stiffly to his feet, offering his hand to Sunny.

"Thank you."

"Right this way," Echo said in a formal tone. But then she led them past what looked like a dining room and on through the kitchen and finally out a door and onto a deck where a table and chairs were set up with a tablecloth, flowers, votive candles, and pretty dishes.

"Wow, this is beautiful," Sunny said.

"It was Echo's idea," Cody said. "We might want our coats, although I've got the firepot going to take the chill off."

"It's lovely," Sunny told Echo.

"Thanks." Echo smiled happily.

Once they were seated, Cody bowed his head and asked a blessing. The sincerity in his tone made Sunny think this was more than just a habit, more than just a show. Right then something in Sunny's heart clicked—almost like she could hear the sound, like a key turning in a lock. *Click.* And yet, as quickly as it happened, she dismissed it. *Pure emotion,* she told herself. *Who wouldn't be touched by such a homey, sweet setting?* It was like a scene from an old-fashioned movie.

"Don't be fooled by this elegant table," Cody said as he ladled out stew. "I think it was Echo's way of making up for our humble fare." He handed Sunny a bowl.

"And don't be fooled by Dad's humble speech," Echo said. "Everyone knows he makes the best elk stew on the reservation."

"His mama taught him well," Hank added as Cody handed him a bowl.

"And how do you have time to work and cook?" Sunny asked as Echo handed her a basket of what looked like freshly baked corn muffins.

"Oh, the stew's easy. I throw it all in the slow cooker in the morning and come home and it's done."

Hank chuckled. "He makes it sound easy, but I've attempted it a time or two and can assure you it's not that easy. Although I'm pretty sure his mama taught him a few tricks that she never told me."

Sunny waited until everyone was served, and only when Echo picked up her spoon did Sunny follow. It wasn't only good manners that made her wait, but apprehension as well. She had never eaten wild game of any kind. Cautiously, she dipped her spoon and saw that it contained a small piece of potato and meat. Bracing herself, she tasted it and was stunned at how good it was. "This is delicious," she told Cody.

"You look shocked."

She smiled. "I am a little surprised."

He just laughed. And then they all loosened up and Echo told them about a school play that she wanted to try out for and Hank started telling a story about when Cody was in junior high and got talked into being in a play. "I think it was Lenora who got you to agree, wasn't it?"

"Oh, Dad," Cody said, "you're not telling that old story, are you?"

Hank chuckled. "Poor Cody, he'd just gone through a growth spurt. I think he was about fourteen at the time and nearly six feet tall. It was a Shakespeare play, as I recall, and on opening night, Cody was doing something backstage when he tripped. The next thing we knew the whole castle scene fell down with a boom, and poor ol' Cody was sprawled across the top of it. Fortunately, no one was seriously injured."

"Except that my acting career was ruined." Cody winked at Echo. "Hopefully you'll redeem your old man if you decide to take up the theater."

Sunny felt a strange sense of belonging as she sat at the table with these three generations of people, almost as if she'd known them for years. Like they were old friends, or even family. The food, the crackling fire pit, the crisp night air, the candles, the laughter—all was delightful…and something she would store inside of her for a long time to come.

Chapter Twelve

....

Sunny begged to help clean up, but Cody and Echo wouldn't have it.

"You go talk to Grandpa," Echo insisted.

"That's right," Cody said. "This is supposed to be a research night for you."

"And, if you're not afraid to accompany me to my bachelor pad, I have some things I'd like to show you," Hank told her.

She exchanged a quick glance with Cody, but his nod assured her that this was perfectly acceptable. "I'm not afraid," she told Hank. "Lead the way."

Soon they were comfortably seated on his navy blue velvet couch. And while his living room may not have been as fashionable as the other house, it was equally comfortable. Hank opened the trunk that served as a coffee table and pulled out what looked to be a very old photo album.

"This was my mother's," he said as he placed it between them. "She was born a couple years before your grandmother, back in 1910. Her name was Bertha Hopping Crow, and I wouldn't be surprised if she knew some of your family. You say your grandmother was born in 1912. Did she live on the reservation for long?"

"Until she was eighteen. Then she married a man she barely knew. He was a white man and not a very good person, but she thought he was her ticket off the reservation."

"So she lived here until 1930." Hank flipped a page to where photos similar to the one of Polly were attached with dates ranging from 1910 to the 1930s. "Chances are, your grandmother knew some of these people."

"Or maybe she's in some of these photos." Sunny peered closely at one of the group photos of schoolchildren, straining her eyes and brain to see if she could spot her grandmother as a child.

"I have an old aunt," Hank told her after they gave up on the photo album. "Lulu is in her nineties and unable to walk much, but her mind is still fairly sharp. Would you like me to introduce you to her?"

"Yes, if you don't mind. I'd love to meet her."

"How does tomorrow sound?"

"Wonderful."

He smiled as he set the album on the trunk. "Heritage is a tricky thing, Sunny. A bit like a coyote."

She studied him. "Why do you say that?"

"Well, we want to know where we came from, but when we find out, we can be disappointed. Kind of like how a coyote can seem friendly almost like a dog, and then—just like that—he can turn on you."

Sunny slowly shook her head. "I don't mean to disagree, but I honestly doubt that anything I find out would be any more disenchanting than what I've lived with my entire life."

After some prodding, she told him a bit of her story—about being raised by a slightly paranoid old woman, being taught to be fearful, cautious, wary.

"Nobody's upbringing is perfect, Sunny."

"I'm not trying to say my grandmother did everything wrong. I know she loved me wholeheartedly, and I honestly don't know what I would've done if I'd been in her shoes. But I know I learned things from her that my parents would not have approved of. My parents were fearless. They embraced all cultures equally and celebrated differences. I'm sure they expected me to grow up doing the same." She gave a sad little laugh. "Ironically, I grew up in a fairly whitewashed, overly protected, homogenized, and somewhat fear-driven environment that did little to prepare me for real life."

"Yet here you are—a lovely, intelligent young woman. Your grandmother didn't do too badly."

"Thank you. But I think being here, in Pendleton and on the reservation, has already started changing me. Just riding horses with your granddaughter—well, it's like I'm someone else...someone I think I was supposed to be, but never knew how."

He nodded sagely. "It's clear your heritage is a good one, Sunny. And I think I know your secret."

"My secret?"

He smiled.

"What do you mean?"

"Your grandmother's name was Sunrise?"

"Yes. Mary Sunrise."

"And your name—Sunny—is that short for Sunrise too?"

"Yes."

"Sundown. Sunrise. A baby born nine months after Jackson Sundown becomes a legendary cowboy at the Pendleton Round-Up."

"But I don't really believe it," she said quickly. "Most of all, I just want to know the truth." She reached for her bag now, removing the old wooden box, opening it, handing it over to him. "My grand-mother kept this hidden from me. My father mentioned something about this connection before my parents died. But my grandmother vehemently denied it."

Hank was looking at the memorabilia now, nodding as if none of this surprised him in the least. And then he handed it back to her. "I've heard a story like this."

"Really?" Sunny's heart was starting to pound a little harder. "Then you think it's true?"

"True?" He smiled. "The only truth may be deep inside you."

Sunny thought about DNA now. Certainly that held the truth. Not that she could ever link it that far back.

"But remember, heritage is like a coyote."

She nodded. "Tricky."

Just then there was a knock on the door and Echo came in. "Okay," she said, "we have dessert at the house." She grinned at her grandfather. "And it's sugar-free."

He made a disappointed face.

"Come on, Grandpa." She reached for his hand. "It's really good. Blackberry cobbler with sugar-free ice cream. You'll like it."

"Hmm?" He smacked his lips. "Okay, honey, just don't keep going on about the sugar-free stuff and I'm on board."

Sunny was disappointed to end her conversation with Hank. He seemed to understand her situation better than anyone so far. But as they went into the house, she reminded herself that he was going to introduce her to his aunt tomorrow. Maybe that would turn over some stones.

"So did you have any luck with the old photo album?" Cody asked as they sat in the living room with their dessert.

"I saw some school photos that my grandmother might've been in," Sunny admitted. "They were the right years. But it was hard to pick out exactly which one might've been her. I've never seen a picture of her as a girl."

"It doesn't help that those old photos are pretty blurry," Cody added.

"So did you grow up with any family around you?" Echo asked her.

Sunny forced a smile. "Well, I had both my parents until I was ten. Those were happy times. After that, it was just my grandmother and me."

"And that was all?" Echo looked stunned. "No other grandparents, no aunts or uncles or cousins or anything?"

Sunny shook her head. "My grandfather was from the East Coast. My grandparents only had one child—my mom. My dad's family had problems, and he was raised in foster homes. He put himself through college, and we were his only family."

"Wow. That must've been hard."

"So you must have family here," Cody insisted. "Even if it's second or third cousins, it stands to reason that if your grandmother was born on the reservation, then she would have relatives here."

"I'm taking Sunny to meet Aunt Lulu tomorrow," Hank told them.

"Did you tell Sunny that Aunt Lulu is mean?"

"Mean?" Sunny glanced at Hank.

He shrugged. "Oh, sure, she's got a sharp tongue, but it matches her sharp mind. You don't make it to her age by being pushed around."

"Just make sure you take Aunt Lulu with a grain of salt," Cody warned. "And don't tell her I said so, but she can be a bit of a drama queen."

"She likes attention," Echo said, "and respect. If you don't show her respect, she might pinch you."

"She wouldn't pinch Sunny." Hank shook his finger at Echo. "Just naughty great-great nieces who sneak her lemon drops."

Echo grinned at Sunny. "Yeah, keep your hands off her lemon drops."

As much as she hated to go, Sunny knew it was getting late and Echo probably had homework. So she thanked them all for their generous hospitality, agreed to pick Hank up tomorrow at ten, and said good-bye. It wasn't until she was in her car and driving down the dark country road that she realized she wasn't too sure of where she was, and when she looked for Cody's business card with his directions, she couldn't find it anywhere in her purse or car.

She knew she should be able to figure this out. Just do the opposite of what she'd done to find the Barretts' house and she would find her way back to the Lowensteins'. But after twenty minutes, she was feeling not only lost, but desperate. Every road looked the same as the last, and the names all sounded unfamiliar. Not only that, but she felt like she was on the verge of a serious panic attack.

Finally, she pulled over to the shoulder of the road, and forcing herself to relax and to just breathe, she told herself to get in control. She could do this. Then she bowed her head and prayed for help. As she was praying, she saw a set of headlights behind her. A car pulled up and stopped. Suddenly she imagined the scene that Aubrey had suggested earlier today—a car full of drunken guys, out of control and wanting to be crazy. Or else this might be a good Samaritan stopping to offer help and give directions.

She peered in her rearview mirror to see that the car, which looked like an old junker, did appear to have a number of passengers. Just then a jolt of fear rushed through her. What was she doing here, out in the middle of nowhere, like a sitting duck? But as she stepped on the clutch, attempting to put her car into gear, she did something wrong and suddenly the engine went dead. She fumbled, but it was too late. Several of the people from the other car were approaching hers. Her head buzzing and her hands shaking, she tried to start the engine again.

Someone was knocking on her window now. Bracing herself, Sunny looked up, expecting to see a crazed face or even a club or a gun aimed at her head. Instead, she saw a smiling young Indian woman, along with a couple of others. Although her heart was still pounding, Sunny managed to put the window down a few inches and mutter a shaky "hello."

"Are you okay?" the young woman asked.

"Did you break down?" another girl asked.

"Actually, I'm lost," Sunny admitted. Then, feeling that these girls were trustworthy, she got out of her car and started to explain. "I lost my directions and got all turned around. And I have no idea where I am now."

"We're on our way home from dance class," the first girl explained. "But how about if we lead you back toward the casino junction? You can get on the freeway and head west from there. Do you think you can find your way then?"

"Yes, of course," Sunny said eagerly. "Thank you so much."

"I like your car," one of the girls told her.

"Thanks."

"So what are you doing here anyway?" the first girl asked curiously. "Visiting family?"

"Trying to *find* family," Sunny admitted. "My people are from here, but I've never really known any of them."

"What are their names?"

Sunny gave an uneasy smile. "That's the problem. I'm not really sure."

The girls thought this was funny and teased her a little, but it was good-natured. Then they realized they needed to get going. "Just follow me," the first girl told her. "When we get to the casino junction, you'll know where to go."

And so Sunny followed them, making several turns and traveling a few miles until, sure enough, there were the bright lights of the casino and all the other buildings. Sunny tooted her horn in thanks and the other car did a U-turn, heading back in the opposite direction. They really were just good Samaritans.

Even so, Sunny thought she might try to find a phone charging cord. Not because she was afraid of people on the reservation, but simply because it was the grown-up and responsible thing to do. Still, she looked forward to telling Aubrey this story. Maybe it would help to counterbalance some of the other stories she'd heard.

Chapter Thirteen

....

On Friday morning the sky was cloudless, and the day promised to be warm and summer-like. Aubrey and Sunny took their coffee outside, sitting on the porch of the bunkhouse. "How was your evening with friends last night?" Sunny asked.

"Really fun. We started out at the Rainbow."

"The Rainbow?"

"It's the oldest bar in Pendleton—a real cowboy hot spot. You should've joined us. It was really a kick."

"Thanks, but it was fun meeting Cody's dad. And Hank's going to introduce me to his elderly aunt this morning. It's possible she might know something about my family."

Aubrey let out a lazy yawn. "I just plan to veg with my friend Casey today. She's staying at her parents,' and they have a lovely pool that we used to practically live at during the summers in high school."

"Sounds fun." Sunny nodded like she could relate to this, but she couldn't. She'd never had friends like that. Chances were, outside of Aubrey, she never would. Sunny told Aubrey about getting lost last night, making it all sound as if it had been a delightful adventure.

"Weren't you scared?" Aubrey asked.

Sunny smiled. "Well, yes, but it all turned out okay." She glanced at her watch. "However, I will try to get a phone charger cord before I go driving around again. Your mom told me where I might find one, and they open at nine, so I should probably get going."

"Well, have a good day. And if you get tired of sniffing around the reservation and need to come cool off at Casey's pool, give me a call. She promised to make a pitcher of margaritas." Aubrey wrinkled up her nose. "She could probably make you a virgin one."

"Thanks." Sunny stood. "I'll keep that in mind."

By ten o'clock, with her new phone charger plugged into her car, Sunny pulled into the Barretts' driveway again. The ranch looked different in the light of day. The house and traditional-looking barn out back were both painted a brick red and trimmed in white, giving the place an old-fashioned feel. White post and rail fences looked crisp and neat against the green lawn that wrapped around the house. All in all, it was a sweet little ranch—and a stark contrast to a couple of the properties that Sunny had taken time to check out on her way here.

She pulled her car past the house and near where the singlewide trailer was parked behind a grove of poplar trees. As she got out, she heard the barking of a dog. "Hey, Lady," she said as the border collie streaked through the field toward her. "Where's Hank?" She bent down to pet the dog's head.

"I'm right here," he called out as he came around the corner from behind his trailer. "Just checking on the critters' water troughs. Looks like it's going to be a hot one today."

Sunny glanced up. "I heard the weatherman saying it might hit ninety."

"Then let's get moving." Hank grinned. "That your little car?"

"It's a hybrid."

"Hybrid? What's that? Some kind of a tomato?"

She laughed. "Something like that."

He removed his cowboy hat as he got into the passenger seat and looked around. "This one of those cars that runs on cooking oil?"

"Not exactly."

"You got plenty of fuel then?"

"I filled it with gas this morning."

"Can she take some rough roads?" he asked.

"How rough?"

"Oh, about a mile or so of gravel, then a dirt road with some ruts."

"I don't see why not."

It took about twenty minutes and some rough roads to make it to Aunt Lulu's place, which turned out to be a small cabin in the mountains. But once Sunny had parked the car and waited for the dust to settle, she thought the location alone was worth the trip. "This is so beautiful up here," she told Hank. "Are we still on the reservation?"

"On the east side."

But when several scruffy dogs charged out, barking wildly and baring their teeth, Sunny nearly leaped back inside the car.

"Get outta there," a man yelled from the shadows of the house. "Get on back!"

Sunny jumped, then looked at Hank and, seeing he was smiling and waving, decided not to run. "Hey there, Raymond," Hank called out. "How are you doing?"

A man about Hank's age emerged from the porch, yelling once more for the dogs to back off and actually pitching an old pot at them. It clattered loudly, making the dogs scatter in all directions.

"Hello, Hank!" The man came over and clasped hands now, smiling so broadly that his bronze face wrinkled up like an old road map. "Long time no see, cousin."

Hank put his hand on the other man's shoulder. "Raymond, I want you to meet a friend of mine." And then he introduced Sunny. "Raymond is my cousin."

"What are you doing way out here?" Raymond asked Hank.

"Hoping to see Aunt Lulu. I want her to meet Sunny."

Raymond looked curiously at Sunny, then nodded. "Mom's inside. Come on in and say hello."

As Sunny walked up to the house, she got the feeling—again—that she was in a foreign country. And while it was somewhat unsettling, it was also exciting. Inside the house, the light was dim. The air was musty and smelled of wood smoke and cooked food. As Sunny's eyes adjusted to the light, she saw that a tiny woman reclined on an old plaid sofa with a knitted afghan over her legs. Her thin white hair was pulled tightly back into a bun and a pair of dark framed glasses, combined with a hooked nose, gave her an owlish look.

"Aunt Lulu," Hank said respectfully, "I have brought a friend for you to meet." Then he introduced Sunny, saying that she had descended from a family on the reservation. "The trouble is, Sunny doesn't know any of her family names. But she does have some photos and things. We thought maybe you might know who her folks were."

"Come…sit." Aunt Lulu nodded to a straight-backed chair beside the sofa. "Tell me your story."

Sunny sat down and opened her purse, removing her wooden box. She held it nervously in her lap as she quickly recited what little family history she knew, finally handing Aunt Lulu the photo of her grandmother and the tiny newspaper clipping. Aunt Lulu's vision wasn't strong enough to read the faded words, so Sunny read both the caption on the back of the photo and the details of her grandmother's birth.

Aunt Lulu nodded. "Yes. I remember Polly Wikiapi."

"You do?" Sunny almost fell out of her chair. "You really do remember her?"

"Yes. She was my mother's age. But I do remember her." Aunt Lulu frowned at Sunny in a way that almost felt like disapproval.

"My grandmother was Polly Wikiapi's daughter. Her name was Mary Sunrise, and I think she was probably a little older than you. She died several years ago at the age of ninety-three."

"I knew Mary Sunrise too."

"You did?" Sunny couldn't believe her luck.

Aunt Lulu nodded again, but her expression remained solemn.

Sunny filled in more details. "My grandmother, Mary Sunrise, left the reservation when she was eighteen or nineteen, and she rarely spoke of her mother." She paused, studying the old woman's countenance. "I think she was ashamed...of her mother."

Aunt Lulu did not look surprised.

"And my grandmother gave me reason to believe that her mother was a very bad woman. A dishonorable woman. I think my grandmother wanted to push her mother's memories far away from her."

Aunt Lulu put a crooked forefinger to the side of her head now, slowly making circles as if to signify that Polly Wikiapi had some mental instabilities or worse.

"You believe she was crazy?" Sunny asked quietly.

"That's what people said."

Sunny glanced over at Hank now. He and Raymond were sitting at the kitchen table drinking coffee, but she could tell they were listening.

"You're saying that Polly Wikiapi was not in her right mind?" Hank asked his aunt.

"Maybe so."

"Oh." Sunny leaned back in the chair. In a way, she was shocked. In another way, she was not.

"Polly Wikiapi was too beautiful," Aunt Lulu said soberly.

"*Too* beautiful?" Sunny watched the old woman closely.

"Too much of anything is not good."

"Oh." Sunny tried to take this in. "And you think that made her crazy?"

"Maybe so."

"My grandmother said her mother was an alcoholic."

"Yes."

"You knew that too?"

Aunt Lulu shrugged. "Everyone knew. But there was more. Polly Wikiapi was different than other women—not like other mothers and aunts. She held herself high…looked down on others. Yet she did not care for her child. She did not respect her elders. She ran with men. Drank with men. She died young."

"Yes. I know."

Now Aunt Lulu looked closely at Sunny. "You are like her?"

"No," Sunny said suddenly. "I am nothing like her."

Aunt Lulu held up the photo, peering at it and then at Sunny as if skeptical. "Why are you here? Why do you want to know about Polly Wikiapi?"

"I want to understand my family," Sunny explained. "I went to college, and I got a degree in anthropology—" She paused, trying to think of a simple way to explain this concept more clearly. "That's the study of people and society. After my graduation, I taught anthropology to college students. Yet I never studied my *own* people." Even as she confessed this, she felt ashamed. Deeply ashamed.

The scowl on Aunt Lulu's wrinkled brown face intensified. "You teach the study of people? And you never studied your own people? How can you teach what you do not know?"

Sunny had no answer for that. In fact, she was on the verge of tears. Of course, Aunt Lulu was exactly right. Not only was this preposterous, it was arrogant and downright hypocritical. No wonder Sunny had lost her job. She had never deserved it in the first place.

"Aunt Lulu," Hank said gently, "education in the white man's world is different."

Aunt Lulu gave him an even darker look, full of disapproval. Sunny could imagine what the old woman was thinking—that the white man's education wasn't only different, it was foolish and worthless.

"Remember my boy, Cody," Hank continued without intimidation. "You know how he went to the university to learn how to help our people with their problems—problems with alcohol and illegal drugs. But Cody has never had a problem with alcohol or drugs. Yet he teaches classes and helps people get out of that destructive lifestyle and live a better life."

She seemed to consider this. Then she pointed her finger at Sunny. "Why did you not learn of your own people?"

How could she explain? Sunny wondered. "My grandmother left everything behind," she said. "Her shame was so deep that she pretended she had no family. She never spoke of it. She lived as a white woman with no past. She taught me to do the same."

Aunt Lulu nodded sadly, as if she understood but didn't approve.

"Because if you're right," Sunny said, "if Polly Wikiapi *was* crazy, it would be very painful for her child. I can understand why my grandmother would want to escape that kind of life."

"There were other mothers…other women who helped raise Mary Sunrise, including her grandmother."

"And I'm sure my grandmother was grateful to them. But for some reason, when she left the reservation, she left all her memories and everything else behind her."

Aunt Lulu sighed with a faraway look. "Some of our people leave."

"Like Myrtle," Raymond said quietly.

Aunt Lulu looked down at her hands.

"Myrtle is Aunt Lulu's youngest daughter," Hank told Sunny.

"She left too," Raymond supplied. "More than forty years she's been gone with no word, no letter, nothing."

"I'm sorry, Aunt Lulu," Sunny said gently. "That must hurt. And you seem like such a good woman. I don't know why your daughter would want to leave you."

Aunt Lulu picked up the photo of Polly again. Once more she held it up, comparing the image to Sunny. "Are you married?" she asked Sunny. "Do you have children?"

Sunny shook her head. "No. I've never been married. No children."

Aunt Lulu looked surprised now. "How old are you?"

"Thirty-six."

"And not married? No children? What is wrong?"

Sunny held up her hands with a forced smile. "I went to college, and I worked and took care of my grandmother in her elderly years. I guess I just didn't have time to marry and have children."

Aunt Lulu frowned. "You are very old, not to be married."

Growing more and more uncomfortable, Sunny decided to change the subject. "Did Polly Wikiapi have any brothers or sisters? Do you know if I have any relatives still living here on the reservation?"

Aunt Lulu's brow creased and her eyes closed, as if she were thinking hard. Finally, she said, "Yes. I remember an older brother and an older sister. I cannot remember their full names. The family name was Blue Crow, and also there were some Staffords. The sister married a Stafford. I don't know if you'll find any Blue Crows around, but there are still some Staffords."

"Pete Blue Crow was about my age," Raymond told Sunny. "But he never married. Lived a rough sort of life. He died about ten years ago."

"There's Bill and Ellie Stafford and their kids," Hank offered. "They don't live far from me. And they're a real nice family too. Tina Stafford was a Happy Canyon Pageant Princess a couple years back, and there's a son who's older and the youngest girl, Misty, is a friend of Echo's."

"And you think they might be relatives?" Sunny asked hopefully.

"More'n likely," Hank assured her.

Sunny reached over to take Aunt Lulu's hand now. "Thank you for remembering my family," she told her. "I really appreciate it."

Aunt Lulu looked deep into her eyes. "That is our job—to remember, to tell our stories, to teach the young people to remember, so they can tell our stories to their children...so that we never forget."

"I promise you," Sunny swore, "I will learn my story. I'll even write it down."

Aunt Lulu tapped her chest. "Write it down inside you. And then tell it. Tell it to your children and your children's children so they never forget."

Sunny smiled. "Yes. I will do that too…if I get the chance to have children."

Aunt Lulu nodded. "You will have children. I can see it in your eyes."

Sunny squeezed the old woman's hand and thanked her again. Then she and Hank left.

"Your aunt Lulu is a sweetheart," Sunny told Hank as she drove down the dirt road away from the cabin.

He chuckled. "I think she must've liked you, Sunny. She was a lot nicer than I expected her to be."

"Even though she said some hard things, they weren't untrue."

"Aunt Lulu speaks the truth as she sees it. Sometimes it's not a complete truth." He took a deep breath. "What she said about your great-grandmother being crazy…I would do as Cody advised."

"What's that?"

"Take her words with a grain of salt."

"I don't know," she said thoughtfully. "It wouldn't surprise me if Polly Wikiapi *was* insane. In fact, it would explain my grandmother's deep aversion to her own mother. And it's no secret that alcoholism is often a form of self-treatment for other forms of mental illnesses or chemical imbalances."

"So would that be your explanation in regard to Jackson Sundown? Your reason for dismissing him as an ancestor?"

"I think it's feasible that Polly Wikiapi—in a delusional state of mind—may have thought that Sundown had fathered her baby."

"Does it make you more comfortable to believe that?"

"That theory helps to preserve Jackson Sundown's larger-than-life image—preserving the hero legend."

Hank slapped his thigh and laughed. "Well, that shows how much you don't know about cowboys or Indians, Sunny Girl."

"What do you mean?"

"I mean it takes all kinds. Just because a man is legendary and he can ride broncs and bulls and impress the fans, that doesn't warrant the man has morals or character."

"Yes, I'm aware of that."

Hank's silence suggested he doubted this.

"So are you suggesting Jackson Sundown was a cad?" she challenged.

"No, not at all. But, on the same token, I'm willing to bet he wasn't a saint, either. He was human, Sunny, a flesh-and-blood man. Surely you've heard the old story about graven images with feet of clay?"

"Of course. And I've done enough research to know that Sundown did some wild things in his time," she admitted. "But that doesn't prove he got my great-grandmother pregnant, then left her behind and married another woman."

"Aha," he said in a knowing tone. "So is that your secret fear? That maybe the legendary Jackson Sundown may have mistreated your great-grandmother? That he's not the hero you'd like him to be?"

Sunny didn't want to be insincere or dishonest with Hank or with herself, yet she hated to concede that he might've just hit the nail on the head. "I don't know for sure," she finally admitted. "I'd like to believe that I'm searching for the truth—that I'm not going to settle for anything less than truth."

"The truth." He nodded. "Well, I can't fault you for that, exceptin' the truth doesn't always reveal itself all at one sitting. Sometimes it's like digging a well, pulling out one bucketful of dirt at a time."

"Hoping that you eventually hit water." Even as she said this, she knew she'd be lucky to find her truth as easily as finding water. But maybe it was like that old saying: it was more about the journey than the destination.

Chapter Fourteen
....

It was close to noon when she turned onto the Barrett driveway, but Cody's pickup was already parked in front of his house.

"You got me home just in time," Hank told her as she stopped her car.

"Just in time?"

"Cody usually comes home for lunch," he explained. "Checking up on me, I suspect, although he says it's for other reasons."

"Oh." Sunny remembered about the diabetes now. "Well, thanks again for your help, Hank. Today meant a lot to me."

"Hey, you can't leave yet, Sunny."

"Why not?"

"Because I got to introduce you to your other relatives."

"But I—"

"No buts." He put on his cowboy hat and opened the door. "You come on into the house and have a bite of lunch, then we'll continue on our detective work."

"Detective work?"

He chuckled. "Oh, you'll have to excuse me. I like reading mystery books, and I suppose I'm pretending that we're out to solve the mystery of whether or not you're a descendant of Jackson Sundown. You'll have to humor an old man."

"I'll humor you as long as you don't go around bringing up Jackson Sundown, Hank."

"I didn't say a single word to Aunt Lulu," he said defensively. "You saw that. She already knew the story."

"Yes, but she's very old. And I think she doubted the story right along with my great-grandmother's sanity."

"Maybe so." He nodded. "Now, are you going to come on into the house, or are you going to make me sit here until Cody comes out to fetch me? He gets a mite bit grumpy when I'm late for lunch."

"But I don't want to intrude."

"Then I reckon you didn't notice that big old pot of elk stew last night. My best guess is that's what we're having for lunch. Leftovers." He smacked his lips. "But if you thought it was tasty last night, I can promise you it'll be even better today."

Cody was out on the porch now, waving at them. Sunny put down her window and waved back.

"You guys better get yourselves in here before the stew gets cold," he called out.

"See," Hank said with satisfaction. "You should've listened to me in the first place."

Still feeling like an intruder, Sunny followed Hank into the house where, sure enough, she could smell food cooking. "I really didn't mean to invite myself to lunch," she told Cody as she joined him in the kitchen.

"You didn't invite yourself," he said. "I invited you."

"I invited her first," Hank declared.

"But I had dinner with you last night, and here I am again today. You'll think that I'm trying to move in on you." Of course, no sooner had she said this than she realized how wrong it sounded.

But Cody just laughed.

"Well, after the way Aunt Lulu took to you this morning, I'm thinking maybe you are one of the family."

"Aunt Lulu liked you?" Cody asked as he filled a bowl with stew and handed it to Sunny.

"She took right to her," Hank answered as Sunny set the bowl on the table and went back to get the next one.

"She knew both my great-grandmother and my grandmother," Sunny said as she took the next bowl. "Do you think it's possible that I am related to you?" she eagerly asked Hank. "Is it possible that your mother is related to my family? Didn't you say her last name was something Crow and my family name was Blue Crow?" She grinned at Cody. "Maybe we're long-lost cousins."

He appeared thoughtful, then frowned as if it weren't too likely.

"I felt such a kinship with Echo when I first met her," Sunny said with enthusiasm. "Like she could've been a relative."

Hank chuckled. "Well, if you go back far enough, we're all related. But didn't you say your great-grandmother was Cayuse?"

"Yes." Sunny waited.

"My mother was Umatilla."

"But didn't they ever mix? I mean Jackson Sundown was Nez Percé and—" Sunny stopped herself, glancing over at Cody, who was getting down water glasses. "Well, I remember reading that he married someone from another tribe." She went over to help fill the water glasses.

"You're right. There is intermarrying amongst tribes. But from what I can remember, my mother was mostly Umatilla, maybe some Walla Walla."

"Sounds like we're not cousins," Cody said as they carried the water glasses to the table.

When they were all seated, Cody said a quick blessing, then encouraged his father to start eating.

"Cody is like a mother hen," Hank said as he stuck his spoon in his stew. "But lucky for me, he can cook like a mother hen too."

"Hens can cook?" Cody questioned him.

"You know what I mean."

"Dad's a good cook too," Cody told Sunny. "You should taste his barbecued salmon sometime. He's got this killer huckleberry glaze, and he won't give out the recipe to anyone."

"I'll teach it to Echo someday," Hank said with his mouth full.

"That's a relief." Cody winked at Sunny. "In case he kicks the bucket, you know. Might be nice to keep it in the family."

Hank laughed.

"It's possible that some of your neighbors are my relatives," Sunny told Cody.

"That's right," Hank added. "The Staffords might be related."

"Nice folks." Cody reached for a corn muffin. "Misty is a good friend of Echo's. They're less than a mile down the road from us."

"I'm going to take Sunny over after we finish up lunch," Hank explained, "to see if Ellie's home and if she wants to visit a bit."

Cody nodded, but Sunny could see concern in his eyes as he glanced at his father. Was he worried that Hank was overdoing it? Or was it something even more?

"Do you think we should wait until tomorrow to visit the Staffords?" she asked Hank. "Today's been pretty full already. And maybe Mrs. Stafford would prefer if we phoned ahead rather than just showing up."

"Oh, I doubt that Ellie would mind—"

"I have an idea," Cody interrupted. "How about if I take Sunny with me to Crow's Shadow after lunch. She might be interested to see what they're doing over there. In the meantime, you give Ellie a call, have a little rest, and then when we get back, you and Sunny can head over to Staffords'."

Hank frowned, then nodded. "Yeah, I reckon that's a good plan."

So, after lunch, Cody went to check on a horse with colic, Hank went over to his house, and Sunny cleaned up the lunch things. She wasn't trying to snoop, but she could tell that it was a fairly well-organized kitchen and suspected this was Lorena's doing. And, not for the first time, she was curious about this woman. Curious beyond the pretty smiling girl in the rodeo photos. Who had she really been? What had she really been like? Not that it was any of Sunny's business, but she just wanted to know.

"Hey, thanks for cleaning up in here," Cody said as he washed his hands in the sink. "Good ol' Joker is looking as good as new."

"Is that the sick horse?"

"Yeah. I've had him since high school. And I should've known better than to let him out on a green field. He's always been a greedy eater and prone to colic. Fortunately, he's resilient. But I still need to be careful. The old guy is in his twenties."

"Is that old for a horse?"

"Pretty old." He wiped his hands on the towel and looked at her. "Hope you didn't mind me running interference on my dad. It's just that he's kind of like Joker. He gets going and forgets his age…and that he needs to pace himself. I could tell he was tired, so I kind of jumped in."

"Oh, no, that's fine. I wondered if that was the problem." She glanced at her watch. "And, really, don't feel like you need to baby-sit me. I'll be fine on my own. I can come back in a few hours and—"

"I'm not baby-sitting you." Cody grinned. "I just thought I could show you around the reservation a bit—something beyond the casino, hotel, and golf course."

"Yes, I already saw those."

"Did you make it to Tamástslikt yet?"

"No, what's that?"

"Our cultural center. It's near the casino, but it's tucked way back so you might've missed it."

"Yes, I'm sure I did."

"And there's Crow's Shadow, our art center. They have a great print exhibit going on right now. Then I thought I could direct you to our radio station, KCUW. I won't have time to do much more than point these things out because I teach a class at Yellow Hawk at two. But if you don't want my help—"

"No, I'd love to see some things and possibly meet some people. I just hate feeling that I'm putting you out. You and your dad and Echo—you've all been so nice to me. I don't want to take advantage of your hospitality."

He laughed as he reached for his hat. "Hey, we Barretts are a tough bunch. You can be sure we'd tell you where to get off, if we thought you were taking advantage of us."

"Oh, okay." She nodded and reached for her purse.

"Maybe we happen to like your company."

She smiled. "Thanks. You've made me feel really welcome and at home…almost like family."

"You haven't had too much of that in your life, have you?" He opened the front door, waiting for her to go out.

"Not too much."

"Must've been hard."

She shrugged. "I don't know. It almost seems harder now—like I'm suddenly discovering all I've missed out on. I was so used to my quiet, little, controlled urban life...just my grandmother and me. I suppose it's true that ignorance is bliss. Then you wake up." She glanced at his pickup. "Maybe I should follow you since you have your work to do and all."

He nodded. "Good idea. How about if we go to Yellow Hawk first? We can leave your car there. Then I'll take you around so you can get the lay of the land. When it's time for my class, we'll come back for your car."

She followed him to a complex of yellow buildings, parked her car next to his, and got out.

"This, as you can see, is Yellow Hawk." He pointed to the biggest building. "The clinic and classrooms and social services offices are in there, and that's where I spend most of my time, either doing counseling or diversion classes, unless I'm off-site doing home visitations or probation hearings." He pointed another direction. "That's the day care center and Head Start classroom. Over there is where we have community classes like the one Dad goes to for controlling his diabetes."

"That's great to have all those services available," Sunny told him.

He glanced at his watch. "Now, if you want to ride with me, I'll take you to the other spots you might like to visit."

She locked her car and got into the pickup. "Thanks, Cody. I really appreciate you taking this time for me."

He turned and grinned. "My pleasure."

Warmth rushed up her neck, flushing her cheeks. What was it about this guy that got to her? Maybe it was simply the romantic combination of being in the company of an attractive gentleman while in the land of her ancestors. Anyway, that was what she told herself as he drove. Still, she wondered.

"Over there"—he pointed to his right—"is a fairly new housing development."

She glanced over to see what looked like a nice neighborhood, especially compared to some of the other areas she'd seen on her first trip through the reservation. But this one had attractive two-story homes, trees, paved streets, landscaping. Really, it wasn't much different from the newer developments she'd noticed popping up in some of the Portland area suburbs.

She took in the landscape as he drove away from the populated part of the reservation. Graceful golden hills, dry grasses swaying in the wind, an occasional tree, and always the wide open skies. "I feel so strangely at home out here," she told him. "As if a part of me is a part of this land."

"That's how I've always felt too."

"That makes sense, because you grew up here. But with me, it seems odd. I mean, since this is my first time here."

"I believe God made us with special gifts." Cody paused to glance at her. "It probably sounds weird, but I think we have a lot of hidden senses that most people never tap into. Kind of an extrasensory perception or sixth sense, but even more so. Maybe that's why you feel the familiarity of this land—because of your ancestors."

Sunny nodded eagerly. "I believe that too. Like intuitions that are unexplainable, but turn out to be correct."

"It might be God's way to communicate with our spirits—to lead us to places where we might not otherwise go."

"Yes. I think you're right."

Cody turned off of the main road now. "And this is Saint Andrew's Mission," he told her. "It was established around 150 years ago."

"Really? That long ago?"

"Yes. It was a Catholic mission." He pointed to a pale stucco building that looked like it could've been built in the Southwest. "The goal of the mission evolved over the years, but back in the early part of the past century, it housed a school where Native Americans were boarded and educated in the hope that they would assimilate into white culture. Of course, the assimilation program was initiated by the government, and when the church cooperated, they received federal aid to run the school."

"Oh." Sunny frowned. "I've read about government assimilation programs. A lot of heartaches resulted."

He just nodded. "Crow's Shadow is housed in that building now. I encourage you to come back here and take some time to look around. I checked the schedule, and there should be a moccasin-making class going on here later this afternoon."

"That sounds interesting."

He turned the pickup around now, heading back out. "That's the church," he said as he pointed to a tall building. "The stained-glass windows in there are worth seeing too. They depict biblical stories with Native American characters."

"I'll be sure to take a look."

He pointed to a small cemetery now. "The old graveyard might interest you as well. It's one of several, and most people on the reservation can find a relative's name here or there."

They drove around for about thirty more minutes while Cody pointed out the radio station, the museum, and several other places of interest. Then it was time for him to return to Yellow Hawk for his diversion class.

"Thanks so much for showing me around," she told him as he parked. "I feel like I can find my way now."

He pulled out his business card. "Feel free to call if you have more questions or need any help. Or just call my dad. I'll jot his number on the back for you." He grinned as he handed her the card. "I think he's got a crush on you anyway."

She laughed as she got out of the pickup. "Your dad is a real sweetheart."

"You take care now." He reached for a tooled leather briefcase. "And just because you feel at home on the reservation doesn't mean that it's perfectly safe here. I'm not trying to scare you, Sunny, but you need to be as street smart here as you are in Portland." He looked into her eyes. "Does that make sense?"

"Yes." She nodded. "I'll keep that in mind."

Then they said good-bye, she got into her car, and drove back to Saint Andrew's Mission.

Chapter Fifteen

....

Sunny parked her car in front of the stucco building at Saint Andrew's Mission, then got out and walked around to look at the architecture. The building appeared to be fairly old and in some disrepair, but the marker by one of the front entrances was dated 1931.

"Hello?" called a woman's voice. "Are you here for the moccasin class?"

Sunny turned to see an older woman waving from the side of the building. "Mostly I just wanted to look around Crow's Shadow. I heard there's a good print exhibit to see."

"Come this way," the woman called as she disappeared around the back side of the building.

Sunny walked on around to where several cars were parked in back. An open door led into what appeared to be a gallery with pale hardwood floors and white walls, where a number of attractive Native prints were displayed.

"The class is back here," the woman called as she went into another room. "Come on in if you like."

Sunny thanked her, then took some time to examine the prints. Again, she got that feeling—like she was connecting to this artwork in a way that was unexplainable but very real. She studied the names of the artists, but none of them sounded familiar. Finally, lured by the quiet voices of women, she went into what looked like a craft room to see five older women intently working with leather and beads.

"Are you here for the class?" a different woman asked.

"No, she's just looking at the prints," the first woman answered for her.

"You don't want to make moccasins?" another woman asked.

"She's not here for that."

Sunny came closer to the first woman now, looking over her shoulder as she laid out some cut pieces of leather with beadwork on them. "That's very pretty," she said as she studied the flower design. "I have a really old buckskin jacket with some interesting beadwork on it."

"Was it in your family?"

"I believe so. I'm not totally sure. But I do think it's quite old. Maybe even a hundred years old."

The oldest woman nodded with interest. "You don't look familiar. Are you new?"

Sunny introduced herself, explaining that this was her first time to visit the reservation. "But my grandmother was born here. She left back in the thirties."

"My mother left back in the thirties too," the oldest woman said. "Left me with my aunt. She raised me."

"What was your mother's name?" another woman asked.

"Polly Wikiapi Blue Crow."

And although none of them were old enough to know her, they were soon telling her about other people somehow connected with the Blue Crow family and how they were either friends or relatives. "I think my cousin's daughter married a Blue Crow…unless it was a Yellow Crow, but he turned out to be no good. Left her with three little kids."

"You mean Tulip?" another said with a creased brow. "My daughter can't stand that woman. You know Tulip is Walla Walla. Mimi told me Tulip would drive any man to run off."

"So does everyone know *everyone* on the reservation?" Sunny asked.

They all nodded as if this were a given and not the least bit unusual. And then they began talking about what must've been the most recent scandal—a young man who'd been involved with two girls at the same time—and now both girls were pregnant.

"Starla should've known better than to trust that boy," Mimi's mother said. "I would've thought she was too smart to fall for his tricks."

"Starla is just like her mother," another said as if this explained everything.

And with the chattering gossip of these old women ringing in her ears, Sunny quietly said good-bye and went back outside to where the sun was shining brightly. She remembered what Cody had said about looking in the church, so she went inside to see that he was right—the stained-glass windows were remarkable and well worth seeing. She recognized the familiar Bible characters and scenes from years of going to the Presbyterian Church with her grandmother. But seeing the traditional pale-faced figures replaced with Native Americans seemed to make the stories come to life and make more sense. And, really, she decided as she finally left, the Native American features were probably more like the Middle Eastern ones anyway.

Next she went to the little cemetery. Walking around, she read the names and dates and was surprised at how far back some of them went. But the most surprising thing of all was when she found a gravestone with the name POLLY WIKIAPI and dates 1895–1924. Sunny knelt down and put her hand on the stone, which, despite the hot sun, remained cool. Because of the dates, she knew this had to be her great-grandmother's grave. Yet it made no sense that Polly Wikiapi, someone who'd been portrayed as a crazy, alcoholic, wild woman, was buried in a Catholic cemetery. Sunny whispered a quiet prayer just then for her great-grandmother…and for herself. Then she merely stood there and wondered. What did it mean?

* * * * *

"I think I'm feeling a little overwhelmed," Sunny admitted to Hank as the two of them sat sipping lemonade in the shade of the locust trees. She'd just told him about finding her great-grandmother's grave and how it made no sense.

"Not surprising. It's a lot to take in."

"Going from knowing next to nothing about my culture and my ancestors and this whole place, then trying to absorb so much in one day."

"I can understand how you feel."

Sunny appreciated his sympathy, but how could he possibly understand? "It's different for you. You've had this and been here all your life—"

"Hold on a minute," he told her. "What are you insinuating?"

She blinked. "Well, just that you've lived here your whole life and—"

"See, there you go again." He shook his finger at her. "Making assumptions. Have you ever heard about that definition of the *assume* word?"

She forced a smile. "Yes, but what is it you think I'm assuming?"

"That I grew up right here on the reservation."

"You didn't?"

"Nope." He held his chin up.

"Oh?"

"You know that my mother was Umatilla and that my dad was white. But I guess you didn't know that the whole time I was growing up, my parents lived *off* the reservation. I was a town kid."

"I didn't realize—"

"I know. You assumed."

She nodded. "Sorry about that."

"Funny thing is, I grew up much like you did, Sunny. We lived in town and, for the most part, I was fairly ignorant about my Indian roots. My mother had some of the Indian looks, like her big dark eyes. But she wore her hair short, always got her permanents, and dressed white, acted white, and mostly passed for white. We were regular working-class folks. I went to public school, played sports, and like a lot of local boys, got interested in rodeo and farming. After high school, I enlisted in the navy, did two tours of duty, and saved up my money with the intention of getting my own place. When I got home and had the opportunity to get my hands on some farmland, the best deal just happened to be on the reservation. I bought a lease from a white guy who was getting too old to farm anymore."

"So you don't actually own this land?"

He shook his head. "It was a ninety-nine-year lease that he'd had for nearly fifty years, and I bought it from him. The lease actually expires in 2016."

"What happens then?"

"Hopefully Cody will get the chance to lease it back again or maybe even buy it."

"Get the chance?"

"It's up to the tribe."

"But you're part of the tribe," Sunny pointed out. "Don't you have a say?"

"Not about this particular piece of land. It originally belonged to some other family and when the lease expires, it returns back to them."

"Oh." She thought for a moment, trying to recall what they'd been talking about. "So you didn't move out to the reservation until you were an adult. Did you start connecting with members of your family then? I mean, the ones on the reservation?"

His eyes looked sad. "Not really."

"But you did know you were half Native American by then, didn't you?" She studied him closely as he sipped his lemonade.

"Oh, sure." He set his glass down. "I always knew I was a half-breed, but like I said, my folks never talked about it. And it wasn't until I was a grown man about Cody's age that I got to know anyone on my mom's side of the family."

"So how did that happen? When did you connect with your aunt Lulu and Raymond?"

"Well, when I first started working this farm, after the navy, my neighbors, like you, made their assumptions. They regarded me as a white man, a foreigner, and for a while I went along with it. Eventually, I married Helen. As you know, she was a white woman. I brought her out here, and together we built this house. After a while, Cody came along. For years, the three of us lived here like we had nothing to do with the Indians. Sometimes Helen and I would put the Indians down—but not to be mean. We just didn't like to hear about them drinking and carrying on and being irresponsible toward their families. I s'pose we thought we were better than them—some of them anyway."

"Did Cody know about his heritage?"

Hank let out a long sigh. "That's where we made our biggest mistake. For quite some time, Cody had no inkling he was a quarter Indian. Helen and I didn't think much of it. Truth be told, there are a lot of folks with Indian blood running through them who don't know about it. We figured, what did it matter? We were who we were. Didn't matter what you called us, did it? We were the Barretts—simple, hardworking people who tried to live according to the Good Book. Oh, sure, I drank a bit in my younger day, but not like some of them did. And Helen was a good Christian woman, a good wife and mother. Cody was a good boy, a good student, well liked in his class. So why should anyone care about anything beyond that?"

Sunny merely nodded, trying to take this in.

"But Cody was about twelve when he became friends with Larry Strong Horse."

"Was Larry an…an Indian?" She winced slightly to hear herself say the *I* word, but out of respect for Hank, and wanting to fit in, she was trying to work it into her vocabulary.

"Yep. And he and Cody really clicked. Both of them were big into horses and rodeo, and both of 'em as smart as whips. Real good boys."

"And you and your wife were okay with Cody being friends with a full-blooded Indian?"

"To be honest, Helen wasn't too sure at first. But I encouraged her to give it a chance. The more we got to know Larry, the more we knew he was a really good kid. And by then, times were changing. A lot of the Indians, including the Strong Horse family, were starting to take pride in their heritage. One day I was in town getting some feed and picking up Cody from school when I saw something that changed me. Changed me for good."

"What happened?"

"I had just pulled up at the junior high, 'round the back side, and noticed a small crowd of boys. I could tell they were up to no good. So I quietly walked up from behind and heard some of the boys calling Larry names—you know, the dirty Injun garbage…and worse. I was ready to step in and then I saw Cody standing by Larry—sticking up for his friend. Let me tell you, I couldn't have been prouder of my boy. Then the other kids started calling Cody an Injun lover and going after him. I could tell it was about to break into a fight, so I made my presence known and the kids scattered like scared rabbits. But right then and there, I knew it was time for me to speak out. So it was that night that I dug out my mother's old photo album and told Cody the truth."

"How did he take it?"

"At first he was pretty surprised. I was worried he was mad at us for keeping it from him because he went to bed without even talking much. But I think he needed to let it sink in. A few days later he was happy as a clam, and he and Larry were best friends again."

"Did it change things for him? With his friends or at school? Was he treated differently?"

"Not that I ever heard about. But I suppose you'd have to ask him."

"And what became of Larry? Are they still friends?"

"Larry enlisted in the army right out of high school, went through the whole ROTC program in college. and made it as an officer. Can't remember what his rank was, but it was impressive."

"Was?"

"He was one of the first casualties in Afghanistan. Left behind a widow and son."

"Oh." Sunny shook her head. "Sad."

"Yeah. It was hard on everyone."

"Do his widow and son live on the reservation?"

"Yeah. They'd been on an army base but moved back here after Larry's death. Trina works at Tamástslikt and Jackson is a year older than Echo. Cody made a promise to Larry the first time he went into active duty: that he'd help out if anything happened." Hank leaned forward and said softly, "Larry's mom and siblings are what you might describe as dysfunctional. Anyway, we consider Trina and Jackson as family."

"I'm sure they must appreciate it."

"You'll probably meet them if you stick around long enough. In fact, I know they'll be over here next week. We always have a little shindig the evening of opening day of Round-Up. That's next Wednesday. Would you like to come?"

"I wasn't sure if I'd stay for the rodeo."

"I thought you said you didn't have a job to go back to."

Sunny smiled. "Well, that's true."

"So why not stick around until Wednesday? For that matter, you should stay and enjoy the whole week of Round-Up. There's nothing quite like it anywhere else in the world. And remember what Aunt Lulu said about learning about your own people?"

"Yes." She nodded. "Okay, you talked me into it, Hank. I'll stick around for rodeo." She remembered the time now. "And if you'll excuse me, I was hoping to go ride with your granddaughter again."

"I know Echo would appreciate the company."

"Do you mind if I ask why she rides over there instead of over here?"

"After Lenora passed, Echo's grandma, Cindy, well, she got in a real bad place. So depressed she was hardly even getting out of bed. Echo seemed to be the only one to pull her out of that slump. It just made sense to let her spend more time there. Plus Lowenstein's got that great arena over there, and the school bus drops Echo right at their ranch, which is a shorter ride than out here. And Cody doesn't mind going over to pick her up at five. It's a good situation for every-one...for right now anyway."

"I know Cindy appreciates having Echo around."

"You probably already heard that Cindy and Doug are grooming Echo to be a Round-Up princess someday." His dark eyes twinkled. "As good as that little girl is on a horse, and as pretty as she is, well, it's not outside the realm of possibility either. It's one of the reasons I'm trying to watch out for my health these days. I want to be around to see our little girl wearing that crown."

Sunny had to bite her tongue. She didn't want to give Echo's secret away. And she suspected that if and when the time came, both Hank and Cody would be understanding and supportive of Echo's opinions. Or perhaps Echo might even change her mind by then. Whatever the case, it wasn't Sunny's place to intervene.

"Well..." Sunny stood. "I really should head on over there if I want to get in some riding time with her." Then she thanked him for the lemonade and left. As she drove back toward the Lowenstein ranch, she tried to make sense of her day. The truth was, she did feel overwhelmed. And even though she'd managed to learn a few things about her family, she was just as lost—maybe even more so—than ever.

Chapter Sixteen

....

Sunny was surprised to find both the corral and arena empty when she got there. And yet it was only 3:30. She walked over to the horse barn and glanced in to see what looked like a pair of boots sticking out from the shadows. Waiting for her eyes to adjust to the dim light, Sunny realized that the boots belonged to Echo. The girl was sitting on a bench with her head leaned back and her eyes closed.

"Are you okay?" Sunny asked quietly.

Echo jerked to attention, sitting up straight. "Sure."

"Oh." Sunny sat down on the bench next to her. "Not riding today?"

Echo shrugged.

"Is something wrong?"

"It's no big deal."

"Okay." Sunny suspected by Echo's creased brow that it was a bigger deal than she was showing. "I've had a weird day today myself."

"What happened?"

So Sunny told her about meeting Aunt Lulu and then finding her great-grandmother's grave. "But the weird thing is, I feel more lost and confused now than I did before I started looking. It's like I know I have these roots, this heritage, but I can't access them, and I don't know much of anything for sure. Like it's gone and buried and maybe I just need to let it go." She sighed. "Yet it makes me feel more cut off and, in a way, more lonely than ever."

"I know how you feel."

Sunny glanced over at Echo, noticing how sad the girl's eyes looked. "You feel lonely too?"

Echo nodded sadly.

Sunny reached over and placed her hand on Echo's shoulder. "Maybe you and I need each other. You sure you don't want to go riding?"

Echo brightened. "Yeah, let's saddle 'em up and go."

So they saddled up the horses and soon were riding along the fence line. Sunny was surprised at how much happier she felt—and free— like a load had been lifted from her. When they reached the creek, pausing to let the horses drink, Sunny smiled at Echo. "I can't believe how much I love to ride. I'm a different person when I'm on the back of a horse. My worries and troubles just disappear." She shook her head. "I can't even imagine how much I'll miss this when I go back home."

"Can you get a horse there?"

Sunny laughed to imagine a horse in her tiny backyard. "No, I don't think so."

Echo broke off a piece of dried grass and stuck it in her mouth. "You know why I'm feeling so bad?"

Sunny shook her head. "No, why?"

"Because my best friend kind of dumped me this week."

Sunny made a sad face. "Why?"

"I don't even know why. Kendra and I have been best friends since second grade. But now she's hanging with Hadley Epperson, who is totally boy crazy and dresses like she's in high school. Kendra won't even talk to me anymore. Like she's so much better than me now. I just don't get it."

"That's got to be hard."

Echo nodded with moist-looking eyes.

"Something like that happened to me in junior high too. It hurt a lot. I'm sorry."

"And Kendra and I had signed up to be in the Dress-Up Parade together. Now she says she doesn't even want to do it. She says it's lame."

"What's Dress-Up Parade?"

So Echo explained that tomorrow was the kick-off parade for Round-Up and that everyone dressed up however they liked and rode horses. Anyone could be in it. "It's really fun. I've done it every year since I can remember. I used to do it with my mom. When I was too little to ride a horse by myself, I rode with her. And then, after she got sick, I always rode with Kendra. Sometimes we were Indians. Last year we were rodeo clowns. We were going to be old-time cowgirls this year. I've got my outfit all ready and everything."

"That does sound like fun. Can't you do it anyway?"

"By myself?" Echo frowned.

"Maybe your dad could ride with you?"

"He's helping to do a float with some guys from the diversion program from Yellow Hawk."

"Oh. I'd offer to go with you, but I'm not really that good on a horse."

"You're better than Kendra."

"Really?"

"Yeah. She hardly ever rides anymore."

"But I don't have an outfit."

"You could wear your fringed jacket. That's old."

Sunny nodded. "I guess so."

"And I'll bet Grandma could help find some things. She's got all kinds of cool cowgirl stuff."

Part of Sunny felt like she was thirteen years old and she definitely wanted to participate in this parade. But another part of her felt like she was as old as her grandmother and she couldn't possibly be in a parade.

"Will you ride with me, Sunny?" Echo's eyes were hopeful.

"What if the horse acts up or tries to run away or something?"

Echo giggled. "Brownie Anne? Trust me, if there was ever a bombproof parade horse, it would be Brownie Anne."

"But you'd help me if I had a problem?"

"Of course. But you won't."

Sunny nodded. "You're right. I won't."

"So you'll do it?"

Sunny laughed. "Yes. I will."

Echo hugged her. "It'll be so cool. Let's go tell Grandma and see what she's got for you to dress up in." And just like that, they were back on their horses and galloping toward the horse barn. Once again, Sunny felt like she was thirteen years old. And it felt good!

* * * * *

"I can't tell you how glad I am that you're riding in the parade with Echo," Cindy quietly told Sunny. Echo had gone to look through her grandpa's things for the perfect old-fashioned cowboy hat and belt, while Cindy helped Sunny with an old split skirt that was a bit too large around the waist.

"I think it'll be fun," Sunny said as Cindy pinned the waistband.

"She was so brokenhearted that I got worried, thinking I'd have to ride with her, and goodness knows I haven't been on a horse in ages." Cindy chuckled. "I'm not so sure Echo would want to be seen in the parade with her old grandma by her side anyway. I wanted to strangle that smart-aleck little Kendra. When I think of all that we've done for her and, at the last minute, she pulls a stunt like this."

"I found some great stuff," Echo announced as she came in with an armload of things. Soon Sunny was standing in front of the mirror in the sewing room, dressed in what actually looked like a somewhat traditional old cowgirl's outfit. An oversized felt hat and a large red silk bandana completed the picture.

"Now I'll just take this skirt in and you'll be all set," Cindy told Sunny.

"Can I spend the night here?" Echo asked her grandma. "So I can help Grandpa load up the horses in the morning?"

"It's fine with me as long as your dad doesn't mind."

"Can I sleep in the bunkhouse with Aubrey and Sunny?" Echo asked hopefully.

"I don't see why not," Cindy told her as Sunny handed her back the skirt. "Unless Aubrey or Sunny have objections."

"I think that sounds like a great idea," Sunny told Echo. "It'll be like a slumber party."

Echo's eyes lit up. "Yeah, we can watch movies and have popcorn."

"Sounds fun."

"Now I think I'm jealous," Cindy told them.

"Why don't you join us?" Sunny suggested as she zipped her jeans.

"I would except that Doug and I have a dinner to go to tonight."

"Hello up there?" called a male voice.

"That's Dad." Echo was already out the door. "I'll go see if it's okay to spend the night. But I'll have to go home to get my stuff for the parade first."

Cindy's sewing machine was already whirring. "I really do appreciate you spending time with Echo, Sunny. I think this is just the ticket to help her forget about that silly Kendra."

"I remember…it wasn't easy being thirteen."

"You run along," Cindy said. "I'll have this skirt fixed up in no time."

Sunny thanked her, but before she could leave, Cindy let out a hoot of laughter.

"What is it?" Sunny asked.

"Oh, I just got to thinking that here I am helping Jackson Sundown's great-granddaughter to dress up like an old-fashioned cowgirl. Isn't that something! I only wish you'd let me tell my friends about it."

"Oh." Sunny wished there was an easy answer. "Well, I'm trying to search out my roots, but it's tricky. And the more I discover in regard to my great-grandmother, the more sure I am that I'll never really figure out whether there's any truth to the Jackson Sundown connection."

"I don't see why you're so worried about it, Sunny. Sometimes you simply have to go with something…have fun and enjoy the possibilities."

"Maybe so," Sunny murmured. But even as she said this, she knew she was only trying to be polite. Echo and Cody were both still in the living room when Sunny came down.

"Echo tells me you're going to ride in the parade with her tomorrow." Cody looked curiously at Sunny.

"She talked me into it," Sunny admitted. "I sure hope I don't mess it up. I'm not that experienced on a horse."

"All you do is stop and go," Echo pointed out. "And Brownie Anne will probably follow Sylvester's lead anyway. Besides that, I'll ask Grandma to make sure we're not placed around anything too noisy during the parade."

"Bill Stafford called me up about buying some hay this afternoon," Cody told Sunny.

"Bill Stafford?" Sunny tried to remember why that sounded familiar.

"He's your cousin," Cody reminded her. "Well, second or third cousin anyway. His mom is your grandmother's cousin."

"Right." Sunny nodded. "Lulu mentioned the Staffords."

"So I told Bill about you, and he invited you to stop by their house this evening. They're having a little barbecue, and he said you'd be welcome to come."

"Oh, but we're having a slumber party." Sunny glanced at Echo. "Right?"

"Bill invited us to come too," Cody told her. "But I can tell him you have other plans."

"Oh, let's go to the barbecue," Echo said suddenly. "Misty will be there, and it'll be fun. We can still have the slumber party later." She looked at her dad. "If that's okay with you."

"It's fine with me. How about you, Sunny?"

She smiled. "Fine with me."

"Okay, then we better get going," Cody said to Echo. "I told Bill we'd bring a side dish, and we still need to swing by the store."

"Can I bring something?" Sunny asked.

"Sure, if you want. Even chips or soda would be fine."

She nodded. "Great. I'll pick something up on my way over."

"Starts at six thirty." He gave her some quick directions, which were simple since the Staffords lived only two farms west of the Barretts, then headed for the door with Echo on his heels.

"And I can ride back here with Sunny afterwards, okay?" Echo asked.

"Sounds like a plan."

Sunny felt a rush of anticipation as she headed back to the bunkhouse to clean up. She was going to meet a real live relative tonight. Okay, a second or third cousin perhaps, but it was someone who shared the same ancestry as she. That in itself was exciting. She took a quick shower, put on her jeans and one of the new shirts she'd purchased at Hamley's a few days ago, and left Aubrey a note. With time to spare, she headed into town to find a grocery store, where she bought a carton of potato salad, a couple bags of chips, a six-pack of root beer, and a bouquet of fresh flowers.

Then, feeling nervous and happy, she drove out to the reservation again and, following Cody's directions, turned into a driveway that already had several cars parked in it. Sunny had braced herself for the possibility that this house might be one of the derelict ones with broken windows and junk in the yard, but to her relief it looked nice and neat. The split level house was somewhat plain and the landscaping minimal, but as she got out of the car, she could hear laughter and music and voices, as well as the ring of what she suspected might be a horseshoe game.

Gathering up her food and flowers, she walked around to the backside of the house to see about twenty people already milling about. And, sure enough, there was a horseshoe game going on.

"Sunny," called out Echo as she hurried over to join her, helping to carry a bag. "Come meet Ellie and Misty."

Echo did the introductions. Ellie was Bill's wife and probably in her forties. Misty was their daughter and in the same grade as Echo. Ellie's dark hair was wavy and full and Misty's was pulled back into a sleek ponytail. But they looked very much like mother and daughter.

Ellie thanked Sunny for the flowers, handing them to Misty to put in a vase. "Cody told me that you're Bill's cousin."

"According to Lulu." Sunny quickly explained the old woman's recollection.

"Well, Bill's outside supervising the barbecue," Ellie told her. "But I'd like you to meet Bill's mom." She nodded toward the living room. "She's in here." Then Ellie introduced Sunny to an old white-haired woman named Gert. Her bronzed face was creased with wrinkles, but her black-brown eyes looked sharp and alert. She was seated in a recliner. Sunny sat down in the chair closest to her, and Ellie returned to her work in the kitchen.

"I understand that you are the great-niece of my great-grand-mother Polly Wikiapi," Sunny began carefully. She had no idea what Gert's memories or impressions of Polly might be, but she was prepared for the worst.

Gert nodded as if this was not news to her.

"And perhaps you remember my grandmother, Mary Sunrise."

Gert's eyes flickered. "I remember the name well. But I was a small child when Mary Sunrise left. She and my mother were about the same age. But I recall my mother missed her greatly when she was gone. I think they had been close."

"Really?" Sunny was surprised by this. "Did your mother ever talk about my grandmother to you?"

"Oh, yes." Gert folded her hands together, laying them over her ample midsection in what seemed a self-satisfied way. But the way she narrowed her eyes appeared as if she was deciding whether to continue talking to Sunny or not.

"I was named after my grandmother," Sunny tried. "And after my parents died, my grandmother raised me."

"Oh?" Gert nodded.

"But for some reason my grandmother never talked about her past. She never told me anything about her life on the reservation."

"Really?" Gert looked interested now.

"No. She seemed to want to forget it."

"Yes, I can understand."

Now Sunny waited, observing Gert's dark eyes.

"Mary and my mother were forced to go to boarding school." She shook her head. "Bad memories. Unhappy times."

"Do you mean the school at Saint Andrew's Mission?" Sunny queried.

Gert shrugged. "I don't know for sure. My mother did not like to talk about it. It was not good."

"I went out there today," Sunny said eagerly. "I saw that my great-grandmother Polly Wikiapi was buried there. Do you know anything about that?"

Gert smirked…or frowned. Sunny wasn't sure which.

"Maybe your great-grandmother went to the mission for help," Gert suggested.

Sunny nodded. "Maybe so. She was young when she died. Maybe she was sick and went there for medical assistance."

"Maybe."

"My grandmother didn't have good memories of her mother." Sunny waited.

Gert nodded as if she were aware of this.

"And I've heard that Polly Wikiapi might have been crazy."

Gert's eyebrows arched. "Yes?"

"And that she drank." Sunny watched for Gert's reaction.

"There were many stories about Polly Wikiapi."

"Do you recall any of them?" Sunny leaned forward.

Just then Echo and Misty came into the room. Sunny didn't know if she wanted to continue this conversation, but it seemed to be too late.

"I remember one story," Gert began. "A story my mother told me about Polly Wikiapi."

Echo and Misty sat down on the sofa now, as if waiting to hear this story.

"Polly Wikiapi had a baby girl—your grandmother, Mary Sunrise—the year after Jackson Sundown came to the 1911 Round-Up."

Sunny's cheeks grew warm now. She considered stopping Gert, but she really wanted to hear this.

"Polly Wikiapi told everyone that the baby was Jackson Sundown's."

"Jackson Sundown?" exclaimed Echo.

"That's right." Gert nodded. "Polly said Jackson Sundown was the father of Mary Sunrise."

"Was he?" asked Misty.

Gert shrugged. "How would anyone know?"

"But if he was"—Echo gazed at Sunny with wide eyes—"that would make you Jackson Sundown's, uh, granddaughter?"

"Great-granddaughter," Sunny told her. "I mean, if it were true."

"It's not true?" Echo looked disappointed.

Sunny held up her hands. "Well, no one knows for sure."

"But it could be true?" Echo was standing now.

"That is so cool," Misty said with excitement. "You could be Jackson Sundown's great-granddaughter. Do you know how cool that is?"

"It would be very cool," Sunny admitted. "Except that I don't know it's true."

"What do you think, Grandma?" Misty asked Gert hopefully. "Is it true or not?"

Gert shrugged again. "Some people thought Polly Wikiapi was crazy."

"Is that what your mother thought?" asked Sunny.

Gert got a faraway look in her eyes. "My mother believed Polly Wikiapi's story."

Sunny was too stunned to respond. She just stared at Gert and wondered if she'd heard her correctly.

"So maybe it is true?" Misty turned to Sunny with arched brows. "Do you think it's true?"

"Of course it's true," Echo proclaimed. "It makes perfect sense."

Sunny couldn't help but smile at this youthful confidence. "Why is that?" she asked Echo.

"The first time you got on a horse," Echo told her, "you acted like you'd been riding for years. You were a total natural. This explains everything."

"And Jackson Sundown was the greatest horseman ever," declared Misty. "You have to be his great-granddaughter. Oh, I can't wait to tell everyone."

And before Sunny could say a word, Misty dashed from the room yelling, "Let 'er buck!"

"Echo," Sunny said quietly, "we don't know this for sure."

"Woo-hoo!" Echo cried out. "This is so cool. Let 'er buck!" she cried as she took off after Misty.

"Oh, dear." Sunny just sat there.

"What is wrong?" Gert asked.

"I don't know if it's true," Sunny confessed. "I hate having this spread around and it's not even a fact."

Gert looked dismayed. "Jackson Sundown was a fine man."

"I know that."

Gert pointed her finger at Sunny with a somber expression. "You should be proud."

Sunny wanted to be proud. She really did. But all she could think of was how foolish she might look in the eyes of others—those who would surely doubt this farfetched tale. Worse yet, those who would see this as Sunny's attempt to gain recognition or attention here on the reservation. Nothing could be further from the truth.

Chapter Seventeen

....

"Is it true?" Cody asked Sunny as she went outside for some fresh air.

"So you've heard?" Sunny frowned.

"Everyone heard. But is it true?"

She shrugged. "Who knows what's really true?"

"Of course it's true," Hank said as he came up from behind his son.

Sunny gave him a warning look.

"Why wouldn't it be true?" he persisted. "You've got the photos and memorabilia. Your great-grandmother named her child Sunrise. The birth date lines up. I'd be willing to bet it's the truth."

Soon others were clustering around her, treating her like she was some kind of a celebrity, and a couple of the younger guests even took photos with their cell phones. While a small part of her enjoyed this attention, another part of her wanted to shove it all away.

When it was time to eat, she found herself surrounded by Misty and Echo and several other young people. All eagerly asked her questions, most of which she had to admit she didn't have the answers to. Not that it stopped them. Her most eager admirer seemed to be a teenaged boy named Jackson.

"Jackson was named for Jackson Sundown," Echo told her. "His dad was my dad's best friend."

Just then Sunny remembered. "Was your dad Larry?"

Jackson nodded.

"Hank told me about him. He must've been quite a guy."

"Yeah." Jackson looked down at his plate.

"Jackson is a really good horseman too," Echo told her.

Jackson looked up now, a slow smile lighting his face. "I'm going to be in the Indian relays when I'm sixteen."

"The Indian relays?" Sunny was curious. "What's that?"

"It's this really cool rodeo event," Echo began.

"Yeah," Jackson added, "a race where one rider has to switch horses. You have to be really quick."

"You switch horses?" Sunny was trying to grasp this. "In the middle of a race?"

He nodded eagerly. "Yeah, it's amazing. Sometimes it goes really smooth and sometimes, well, it doesn't."

"And it's an event in the rodeo?"

"Yeah." He grinned. "You'll have to make sure you come see it."

"I don't have tickets yet," Sunny admitted. "But maybe I can—"

"No way," said Misty. "If you don't have tickets by now, there's no way. The hundredth celebration has been sold out for ages."

"My grandpa always has extra tickets," Echo assured her. "Don't worry, we'll get you one."

Then the talk switched over the Dress-Up Parade and, to Sunny's relief, she was out of the spotlight. She listened to the youths chattering amongst themselves and suddenly realized that she felt like she was sitting at the kids' table. And while it was amusing, she would much rather be sitting with Cody and Hank. Or even her cousin Bill, whom she'd barely met. She glanced across the yard where chairs and tables were randomly placed and noticed that Cody was sitting at a small table with an attractive Native American woman and Bill and Ellie. The foursome chatted amicably as if they were old friends. And, as much as she hated it, Sunny felt an unexpected jolt of jealousy.

She blinked and looked away, wondering what had brought that on. She tried to convince herself she was simply feeling slighted because she wished she was the one visiting with Bill and Ellie. But she suspected that was only a partial truth.

"Hey, you should wear something in the parade tomorrow," Jackson was telling Sunny, "that shows you're Jackson Sundown's great-granddaughter."

"Yeah," Echo agreed. "And maybe we can ride with Jackson—he's dressing up like Jackson Sundown."

"Really?" Sunny smiled. "That should be interesting."

"Yeah, I got the spotted shirt and chaps and everything," he said with enthusiasm. "It'd be really cool if we could all ride together."

And then he and Echo were plotting how they could accomplish this and where they would meet. Realizing this was her chance to slip away, Sunny excused herself, dumped her plate, and went around to the front of the house, where she sat on the porch and just wondered. She felt like she was on a runaway horse tonight. Or like someone had set a wildfire, and there was no stopping it. She looked out to the western horizon, where the sun was sinking low in the sky and ripples of pink and red slowly began to glow.

"Jackson Sundown," she said quietly, "I wish you could pop down here for a minute or two and clear this thing up for me." She sighed. "Are you my great-grandfather or not?"

Of course, there was no answer. And she was guessing there never would be an answer. She slowly stood, knowing she wasn't being a very polite guest to be hiding out like this. If she hadn't promised to give Echo a ride back, she would simply have thanked her hosts, excused herself, and driven back to the Lowenstein ranch by now. As it was, she'd probably need to stay awhile longer.

Just smile, she told herself as she walked back around. *Act like you're having a great time. And if you see Cody with that woman, act like you could care less.* So what if she felt like a fake? After all, here she was, masquerading as Jackson Sundown's great-granddaughter. How much more of a phony could she be?

"There you are," Echo said as she spotted Sunny. "Bill was looking for you."

"Oh." Sunny smiled brightly. "Where is he?"

Echo pointed to where he was still sitting with his wife and Cody, as well as the petite, pretty woman Sunny was desperately trying not to dislike. "Come on." Echo tugged on her arm. "He wants to ask you about Jackson Sundown."

Sunny suppressed the urge to groan as she let Echo lead her over to the table.

"Here she is," Echo proclaimed.

"Take my chair," Cody offered, and before she could decline, she was seated.

"Hey, cousin," Bill said to her. "I hear there's a rumor going 'round that you're Jackson Sundown's granddaughter."

"*Great*-granddaughter," Echo corrected.

He grinned. "So, is it true or not?"

Sunny held up her hands in exasperation. "Ask your mother. She's the one who got this whole thing started tonight."

"So it's the first you've heard of this?" he questioned.

"To be honest, it's not." She sighed. Then, as Cody returned with another chair to join them, Sunny explained to Bill about her recent findings and some of her childhood memories. "But it's not a lot to go on, and I honestly never planned to tell anyone without real evidence."

"Real evidence?" Bill frowned. "Like what?"

She shrugged. "I don't know."

"Well, I must say, my son is totally enamored with you," the strange woman announced. "You are all he's been talking about."

Sunny looked evenly at this woman. She was undeniably pretty. Her sleek dark hair was cut in a fashionable bob, and her perfect clothes and makeup suggested she worked someplace where appearances were important. "I'm sorry," Sunny said. "I don't believe we've met."

"Oh, I'm so sorry," Ellie said suddenly. "Sunny Westcott, this is Trina Strong Horse."

"Trina is Jackson's mom," Echo explained.

Sunny nodded with realization sinking in. So this was Cody's best friend's widow. Of course. It made perfect sense. Hank had said Trina was almost like family. It was only natural that Cody would be with her.

"And Jackson was just over here telling me that you and Echo are going to ride with him in the parade tomorrow." Trina smiled. "He couldn't be happier."

Sunny smiled back. "Yes, I think it's going to be quite a day." She glanced at Echo now. "Speaking of the parade, do you think we should be heading back to the ranch? I mean, if we're still having that slumber party, we might not want to stay up too late if we have to get up early for—"

"Yes," Echo said eagerly. "You're right." She leaned down and kissed her dad on the cheek. Good-byes were said, and to Sunny's relief, she and Echo were on their way.

Echo chattered happily about the Jackson Sundown news and about how fun it would be to have Jackson Strong Horse with them in the parade tomorrow. "It's going to be the best Dress-Up Parade ever," she proclaimed as Sunny parked her car in front of the bunkhouse.

"Looks like Aubrey is home," Sunny said as they got out. "I left her a note about our slumber party plans."

"And I brought movies and popcorn for us," Echo told her.

"Let the fun begin," Sunny announced as she opened the door.

"Let 'er buck!" Echo exclaimed as they entered the bunkhouse.

"That's right," Aubrey whooped, "let 'er buck, cowgirls!"

With pajamas on and popcorn popped, they started the first movie, an old western, but midway through Aubrey suggested that Echo and Sunny should try on their Dress-Up Parade outfits. "It'll be like a dress rehearsal," she urged them. But as Sunny gathered her clothes and things to change, she realized her split skirt was missing.

"It's probably still in Grandma's sewing room," Echo said. "Run over and get it."

"I'm in my pajamas." Sunny wrinkled her nose. "I'll get it in the morning."

"But you need to try everything on tonight," Echo insisted.

"It's okay," Aubrey assured Sunny. "Mom and Dad aren't even home."

"Okay." Sunny wrapped a blanket over her shoulders and headed out into the darkness. Letting herself into the still house, she quietly went to the sewing room and found the altered split skirt, but on her way down the hall, she noticed a light on in the pink memorial bedroom. Naturally frugal about conserving electricity, she went in to turn off the light, but instead of turning it off, she stood there looking at the cowgirl memorabilia and old photos of Lenora. What was she really like? And why did it matter so much to Sunny? She picked up the framed close-up photo of Lenora wearing her Round-Up princess outfit and stared at it. Those fluffy blond curls, a sweet sparkling smile, big blue eyes…she must've turned a lot of heads. No wonder Cody had fallen in love with her.

For some reason, Sunny found herself comparing Lenora to the woman she'd met tonight, the one Cody had been engaged in conversation with. Trina Strong Horse. Of course, Trina, being Native American, was darker and different looking than Lenora. Yet there were similarities too. Both women possessed a beauty, style, and poise, a similar sense of self-assurance—all giving the impression that both were perfectly comfortable in their own skin, confident in themselves, and pleased with their position in life. So unlike Sunny. Why wouldn't Cody be attracted to someone like Trina? Plus, she had been his best friend's wife. They were already close—like family.

"What are you doing in here?"

The deep male voice made Sunny almost drop the framed photograph. But instead, with trembling hands, she set it back on the dresser and turned to see Aubrey's father staring at her with suspicion.

"I was just getting the skirt Cindy fixed for me," she stammered, "and the light was on in here. So I came in to turn it off and—"

"What's going on?" Now Cindy was standing behind Doug, looking into the room with a confused expression.

"I found Sunny in Lenora's room," Doug said in a harsh tone.

"I was getting the split skirt," she said again, holding up the skirt. "Echo and Aubrey wanted us to have a dress rehearsal tonight. On my way out of the sewing room, I noticed this light on. Since I'm so used to conserving electricity, I came in here to turn it off and—"

"Well, of course," Cindy said in a warm tone. "I was in here changing the bedding so that Aunt Belle could use this room. She just called this afternoon saying she wanted to come for Round-Up. I'm sure I'm the one who left the light on."

Doug harrumphed. "Well, I'm not used to coming in the house and finding someone prowling around like a thief."

Sunny bristled, but Cindy just laughed. "You better get used to people prowling about, Doug. We'll be crawling with guests in a few days."

He shook his head and left.

"Don't mind him." Cindy put her hand on Sunny's shoulder. "He lost in cards tonight and drank too much, and now he's in a mood."

"I'm so sorry," Sunny told her. "I didn't mean to snoop. I was about to turn off the light when I saw a photo of Lenora, so I picked it up. I found myself thinking about her…wondering what she was like. She was so beautiful. But there's also such a sweetness about her. She must've been a wonderful person."

Cindy nodded sadly. "She was."

"And I can only imagine how you must miss her."

"I know people don't think that mothers and daughters can be close, but Lenora was my best friend."

"I understand." Sunny held up the skirt. "Thanks so much for altering this for me."

Cindy nodded and, moving over to the bureau, picked up the same photo that Sunny had been studying. "Lenora was such a good girl.

I still can't believe she's gone sometimes." She looked at Sunny with moist eyes. "I try not to be mad at God, but sometimes I can't help it."

"I know what you mean," Sunny confessed. "When my parents died, I was so enraged at God. In fact, I quit believing in Him altogether for a number of years. Even when my grandmother forced me to go to church with her, I would just sit in the pew filled with anger and resentment."

"But you did get over it?"

Sunny nodded. "Yes. It was in my late teens that I found myself spiritually bankrupt."

"Spiritually bankrupt?"

Sunny pointed to her chest. "I felt empty inside…and lost."

"So what did you do about it?"

"I gave God a second chance."

"Lenora made me promise that I wouldn't be angry at God," Cindy said quietly. "Before she died, she became very close to God, and she was worried that her death was going to embitter me. I suppose she wasn't too far from the truth."

"You don't seem bitter," Sunny said gently.

"I try not to be. But I'm afraid it's down there inside of me. I'm not even sure how to let go of it." She turned to Sunny with glistening eyes. "How did you do that?"

"It's hard to explain. I think maybe God helped me reach that place. Sort of like I was so worn out, so sad, so weary, that all I could do was give up."

"Yes, I know how that feels."

"And when I surrendered like that, I think that's when God stepped in."

"So you just let go of all those emotions?" Cindy looked hopeful.

"I think it was a process—sometimes I'm still working on it. But, yes, there was an initial letting go. You know what they say: let go and let God. That's what I try to do. But, really, I'm no expert." She shrugged. "I feel like the blind leading the blind."

Cindy replaced the photo and sighed. "Maybe that's okay. A blind person can relate to another blind person." Then she reached out and hugged Sunny. "You know, I have a feeling Lenora really would've liked you."

Sunny smiled. "Thanks, Cindy. That means a lot to me."

"Tell Echo not to stay up too late," Cindy said as she turned off the light and they exited the room. "I'll have breakfast ready for you girls by seven thirty, and then we'll need to get those horses loaded up and ready to head into town by nine."

"Echo is blessed to have such a supportive grandmother," Sunny said as they paused in the kitchen.

"I feel the same way about Echo." Cindy smiled. "Don't know what I'd do without that little angel in my life."

Sunny thought about this as she walked back through the darkness toward the bunkhouse. Hopefully that was how her grandmother had felt about her too. Of course, Sunny still had some misgivings about how her grandmother would feel if she knew where Sunny was and what she'd been doing—or the fact that a number of people in this town now believed that Sunny was the direct descendant of Jackson Sundown. But maybe they would forget about all that in the excitement of this week's rodeo.

Chapter Eighteen

....

Sunny woke up early on Saturday. Since her cowgirl regalia was all laid out and ready to go, she simply got dressed. Afterwards, she took a moment to admire the complete outfit in the full-length mirror on the closet door. The split skirt was a little on the short side, but at least it reached the top of her Old Gringo boots. And the wide western belt with the oversized rodeo buckle really did set it off. Along with her fringed buckskin jacket, a retro cowboy shirt, red silk bandana, and the big tan Gus hat that Echo had picked out, Sunny really might've stepped out of the previous century. Still, she wasn't sure what to do with her hair, finally opting for one long braid down the back.

It was a little past seven when Sunny woke up Echo. "Your grandmother said breakfast is at seven thirty," she reminded her. "I'm going to go over and see if she needs any help."

Echo blinked up from where she'd slept on the couch. "You look pretty, Sunny."

"Thanks." Sunny smiled.

The morning sky was nearly cloudless and the day promised to be another warm one as Sunny went over to the house. She quietly walked across the deck, glancing inside to make sure Cindy was already in the kitchen. She did not want to walk in and catch Doug by surprise again. But Cindy was at the stove, so Sunny quietly tapped on the French door, waiting until Cindy came over to open the door.

"Come on in." She grinned at Sunny. "Well, look at you, cowgirl. Come on now, turn around and let me see the whole effect."

Sunny complied, slowly turning around.

"Woo-hoo!" Cindy hooted. "You look like the real thing."

"Thanks again for the skirt and helping with the outfit."

"I'll bet Echo is excited." Cindy turned back to where she had a large pot of oatmeal simmering. "The Dress-Up Parade is her favorite part of Round-Up."

"She told me she used to do it with her mom."

Cindy nodded as she stirred the pot. "Even when she was a baby, Lenora outfitted her in a little pink-checkered cowgirl outfit and tiny boots and a hat that we practically taped to her head. Then she put her in one of those baby packs, you know the kind, and Echo just slept through the whole thing."

"Do you need any help in here?"

"No, I'm keeping it simple. I know Echo likes oatmeal, and I was hoping you did too."

"I love oatmeal."

"Get yourself some coffee or juice if you want."

Sunny had just poured a cup of coffee when Cindy started digging through the refrigerator. "I thought I had some raspberries in here. Doug must've finished them off." She looked out the window now. "Say, do you want to go down and get some for me?"

"Sure. Where do I get them?"

Cindy smiled and pointed outside. "My garden."

"I'd love to."

"They're almost over, but I think there should be enough for our oatmeal." She handed Sunny a small bowl.

Cindy's garden was much bigger than Sunny's, but it also looked a bit more neglected too. Sunny thought if she had time, she might sneak down and give it a good weeding before heading back home to Portland next week. She found the raspberry vines and after a few minutes managed to nearly fill the bowl. Then on her way back to the deck, she heard someone let out a low whistle.

Thinking it might be Doug and that she could apologize for upsetting him last night, she turned with a smile. Instead it was Cody.

"Don't you look nice," he said as he came closer to check out her outfit.

"Thanks." She took in a quick breath. "I didn't expect to see you here this morning."

"Just stopped by to pick up the old hay wagon. We use it in the parade."

"Oh." She looked at his outfit, which was more contemporary than hers. "You look like a real cowboy today."

He was still studying her, almost as if he was taking some kind of inventory or else simply spacing out.

"Echo and Cindy helped me with my outfit," she admitted.

"Very pretty."

"Thank you." Not knowing what else to say, she held up the bowl of berries. "I need to get these in to Cindy. Do you want to stay for breakfast? It looked like she made enough oatmeal to feed a dozen people."

He glanced at his watch. "Hmmm, I might just do that."

Back in the kitchen, Cindy handed Sunny a tray loaded with bowls and utensils and things. "It's so lovely this morning, I thought we should eat outside."

"And Sunny invited me to crash your breakfast party." Cody gave Cindy a hug.

"Get yourself some coffee," Cindy ordered.

Sunny was setting the table on the deck when Echo came up. "How do I look?" she asked Sunny.

"Perfect." Sunny nodded.

"You think this straw hat looks better than the felt one?"

"Better and cooler."

"How about my hair?" Echo took off her hat.

Sunny studied her loose brown hair. "I think it looks very pretty just as it is."

"But I want a braid like yours." Echo reached in her pocket to pull out a rubber band. "Want to help me?"

"Sure." Sunny took the band. "Have a seat."

Sunny was just finishing up the braid when Cody and Cindy brought out the oatmeal and condiments. "You girls look perfectly adorable," Cindy said as she set the pot on the table. "You stay right there while I run and get my camera."

"I hate having my picture taken," Echo muttered as she and Sunny posed for Cindy.

"Me too," Sunny admitted.

"But you're a model," Echo reminded her.

"A reluctant model," Sunny said.

"Your great-grandpa didn't mind being in front of a camera," Cody said in a slightly teasing tone.

Cindy's camera went down and she stared at Cody. "What do you know about Sunny's great-grandpa?"

"Sunny's great-grandpa was Jackson Sundown!" Echo exclaimed.

"So the cat's out of the bag now?" Cindy asked Sunny.

"You mean, you knew, Grandma?" Echo looked slightly hurt as she sat down to a bowl of oatmeal. "And you didn't even tell me?"

"Sunny swore me to secrecy."

"That's right," Sunny told Echo. "I didn't want anyone to know unless I could prove it was true."

"So you proved it was true?" Cindy asked with wide eyes.

Sunny sat down next to Echo. "No. But one of my relatives—Gert Stafford—brought it up last night, and everyone just assumed she knew what she was talking about."

"Gert is Bill Stafford's mom," Cody explained. "And they're cousins of Sunny's."

"And they knew about Jackson Sundown?"

"Gert seemed to believe that the story was true," Sunny admitted. "But, honestly, she has no proof. It was really more of an opinion."

"You should've seen how excited Jackson Strong Horse was when he heard about it," Echo said with bright eyes. "So much so that he begged to ride in the parade with Sunny and me today."

"Speaking of the parade, you better eat your breakfast," Cody warned. "You'll need to be heading to town soon."

"You too." Cindy pushed a plate of whole wheat toast toward him.

"I've got the wagon all ready to go," he said. "I already loaded up the team before I left, and Dad's driving them to the staging area now."

"Is Grandpa L coming to the parade too?" Echo asked Cindy as she dropped some berries on her oatmeal.

"He said he plans to. But he needed to help Jeremy and Scott relocate the irrigation wheel first."

"I love this day," Echo said happily.

Sunny couldn't help but grin. "Me too. It's really exciting."

"I hope Jackson gets to ride with us." Echo glanced at her dad now. "I forgot to ask Trina if she's riding too."

"She said she plans to pass this year," Cody said. "But I told her she could ride on our wagon if she didn't mind being in the company of a bunch of wild young men."

"Is she really going to do it?" Echo looked skeptical.

"She said she'd get back to me on that."

Echo laughed. "I'm thinking that means no."

He nodded. "I think you're right." He held up his empty bowl now. "Thanks for the grub, Cindy. I hate to eat and run, but I'm taking the back road into town with that wagon, so I better head out if I want to make it on time."

"You get rolling then," she told him. "And you did put a red flag on the back end, right?"

"You bet." He stood and tipped his hat. "See you ladies later."

"The law enforcement 'round here is usually pretty understanding about folks getting their wagons and whatnot into town on parade days," Cindy told Sunny, "but you just never know."

"Ready to go load the horses?" Echo said as they were finishing up.

"I'll go put these things in the kitchen while you girls go get the horses brushed and saddled and ready to go."

* * * * *

Sunny felt like someone from a different world—or another time—as she and Echo sat atop their horses waiting for the parade to begin.

"Hey, there's Jackson," Echo said suddenly as a horse and rider hurried to join them. "Check out his duds, Sunny. He looks just like one of those old photos of your great-grandpa."

Sunny cringed inwardly, but smiled as the boy approached. Sure enough, he did look like Jackson Sundown with his spotted western shirt and full furry chaps. Even the hat was right.

"Well, if it ain't my long-lost granddaughter," Jackson told her in a teasing voice.

"That would be *great*-granddaughter," Sunny corrected. "But the truth is, I'm old enough to be your mother."

He laughed.

"I'm so glad you get to ride with us," Echo told him.

"Yeah, I got here early and got my number changed and everything."

Just then the group ahead of them, a group of Native Americans on horseback and in full regalia, started to move.

"Ready to rock and roll?" Jackson asked Sunny.

"And hopefully stay on my horse," she told him.

"Don't worry about Sunny," Echo said. "She's a natural."

Jackson nodded as he adjusted his hat strings, taking on a serious expression that was probably meant to be an imitation of Sundown. "Well, she oughta be."

Sunny almost felt as if she were experiencing an out-of-body moment, as if she were sitting up above and watching as the three of them slowly walked their horses down the street. She vaguely wondered if the great Jackson Sundown, whether related or not, might be watching as well.

Most of her concentration was on Brownie Anne—not that the horse needed extra attention. But as much for Echo and Jackson as for herself, Sunny did not want anything to go wrong. It wasn't until they approached the grandstand, where the commentator was, that Sunny realized the announcer was talking about her.

"Now, for a real treat today, we have Mary Sunrise Westcott on the brown quarter horse. Note that authentic-looking Indian coat. Well, word has it that this young lady is none other than the great-granddaughter of the famous Jackson Sundown."

The crowd broke into applause and cheers and Sunny, too stunned to respond, simply kept a somber expression as the announcer went on to remind the audience of the times when Jackson Sundown competed right here at the Pendleton Round-Up. "It's an honor and a pleasure to have you with us here today, Mary Sunrise. We hope you enjoy your visit."

After they were down the street a ways, Sunny quietly asked Echo how the announcer possibly could've known about that.

"Well, we had to give our names to register," Echo explained. "But that was all I did—just give your name. Your full name." Echo glanced at Jackson now. "Did you tell them something more?"

He grinned. "Hey, I'm Jackson Sundown today. I got a right to make my family known."

Sunny just shook her head and smiled. Really, how could she get mad at this kid? But hopefully this would be the end of it. Instead of obsessing over what she couldn't possibly control, she decided to simply enjoy herself by smiling and waving at the crowds lining the streets. She had no idea how many people were in town today, but she wouldn't have been surprised if it was the entire population of the town and then some.

"Now the Round-Up rodeo doesn't actually start until Wednesday?" Sunny asked Echo as they stopped their horses for another break.

"That's right," Echo told her.

"And town gets even more crowded then?"

"It'll be packed," Jackson said. "We're supposed to have about twenty people camping at our house."

"We've got about ten relatives coming to stay with us," Echo told Sunny.

"And I heard your Lowenstein grandparents plan to have about seventy at their place." Sunny couldn't even imagine how crazy it would get at the ranch in a few days. She wasn't even sure she wanted to stick around to see.

At the end of the parade, Sunny was surprised when a reporter and photographer came over and asked to get some shots of her and the kids. Naturally, Jackson, fully immersed in his role as a rodeo legend, was thrilled. Even Echo was cooperative. So Sunny agreed to the photos and smiled congenially. Then, when the reporter wanted more information about her link to Jackson Sundown, Sunny's smile faded.

"This is more fable than fact," she told the reporter. "I don't have any actual proof to substantiate it."

"Then why did you claim it?" he persisted.

"Actually, I didn't claim it." Sunny pulled her leg around and slid off the horse, looking the reporter directly in his eyes. "I was trying to get to the bottom of it, but the word got out."

"Sunny never told anyone," Echo added. "She even asked people not to talk about it."

Jackson stepped up now. "It's my fault the announcer knew." He held his chin up. "But I believe that Sunny is Sundown's granddaughter. I can tell."

"Great-granddaughter," Sunny corrected, wondering why she even bothered.

"What was the name of your great-grandmother?" the reporter asked.

Sunny pressed her lips together, unsure of whether to answer or not.

"Look, you say you want to get to the bottom of this, don't you?" he asked in a gentler tone. "Why not tell me all the facts you know, and I can do some research on my end. Maybe we'll figure this out."

"Yeah, Sunny," Echo urged, "let him help you."

"Come on, Sunny." Jackson nudged her with his elbow. "Tell him what you know and see if he can figure it all out."

She shrugged. "Well, I don't suppose it could hurt." She eyed the guy carefully again. "As long as you promise me you'll only print the truth."

"I'll stick to the facts."

"Okay, my great-grandmother's name was Polly Wikiapi Blue Crow. And her daughter—the one who was supposedly the child of Jackson Sundown, which is not a proven fact—was Mary Sunrise Wikiapi." Sunny thought for a moment. "Maybe her last name was Blue Crow too because as far as I know, my great-grandmother wasn't married." Then Sunny told him the date of birth of her grandmother and about how she'd been raised in Portland. "My grandmother cared for me after the deaths of my parents, and she seldom spoke of her past."

He asked a few more questions about Sunny's parents and whether she had any relatives on the reservation. "And if you do find that Jackson Sundown is your great-grandfather, what do you plan to do with that information?"

Sunny was puzzled. "Do with it?"

"Yes. Will you look up other relatives in the Nez Percé tribe?"

She shrugged. "I have no idea. So far I'm a bit overwhelmed finding relatives here on the Umatilla Reservation. I can't even think beyond that."

Then he asked for her phone number and gave her a business card. "I'll let you know if I discover anything that might be helpful."

She smiled at him. "Thank you. And thank you for not printing anything but the facts."

He closed his notepad and grinned back at her. "You got it, Sunny."

"You're like a celebrity," Echo told Sunny as they walked their horses back over to the parking lot where Cindy had parked the horse trailer.

"Not really," Sunny said.

Just then Jackson's mom came over to join them. "So did you kids have fun?" Trina asked.

"Yeah, it was great," Jackson told her. "Sunny just got interviewed by a guy from the *East Oregonian*."

"Whatever for?" Trina asked.

"Because of Jackson Sundown," Echo said as if it were obvious.

"Oh, yes." Trina nodded, then studied Sunny curiously. "But you said you weren't sure it was even true."

Sunny just sighed, then peeled off her buckskin coat. It felt like it was about eighty degrees and far too warm for a leather jacket.

"Anyway," Trina said as if to dismiss her comment, "we're all getting together for a barbecue at my place around two. We'll just throw some hamburgers and hot dogs on the grill, but feel free to join us if you like, Sunny. One more person will hardly be noticed."

For some reason Sunny felt that this invitation wasn't totally heartfelt. "Thanks anyway." She smiled at Trina. "But I think I'll head back to the Lowensteins'."

Trina smiled back, nodding like this didn't surprise her. "Another time then."

"Oh, Sunny," pleaded Echo, "why don't you want to come too?"

"Yeah," Jackson urged. "I want to show you my horses. Besides Joker here, I have a paint and an appaloosa."

Sunny looked at the kids' eager faces and suddenly felt bad. "I don't know...."

"Please." Echo smiled hopefully. "Just come out and see Jackson's horses. That way you can give me a ride over there after we get Sylvester and Brownie Anne put away at Grandma and Grandpa's."

"Okay." Sunny nodded. "I guess I could give you a ride and come out and see Jackson's horses for a bit."

"All right!" Jackson gave Sunny a fist-bump and a grin. "See you around two."

"Is there anything I can bring?" Sunny asked Trina.

"Oh, no, that's okay." Trina frowned at her watch. "Guess we should get moving, Jackson. We've got a lot to get done before all the guests arrive."

Chapter Nineteen

· · · · · · · · · · · · · · · · · · · ·

"You girls looked so cute in the parade." Aubrey wiped a soda can across her forehead. "But weren't you hot?"

Sunny smiled as she took off her hat. "No hotter than that steaming day when we did the photoshoot in the park dressed in winter coats."

Aubrey nodded. "Ah, yes, but we got paid for that."

"Some things can't be compared to making money." Sunny sat down on the couch and pulled off her boots. "The parade was a lot of fun."

"How about when the announcer spilled the beans about you being related to Jackson Sundown?"

"Yes, that wasn't so much fun."

"And she got interviewed by the newspaper too," Echo said as she emerged from the bathroom.

"Ooh, we're living with a real celebrity now," Aubrey teased.

"So what are you doing today?" Sunny asked in hopes of changing the subject.

"Just chilling." Aubrey flopped down on an easy chair. "Then meeting up with friends this evening. How about you girls?"

"We're going to a barbecue." Sunny got a bottle of water out of the fridge.

"Want to come too, Aunt Aubrey?" Echo asked.

Aubrey's eyes lit up. "Where is it?"

"Trina Strong Horse's place."

Aubrey wrinkled her nose now. "No thank you."

Sunny sat down across from Aubrey, curious as to the reason for this reaction. "Don't you like Trina?" she asked quietly.

Aubrey shrugged. "Not so much."

"Why not, Aunt Aubrey?" Echo asked. "She's really nice."

Sunny didn't like to think like this, but she wondered if Aubrey's position was because Trina was a Native American. If that was the reason, Sunny was prepared to be seriously aggravated.

"She might *seem* nice," Aubrey told her, "but it's all just an act."

"An act?" Echo frowned.

"How exactly do you know that?" Sunny asked.

"Because I've known Trina for a long, long time. She was a year ahead of me in school. And, trust me, she was the snobbiest girl in her class."

"Trina was snobby?" Echo looked truly shocked.

"Oh, yeah. She always thought she was better than everyone."

"Seriously?" Sunny frowned.

"Do you think I'd make something like that up?" Aubrey appeared slightly hurt. "Honestly, even Cody and Lenora were surprised when Larry decided to marry Trina. I mean, sure, she was pretty and all, but everyone knows she—" Aubrey glanced at Echo and stopped herself.

"Knows what?" Echo asked.

Aubrey seemed stumped. "Uh, well, that Trina's not as nice as she wants you to think."

"But maybe she's changed since then," Sunny suggested.

"Maybe she has." Aubrey stood and stretched with a skeptical expression.

"So you don't even want to give her a second chance?" Sunny tried.

"Not really." Now Aubrey went into her room and closed the door.

Sunny and Echo exchanged glances.

"I guess we should get ready to go." Sunny peered at the clock in the kitchen. "I want to grab a quick shower. How about you?"

"I'm okay."

As Sunny showered, she tried to grasp Aubrey's dislike of Trina, but she just wasn't getting it. And the truth was, Sunny sometimes thought that Aubrey was a bit on the judgmental side. What about her attitude toward the reservation—and those who lived there? That wasn't exactly compassionate. Even though Sunny's initial reaction to Trina had been negative, that had more to do with Cody, not to mention Sunny's own jealousy issues and something she wasn't proud of.

But after seeing Aubrey's prejudice, Sunny was determined to be more friendly to Trina. After all, life hadn't been exactly easy for Trina. Losing her husband in the war, returning to the reservation as a single mom, raising a teenage son on her own… Really, this poor woman deserved some empathy.

"You look pretty," Echo told Sunny as they went out to the car.

"Thanks." Sunny gestured at the red bandana print sundress. "I wasn't sure I'd ever wear this when I got it with Aubrey in Portland, but it's so hot today." She glanced at Echo, dressed casually in khaki shorts and a white T-shirt. "But do you think I overdressed?"

"No, not at all. You're a grown-up."

But as Sunny drove she wasn't so sure. What if it looked like she was trying to draw attention to herself when nothing could be further from the truth? "I thought I'd pick up something in town to take with us," Sunny told Echo. "Is there somewhere we could find a dessert?"

They stopped at a bakery and quickly picked out a lemon cake, as well as a dozen sugar cookies that Echo wanted. And then Echo directed her to Trina's place. But as Sunny turned down the driveway she noticed that there didn't seem to be many cars there. "I guess we're not as late as I thought." She glanced at the dashboard clock to see it was 2:15. Was her clock fast, or had she gotten the time wrong? "Trina did say two, didn't she?"

"Yeah. But there's real time and reservation time."

"Reservation time?"

Echo laughed as Sunny parked. "Yeah, some Indians have their own sense of time, like it doesn't really matter when you get there as long as you get there."

"Oh."

"Not that Trina has that many reservation friends, but she does work at Tamástslikt. And it could be she invited some friends from there."

"That's the museum, right?" With the bakery goods in hand, Sunny and Echo got out of the car.

"Yeah." Echo pointed back toward a small barn in back. "Looks like Dad and Grandpa are here, though."

"Is this a new house?" She looked up at the light blue modular home as they took a paved path through a yard where it appeared the grass turf had been recently laid…and was in need of watering.

"Yeah. The land was in Larry's family." Echo spoke quietly as if she didn't want to be overheard. "There was a little battle over it, but Trina got it worked out. And there used to be an old trailer here, but she used the life insurance money to buy the new house. I've only been here a couple of times, but Trina is making a lot of improvements."

Now they were at the door and Sunny waited as Echo rang the bell. After a minute, Trina appeared. She looked a little flustered, but pretty in a pink and white sundress. Sunny felt a small wave of relief now, like perhaps she hadn't overdressed after all.

"We brought sweets," she said with a smile.

"Sweets?" Trina frowned as if this was not a good thing.

"Just a lemon cake and some cookies," Sunny explained.

"For dessert," Echo added.

"Oh." Trina nodded as she took the cake box from Sunny. "Thank you. And, please, come in."

The interior of the house had a stiff formal look, like it had come directly from a furniture store. "You have a lovely home," Sunny said as they followed Trina into the kitchen.

"Thank you." Trina smiled as she placed the desserts on a tiled countertop. "I haven't even been in it six months yet. But it's coming along."

"Where are the others?" Echo asked.

"Jackson is showing Cody and Hank a calf that's not doing too well," Trina told her. "Go on out there if you want."

Echo took off, so now it was only Trina and Sunny in the kitchen. Sunny wanted to ask Trina where the other guests were but knew that would sound a bit rude.

"I was just getting some things ready for the grill." Trina picked up a platter with pre-made burgers and hot dogs on one side and buns on the other.

"Do you need any help?" offered Sunny.

Trina nodded toward the sink and what looked like bags of fresh produce. "Would you like to make the green salad?"

"Sure."

"Great." Trina smiled. "I think you'll find everything you need in here." Then she picked up the platter and went outside, leaving Sunny alone in the kitchen. Not that Sunny minded being alone. In a way, it was a relief. In fact, Sunny had been feeling somewhat overwhelmed by all the social activities of recent days. She hummed to herself as she started washing the vegetables, lining them along the counter. She soon located a peeler and knife and a cutting board. Trina's kitchen, like the rest of her house, seemed to be quite orderly. Everything appeared to be new.

But as Sunny chopped tomatoes, cucumbers, green peppers, she wondered just how large she should make this salad. Should she use all the ingredients? Or would that be wasteful? She remembered how Trina had said "one more person wouldn't be noticed." That seemed to insinuate this was going to be a fairly big gathering. Sunny figured the other guests would simply be arriving fashionably late. And so she found the largest bowl in the kitchen and decided to make a huge salad.

She was finishing up when someone came into the kitchen. She turned to see it was Cody.

"Hey, what are you doing in here?"

She rinsed the knife and set it beside the sink, then picked up the oversized salad and smiled at him. "Making a salad."

"Oh?" He frowned slightly. "That's a lot of salad."

She wondered how much salad she was supposed to make.

"I just came in to wash my hands." He went to the sink. "But I think it's time to eat."

"Oh, okay."

"Hey, there you guys are," Trina said as she joined them. "The burgers are done. Are you coming out now?"

"Do you want me to put dressing on the salad?" Sunny set the bowl back on the counter. "Or just on the side?"

Trina stared at the salad. "Good grief, that's an enormous salad."

Sunny looked down at the colorful bowl. "Well, yes, I didn't know what you wanted, so I used all the produce. I assumed you were having a crowd."

Trina laughed, but it didn't seem warm or genuine. "That's okay. Maybe it'll be good for leftovers, or for anyone who likes wilted salad." She picked up a dressing bottle and poured a liberal amount over the salad, giving it a quick toss, then picking it up. "This thing weighs a ton."

Sunny stood a bit straighter now. Not only did she feel insulted, but unappreciated as well. Even so, she forced a smile. Perhaps she would simply eat some token food and then make a quick, polite exit. Because, for whatever reason, she wanted to get away from this place—and fast! Maybe Aubrey was right to refuse to come.

"Well, let's get outside," Trina called as she headed out the sliding door. Sunny returned to the sink, pretending to give her hands a quick wash.

"Are you coming?" Cody called out.

"Yes. I'm right behind you."

On the small deck outside where the sun was beating down, a round umbrella table was set with six places. And while the umbrella afforded some shade, Sunny estimated the temperature out here must've been above ninety.

"Hey, there you are," called Echo. "You're sitting between me and Jackson, Sunny."

"Sounds good to me," she told her.

Hank grinned at Sunny from where he was already seated. "You're looking very lovely today, Miss Sunrise."

"Thanks." She smiled at him, thinking that if anyone else had called her by that name she would've been seriously irritated. Yet, coming from Hank, it was sweet. "I figured it was going to be sweltering this afternoon." She waved her hand like a fan as she sat down in the sun. "And it seems that I was right." The truth was, Sunny was surprised that Trina was forcing her guests to sit out here in the heat like this. Still, maybe they were used to it.

"Can you grab the burgers from the grill?" Trina asked Cody.

"You got it." He went over to open the smoking barbecue.

"Goodness, I don't even know where to put this big thing." Trina laughed as she held up the huge bowl for everyone to see. "I swear, Sunny made enough salad to feed an army."

Hank got up, shuffling around in an attempt to help out, and finally pulled over an extra chair to set the salad near the table. The salad looked like it was already starting to wilt in the sun. Kind of like Sunny. Eventually, Cody returned with the meat and, after a bit of passing and readjusting, they were finally eating. But as Sunny nibbled at her hot dog, she felt a hard rock in the pit of her stomach. Then, as if it might help, she gave herself an overly large helping of salad, then attempted to eat it, although it was drenched in dressing. She envied Aubrey now, relaxing back in the comfort of the cool bunkhouse. Sunny honestly could not remember a more miserable meal.

The talk at the table was mostly about today's parade and other upcoming rodeo events and festivities. For the most part, other than an occasional nod, forced smile, or guarded comment, Sunny stayed out of it.

"And Sunny and Aunt Aubrey are doing another photoshoot on Monday," Echo announced in what seemed a slightly strained effort to pull Sunny into the conversation.

"A photoshoot?" Trina looked confused. "For what?"

"The Pendleton Woolen Mill," Sunny offered.

"And what do you do in this photoshoot?" Trina asked with what almost seemed like disdain.

"Sunny and Aunt Aubrey are models," Echo explained. "It's for the Pendleton clothing catalog."

"Oh." Trina looked unimpressed. "Well, I don't get that catalog. Their styles seem more suitable for older women. I think Cody's mother-in-law wears a lot of Pendleton clothes."

Sunny considered disputing the older woman comment but decided it just wasn't worth the effort as she took a large bite of salad. Maybe Aubrey was right about this woman.

"So is that what brought you to Pendleton?" Trina asked Sunny. "Just to do some modeling?"

With her mouth slightly full, Sunny looked evenly at Trina. While Sunny had never been proud of modeling, she wondered why it sounded so wrong when Trina said it like that. Chewing and swallowing, Sunny dabbed her lips with her napkin and forced yet another smile, albeit a very small one. "Yes, it was the modeling job that brought me to Pendleton. But, as you know, my family originally came from this area. And it's been interesting learning a bit more about them."

"Yes. I understand your great-grandmother was quite an *interesting* person."

Sunny decided not to respond to what felt like a jab.

"Bill's mother, Gert Stafford, told some stories after you left last night," Trina continued with what appeared to be a suppressed smile. "It seems that Polly Wikiapi was a real piece of work."

"Polly Wikiapi was a very beautiful woman," Hank said defensively. "Sunny showed me her photo. She was extremely attractive." He smiled at Sunny. "In fact, she looked a lot like our Sunny here."

"Gert said that Polly Wikiapi had quite a reputation amongst the men too." Trina winked like this was some kind of a group secret.

"I'm surprised that Gert knows so much about her," Hank said. "Gert's not much older than me."

"She's a relative," Trina reminded him. "Apparently the story got passed down several generations." She chuckled. "You know how the best gossip tends to last the longest."

"Mom." Jackson's tone suggested he was feeling embarrassed by his mom's little display.

"What, *Jackson*?" She gave him a frosty look.

He stood and stormed off. Echo, obviously feeling sorry for her friend, followed.

Sunny had never considered herself a combative person, but at this moment she felt such a surge of fury that she wondered if some of her ancestors had been warriors. Instead of throwing something, she squared her shoulders and leveled a gaze at Trina. "I'm aware that my great-grandmother had her problems. Normally, I'd be the last person to defend her honor. But on the same token, unless someone has some authenticated and factual information about the woman, it seems unkind, as well as imprudent, to disparage her name and reputation."

Trina looked surprised but then managed a catty smile. "Goodness, for a model, you do speak rather well, Sunny."

"Sunny was a professor of anthropology," Hank said in a serious tone.

Cody's face paled, as if he wanted to add something but couldn't. For some reason, Sunny was not surprised...or impressed. But she was hurt. She stood, slowly folding and setting her napkin on her plate. "Thank you for your warm hospitality, Trina. And I apologize if I seem a bit edgy. I must be a little worn out from the parade and all. If you'll please excuse me."

"Yes, of course, dear." Trina stood and smiled as if this were all perfectly normal. "I can understand how a city girl like you would find our country way of life to be a bit exhausting. Maybe you should go home and take a nice, long nap."

"Yes, something like that." Then without even saying good-bye to the others, Sunny left.

It wasn't until she was driving on the freeway that she felt the dampness on her cheeks. Even then she was stunned to realize she was crying, because Sunny rarely cried. She took a few deep breaths and then assured herself that she probably was just tired. Really, the past week had been exhausting. And now, despite her promises to remain throughout Round-Up, Sunny felt certain she would go home after the photoshoot. Because, really, if she was this frazzled now, how much worse might it get once Round-Up was going full speed?

Chapter Twenty

Sunny decided to ride around the reservation a bit before going back to the Lowenstein ranch. For one thing, she wanted to clear her head, but besides that, she still had that fascination—that sense that a part of her really did belong here. Eventually she came to what looked like an old church. Standing by itself on Tutuilla Church Road, it was a small boxy building with a steeple. Since there were no cars around, she decided to get out and look around. It was a Presbyterian church established more than a hundred years ago. And behind it was an overgrown cemetery.

She walked around reading markers that dated back to the late eighteen hundreds. Most of them were Native American. Although she didn't recognize any names, she was strangely drawn to the history—in the same way she had been at Saint Andrew's Mission. She felt as if there were many, many untold stories here. Many were probably just as painful as the ones in her own family. Some were probably much worse. And, once again, she felt a deep sadness for her ignorance. These were stories that she should know—perhaps even stories that should be written down and, like Aunt Lulu said, taught to the children.

Yet how could she, a newcomer and virtual stranger to this whole lifestyle, be so presumptuous as to think she should be able to do this? Really, who was she fooling? And with that in mind, she got in her car and drove back to the Lowenstein Ranch.

"You didn't stay very long," Aubrey observed when Sunny came into the bunkhouse.

"No, I didn't."

"But you sure look hot." Aubrey grinned.

"I am hot. We ate outside on a sunny deck, and I'm sure it was over ninety degrees."

"I mean hot as in pretty, Sunny." Aubrey pointed to her dress. "Very nice."

"Thanks." Sunny kicked off her sandals and headed for the kitchen.

"I'll bet Trina didn't appreciate that too much."

Sunny opened the fridge to get a soda. She'd stocked it with some things the other day so she wouldn't feel like such a freeloader during her visit. She noticed that Aubrey was helping herself to them as well. Not that Sunny minded.

"She didn't, did she?" Aubrey followed her, sitting at the small breakfast bar and waiting eagerly as if she expected to hear a juicy story. "I'll bet Trina went after you."

Sunny popped open the can and took a small swig.

"Seriously, Sunny, what happened?"

Sunny shrugged. "Not much. I made a salad that was too big. We sat outside at a table that was too hot. And I decided it was time to leave."

"You can't fool me." Aubrey narrowed her eyes. "Trina said or did something, didn't she?"

"What makes you think that?" Sunny took another slow swig.

"Do you know what Trina's name used to be?"

"Used to be?"

"Well, Indians sometimes have nicknames, you know?"

Sunny nodded. "Yes. I know."

"Trina used to be *Spitfire.*"

Sunny couldn't help but smile at this.

"So what did Trina say to you?"

"It was nothing much. I think I was just tired and hot and impatient."

"Come on, Sunny, give."

"Okay, she said something mean about my great-grandmother. And while it might've been true, it seemed rude for her to say it."

"Of course it was rude." Aubrey hit her fist on the counter. "That's the way that girl is. And she is especially rude to certain kinds of people."

"Certain kinds of people?"

Aubrey's blue eyes twinkled. "Yes. Ones she sees as competition."

"Competition for what?"

"You mean you don't know?"

Sunny let out a loud sigh. "Why do you always want to play these question games, Aubrey? Can't you just get to the point?"

"Sorry." Aubrey gave a sheepish smile. "I guess I enjoy the drama. So, anyway, Trina has had her eye on Cody ever since she moved back here. I assumed you knew that."

"I thought that might be the case."

"And so any single attractive woman who steps into the picture can expect to be targeted by Trina."

"It's too bad that she's so insecure."

"Insecure?" Aubrey frowned. "I think it's plain meanness."

Sunny shrugged. "If Trina felt secure in her relationship with Cody, she wouldn't need to attack anyone."

"Yeah, you'd think so. But I suspect that Cody might not like her as much as everyone is assuming."

"So everyone assumes that Cody likes her?"

"According to Mom, they spend a lot of time together. He's out at her place a lot. People just start to speculate…maybe they'll get married. You know?"

"And how do your parents feel about that? I mean, the idea of Trina being a step-mom to Echo?"

Aubrey made a face. "I suppose they're glad that Trina is into horses and all that. But I don't think they really like her much. I honestly don't think anyone likes Trina Strong Horse that much. Not even her own family."

"Well, Cody seems to." Sunny thought for a moment. "And so does Echo."

"That's because Trina is acting really sweet toward Echo right now."

"Maybe Trina really likes Echo."

"Maybe." Aubrey wrinkled her nose. "Or maybe Trina gets that Echo and Cody are a package deal—you don't get one without the other. Duh."

Sunny gave Aubrey a blank look now. "Maybe so." Then she took her can of soda and headed toward her bedroom. "If you'll excuse me, I think I'll take a little nap."

"Wait a minute." Aubrey was right behind her.

Sunny turned and looked at her. "What?"

"How does all that make you feel?"

"How does *what* make me feel?"

Aubrey laughed. "Hey, you're the one who complained about the question game, and now you're doing it too."

"I guess you're rubbing off on me."

"Come on, Sunny. How does it make you feel?"

"I'm honestly not sure what you're talking about, Aubrey. How does *what* make me feel?"

"Hearing that Trina is after Cody. How does that make you feel?"

Sunny frowned. "Like it's none of my business?"

Aubrey studied her. "Are you sure that's all?"

"Okay, I'll admit it." Sunny pressed her lips together for a moment. "I really do care about Echo. She's a sweet, wonderful girl. And I would hope that Trina would never do anything to hurt her. I think that would make me seriously angry."

Aubrey smiled. "Hey, you and a whole lot of other people as well. Echo has her own fan club. We'd all come to her rescue if a wicked stepmother stepped on our girl. Don't you worry."

Sunny smiled back. "That makes me feel much better. Now, if you don't mind, I'll take a nap."

"And afterwards, do you want to go to town with me and have dinner with my friends? They're dying to meet you, Sunny. And, really, they're a lot more fun than Trina Strong Horse. I guarantee you that."

Sunny was about to decline, but decided why not. "You know, Aubrey, that sounds like fun."

"All right!" Aubrey nodded happily. "It's a date!" She pointed to Sunny's dress. "And you have to wear that, okay?"

Sunny shrugged. "Sure. Why not?" Then, feeling like she'd dodged a bullet, she slipped into her room and closed the door.

* * * * *

Sunny wasn't sorry she'd come with Aubrey tonight. Aubrey's friends Garth and Lucy Burkes were the hosts of this evening's gathering, and the gracious couple had a lovely house on the north hill in Pendleton. As Sunny sat on the deck overlooking the town, she was aware of two things. First of all, Aubrey's friends seemed relaxed and fun and generally happy. Second of all, and as far as Sunny could see, they did not appear to be caught up in any of the who's who in Pendleton. Nor were they uncomfortable with cultural diversity. Whether a guest was Hispanic, Asian, or Indian, it all made no difference to the Burkes. And from what Sunny could see, a broad mix of ethnicity was present. Most were friends that the Burkes had acquired in college, and while some were locals, a few had just arrived early for the Pendleton Round-Up.

"Do you live in Pendleton?" a man named Wesley asked Sunny.

"No, I'm visiting," she told him. "How about you?"

"I'm visiting too. I'm actually from the Portland area."

"So am I."

He smiled. "But Pendleton is quite a place. Where else can you find the quintessential all-American town—with cowboys to boot?"

She laughed. "And Indians too."

"But in a couple of days, this place will be crawling with tourists. Have you ever been here for Round-Up?"

"No, it's my first time here ever."

"It's my second Round-Up," he told her. "After the first one, a few years ago, I made Garth promise me that I could be a guest here for the hundredth anniversary. I think it'll be quite an event."

She nodded, looking out over the town's lights in the dusky evening.

"Are you staying for Round-Up?"

She sipped her iced tea. "I had planned to, but now I'm not so sure."

He frowned. "Did you forget to reserve a hotel? I hear it's impossible to get accommodations anywhere now."

"Actually, I have a room at Aubrey's parents' ranch."

He smiled. "So, what's the problem?"

"I don't know." She sighed. "I've been here almost a week already."

"Do you have a job to go home to? Or a husband and kids?"

"Not really." She swirled the ice cubes in the glass.

"Pets? A boyfriend?"

She chuckled. "No, but thanks for asking."

"Then you should stay, Sunny. It's a once-in-a-lifetime event. I'm actually doing a magazine article on it."

She turned to look at him. "You write for a magazine?"

"I'm a freelancer. But this is an assignment I contracted more than a year ago."

Just then Aubrey and her friend Mitchell joined them.

"What a beautiful night," Aubrey gushed. "The temperature's perfect, the air is sweet." She took in a deep breath. "Delicious."

Mitchell laughed. "Hey, Wesley, are you aware that you're talking to a fashion model?"

Sunny laughed. "I'm not really a model," she said quickly. "I just took on the job to earn some money. I was laid off last spring. Cutbacks at the college I taught at."

"Anyway, these girls are doing a catalog shoot on Monday right here in Pendleton," Mitchell told Wesley. "Maybe you can use that in your magazine article."

Wesley chuckled. "I could try to think of an angle just for an excuse to attend the shoot, but I doubt it would really have much to do with Round-Up."

"Yeah, but we're shooting at the Round-Up grounds," Aubrey persisted.

Wesley nodded. "Well, who knows? Maybe there's an angle after all."

"And"—Aubrey pointed to Sunny with a mysterious expression—"here's a girl with a real Round-Up story."

Wesley's eyebrow lifted in interest.

Sunny tried not to glare at Aubrey.

"Oh, I'm sorry, Sunny," Aubrey said quickly. "You know me. These loose lips are always sinking someone's ship." She made a zipper motion over her mouth. "Mum's the word."

"Great, now you've got me all curious." Wesley's head swiveled from one girl to the other. "You're not going to tell me?"

"I want to hear it too." Mitchell frowned. "Come on, Sunny, what's the story?"

Sunny remembered her conversation with the newspaper reporter and the announcement at the parade. "Were you guys at the Dress-Up Parade?" she asked cautiously.

"Sure. Does it have to do with that?"

"Sunny was in the parade," Aubrey bragged.

"Really?" Wesley looked like he was trying to recall.

"Were you near the announcer's platform?" Sunny asked.

"No, we were clear on the end of town," Wesley said. "We got there late."

"Come on, Sunny," Aubrey urged. "Why not just tell them?"

"Yeah, why not?" begged Mitchell.

She shrugged, realizing it might be easier to get this over with. Besides, she might be able to play it down and move on. "It's not a big deal. Nothing is established with any real proof, but there's a rumor I could be a descendant of Jackson Sundown. However, that would mean Jackson Sundown fathered an illegitimate child nearly a hundred years ago. And that's rather hard, if not impossible, to prove. To be honest, I don't even believe it myself. Unfortunately, there are others who seem to get a thrill thinking it's true."

Wesley nodded as if intrigued. "You have to admit, it's interesting."

"But not the kind of thing you'd want to print, since it's probably not true. It could be embarrassing—especially if the Sundown family tried to dispute it." She thought for a moment. "I'll bet it could even turn into a lawsuit…perhaps defamation of character."

"That's a good point," Mitchell agreed.

"So it's best to just let it go," Sunny finished. "In a way, it's probably not that different from women who claim that famous personalities have fathered their children. A convenient way to gain notoriety and maybe even a few bucks."

"Except that there are DNA tests now," Mitchell added.

"Exactly." Sunny pointed her finger in the air. "And that's just one more reason I'd rather play this whole thing down. That way no one ends up looking stupid."

Of course, they had to kick the whole thing around a bit longer, each adding their own theories, but to her relief the interest slowly waned and they soon began talking about other things. All in all, it was a rather pleasant and benign evening.

"Thanks for inviting me tonight," Sunny told Aubrey as they drove home.

"And thanks for coming. I can tell my friends really liked you."

"And I like your friends."

"How about Wesley?" Aubrey asked. "Did you like him too?"

"Sure. He's interesting. I think being a freelance writer sounds like a great job. He travels all over."

"Well, I got the impression he was interested in you too, Sunny. Do you think you'd want to go out with him sometime?"

"I, uh, I don't know."

"He asked me if I thought it was a good idea for him to ask you out. I told him I didn't see why not."

"Oh."

"Unless you just don't like him."

"He seemed nice, Aubrey. But I don't know..."

"How about if we go out together? You and Wesley and Mitchell and me? Would that make you more comfortable?"

"Maybe."

"How about if we go to Round-Up together?" Aubrey suggested. "If we do some ticket swapping, we could probably even sit together. And that's not even like a real date. It's more just friends doing something together, you know?"

"Okay." Sunny nodded. "It sounds like a good plan."

"Cool. I'll get it all set up then. We'll shoot for opening day. Or maybe Thursday."

"All right." And, as she said this, Sunny realized that she had agreed to stay on a few more days. That's when she remembered her promise to Hank—that she'd come to their barbecue on the first evening of Round-Up. Well, she supposed she could do both. And then maybe she'd head home.

Chapter Twenty-one

....

Sunny slept in on Sunday morning. Then she pulled on her jeans, a T-shirt, and an old Roper ball cap she'd found in the closet. Slipping into Cindy's garden, she spent the next several hours weeding and pruning and generally cleaning the plot up. She knew it was a small thing, but it was her way of thanking the Lowensteins for their hospitality. Plus it was good therapy.

"What are you doing out—" Cindy stopped and slapped her hand over her mouth. "My word, did you do all this?"

Sunny stood up and brushed the dirt from her hands, then smiled.

"Sunny, Sunny, Sunny." Cindy came over and threw her arms around her, holding her in a long, tight hug. "I'd been thinking you were just short from being an angel, and now I think I was wrong. You *are* an angel."

"I love gardening."

"So do I. But I've had my bad back and then I was so busy and…I just had to let it go. I kept thinking of hiring someone to come out here. But, you know, a garden's kind of personal." She paused and looked around with wide eyes.

"I hope I didn't overstep my—"

"No, no. You did it exactly as I'd have done. If I'd had the energy, that is." Cindy walked down the path between the sunflowers and beans. "Just look at this garden. It's lovely, Sunny. How can I ever thank you?"

Sunny's smile grew larger. "You already did, Cindy. You've made me feel comfortable and welcome in your home."

Cindy frowned. "Even after Doug jumped on you that night you were in Lenora's room?" She chuckled. "He did feel bad afterwards, when I set him straight. But you caught him by surprise."

"It probably didn't help that I was in my pajamas at the time."

Cindy laughed. "Yes. I'm sure that didn't."

"My grandmother liked to garden," Sunny said in an absent sort of way.

"Your grandmother must've been a wonderful woman, Sunny. She certainly did a fine job with you."

"Hello?" called what sounded like Echo's voice. "Anybody out here? Grandma?"

"Over here, Sweetie," called Cindy. "In my lovely garden."

"Oh." Echo joined them. "There you both are."

"And just look what Sunny did to my garden, Echo."

Echo looked around as if she expected to see something bad. "What?"

"She weeded it and fixed it up."

Echo nodded and smiled now. "It does look nice."

"I've been of a mind to ask Echo to help," Cindy told Sunny. "But I don't want to distract her from riding."

"I could help here," Echo offered.

"Now you don't need to," Sunny told her.

"Do you want to ride with me today?" Echo's eyes were hopeful.

Sunny grinned. "You don't have to ask twice."

"Great. Let's go get saddled up. Dad's already out there getting Chase ready."

"Chase?"

"Yeah. Grandpa's horse. Dad rides him sometimes."

"Chase needs to be worked with," Cindy explained.

"Oh, if you're riding with your dad…" Sunny paused. "Well, you don't need a riding buddy."

"But you wanted to ride," Echo protested.

"You already have—"

"Sunny," interrupted Cindy, "you already told Echo you wanted to ride. Just because Cody is along isn't any reason not to. Now you two girls get going. And, Echo, tell your dad that I expect you to stay for dinner. I plan to call Hank and tell him to get himself over here as well."

Echo nodded. "Okay."

"Are you planning to go into the foothills?" Cindy asked Echo.

"Yeah. Maybe."

Cindy looked back at Sunny. "You make sure you take a water bottle and wear a cool shirt and a good hat." She pointed to Echo. "And you come inside and get some food to pack with you."

"Is this going to be a long ride?" Sunny asked.

"Might be," Echo told her. "But we'll be back in time for dinner."

"Okay." Sunny nodded, unable to hide her eagerness at getting to go on what sounded like a real ride. "This sounds like it could be fun." And yet, even as she proclaimed this, she felt apprehensive. She hadn't spoken to Cody since that uncomfortable scene at Trina's "barbecue." What if her sudden exit had embarrassed him in front of his friends?

Chapter Twenty-two

Sunny was right. The trail ride was fun, and no one mentioned the barbecue. Cody, dressed in worn Wrangler jeans, roper boots, a faded plaid western shirt, and straw cowboy hat, took the lead. And since Sunny was the inexperienced rider, she followed him, with Echo riding behind her. Sunny didn't mind that they didn't talk much along the way. Other than Cody pointing out an occasional deer, rabbit, or interesting bird, the ride was mostly quiet and peaceful. Delightful.

It was around three when Cody stopped his horse beneath a grove of poplar trees next to the barely trickling creek and got down. "How about a break?"

"Sounds good to me." Sunny reached for her water bottle and took a swig.

"And I've got treats," Echo announced. "Grandma's sugar cookies and some fruit."

They let their horses take a drink, then secured them to a tree before they sat in a grassy area and Echo shared the "treats" her grandmother packed for them. "I wish Sunny could do a cattle drive with us someday," Echo said dreamily.

"A real cattle drive?" Sunny questioned.

Echo nodded. "I just did my first one last year. It was so cool. We come up this way, bringing Grandpa's cattle up to the highlands to graze. It's really fun."

"When do you do that?"

"Later in the fall," Cody said quietly.

"Oh." Sunny tried to hide the longing she felt at the idea of a real cattle drive. "Well, I'll be back in Portland by then."

"Why do you have to go back there?" Echo asked.

Sunny laughed. "Because it's my home."

"But you don't have a job there," Echo pointed out.

"Yes, don't remind me." Sunny forced lightness into her voice. "I've been trying not to think about that."

"Maybe you could get a job here," Echo suggested.

"It's a little late in the year to get a teaching job," Cody told her.

"Maybe another kind of job," Echo said hopefully.

"But my home is in Portland," Sunny said again. "I have to go home, Echo."

Echo stared down at the stick she was poking into the ground and frowned.

"Just because you want someone to stay with you doesn't mean they can," Cody told Echo. "You know that people have their own lives to live. Just be glad that Aunt Aubrey brought Sunny here to visit for a while."

"I am." Echo nodded.

"And maybe you'll want to come to Portland sometime," Sunny told Echo. "You'd be more than welcome to stay with me. I even have a guest room."

"Really?" Echo glanced up. "I could stay with you?"

"If your dad didn't mind. I'd love it. I could show you around Portland, the museums and theaters and things. Or we could call Aunt Aubrey and go shopping."

Echo's eyes lit up. "That would be cool."

Sunny smiled. "It really would."

Cody had stretched back now, with his hat over his eyes, his legs crossed at the ankles, and a grass blade sticking out between his teeth. He looked like a real cowboy.

Sunny couldn't help staring. The way Cody and Echo lived—riding horses, living in wide, open spaces, fresh air, taking it slow and easy—seemed almost unreal. She looked away. For her, it was unreal. Someone else's life…someone else's dream. Not hers.

"I'm going to ride up to Mom's tree," Echo said suddenly. "Do you mind, Dad?"

"No. Don't stay too long, though. We should head back by four."

"Okay." She cocked her head toward Sunny. "You don't mind waiting, do you?"

"No, not at all."

Echo mounted her horse and the sounds of his hooves slowly faded until it was only Cody and Sunny. Even though Cody was ignoring her, Sunny felt uncomfortable. Like she was an intruder, like she didn't belong here. She quietly stood and started to walk away. She wouldn't go far. Just far enough to create some space. She needed some space.

"Where are you going?" Cody was sitting up now, his knees pulled up, elbows resting on them.

"Uh, just stretching my legs." This was partly true—she *was* a bit stiff from the ride. But mostly she was uncomfortable being around Cody.

He adjusted his hat to see her better. "Did I scare you away?"

She forced a smile. "No, of course not. I thought you were napping and I—"

"Look, I was hoping I could talk to you. Alone."

"Alone?" She glanced in the direction Echo had gone.

"I didn't ask Echo to leave, though. That was just convenient."

"Oh." She cautiously walked back and sat on a boulder a few feet from him. Placing her hands on her knees, she gazed evenly at him. "What did you want to talk about?"

"For starters, I want to apologize."

"Apologize?" She blinked and waited.

"I want to apologize for how you were treated at Trina's yesterday. I should've said something then, but I was…well, kind of caught off guard."

She just waited.

"And while it's not my place to apologize for Trina's actions, I can apologize for not speaking out in your defense. My dad was a much better man than I was."

"Your father is a good guy."

He nodded. "I know. And my father thinks you're pretty special too. He was hopping mad yesterday. If it makes you feel any better, he left shortly after you did."

She shrugged.

"At the time I didn't know why Trina acted like that. It seemed so out of the blue. But when I got home, Dad straightened me out."

"He did?"

Cody nodded, pulling up another long blade of grass. "Dad's theory is that Trina was jealous of you."

"Oh."

Cody looked up now. "Not that I said or did anything to make Trina jealous. I honestly don't think I did."

"But maybe she just felt threatened by having another single woman around." Sunny wished she hadn't said this. Really, it was Aubrey's theory, not hers.

"I don't know why." He slowly shook his head.

"No, I don't either."

"I wanted to say something else, Sunny." His eyes were sincere. "I know I don't know you that well. I've only known you for a few days—less than a week. But I can't quit thinking of—"

"Dad!" screamed Echo from up above on the hill. *"Dad!"*

Without another word, Cody jumped on his horse and shot up the hill. And with a bit less grace, Sunny hopped on Brownie Anne and the good horse, without much direction, followed the trail of dust until they came to a clearing where both Echo and Cody were still on their horses, staring at what appeared to be the remains of an old tree. A tree that had been split in half by what only Sunny could assume was lightning.

"It must've been from that storm in late August," Cody said sadly. "Remember how wild that night was?"

Tears streamed down Echo's cheeks. "It was Mom's tree," she sobbed.

"I'm sorry," Sunny said quietly. "It looks like it was a beautiful tree."

Cody nodded. "It was."

"And now it's gone," Echo sobbed. "It's dead. The lightning killed it."

Sunny felt more like an intruder than ever. They did not need her around to witness their grief. So she gently pulled the reins to turn Brownie Anne around, and they slowly made their way back down the trail, back to the creek, where she let the old horse have another drink and waited for father and daughter to return.

But as she stood there, she wondered: what had Cody been about to say to her? She knew he'd been saying he hadn't known her for long, and he'd seemed uneasy about what he was about to say. It was clear their conversation could've gone one of two ways. The first route seemed the most likely, especially following the talk she'd just had with Echo about maintaining their fledgling friendship over the miles. Of course, that had to be it. She should've known that she'd stepped over the line. Really, what sensible adult went around inviting a young girl—someone she barely knew—to visit in a big city? And what kind of parent wouldn't see that as some kind of a warning flag? Naturally, that had made Cody uneasy. And he'd been about to tell her so—that he'd only known her less than a week and here she was acting like it was okay to invite Echo into her life. Really, why had she done that?

On the other hand—and she hardly wanted to allow herself to go this route—what if Cody had been about to express a feeling for her? It seemed possible that the next line coming from him might've been that, although he'd only known her a short while, he was developing feelings for her. Wasn't that possible? Or was that only in movies? And in dreams?

She weighed this against his slightly awkward apology regarding Trina's bad manners yesterday. And he was right: it really wasn't his place to apologize for Trina, unless the two were a couple and seriously involved. Perhaps that was it. Perhaps that was exactly what he'd been trying to tell her. Of course, that made the most sense. And Sunny was simply playing the role of a sentimental fool to try to imagine this in any other sort of light. What had she been thinking?

It was about thirty minutes before Cody and Echo came down, but the tears and all traces of them were gone. Echo actually seemed in fairly good spirits, though Cody was quiet.

"We'll have to head back now in order to make it to the ranch in time for dinner," Cody said as he and Echo gave their horses a quick drink. And just like they'd come, Cody led the way, Echo brought up the end, and stuck in the middle, Sunny let Brownie Anne have her lead and the dependable old horse took her flawlessly down the mountain as if she understood how much Sunny's heart was hurting.

Back at the horse barn, they all hurried to get the saddles off, quickly brushing down the horses, then turning them out to pasture. "I'm going to run ahead," Cody told them, "to make sure Cindy remembered to call Dad."

"You know," Echo told Sunny as they finished up and walked back toward the house, "I was really upset at first, but then Dad helped me understand that it was okay."

"What was okay?" Sunny studied the young girl's face—her sincere brow and serious, dark eyes—as they walked.

"That Mom's tree is gone. It's like everything changes, and that's how life is. And then we looked around until we found a baby tree bravely growing just a few feet away—right in the midst of the rubble from the fallen tree."

"Really?"

"Yeah. Dad and I cleared around it, moving away the branches and cleaning up a space around the tree. Then we got some rocks and made a little circle around the tree." Echo smiled. "I even gave it some water from my water bottle."

Sunny smiled back. "That's so sweet."

"I'll keep checking on the new tree now. Someday it'll be as big as the other one."

"Aren't you glad you went up there now?" Sunny told her as they stood by the bunkhouse. "Otherwise you wouldn't have known the big tree had fallen and the baby tree needed a little help."

Echo nodded. "Yes. You're right." She hugged Sunny. "See you at dinner."

Sunny felt a lump in her throat as she went into the bunkhouse. Thankfully, Aubrey wasn't around to see her quiet tears. She didn't even know why she was crying exactly. But something deep within felt as if it had twisted so hard and so sharp that it hurt, and that pain was making her cry.

She splashed cool water on her face, quickly cleaned up, changed into a fresh shirt, and hurried back to the house in time to hear Cindy ringing the dinner bell. "Hey, there you are." She smiled. "Did you have a good ride? You look a little flushed. Hopefully the heat didn't get to you."

"It was a truly memorable ride," Sunny said. "Can I help you?"

So Cindy put Sunny to work helping to carry food to the massive table in the dining room. Before long they were all seated around it—a dozen of them counting the three Barretts and the other Lowensteins (Aubrey's older brother, his wife, and boys). Doug bowed his head, asked a blessing, and soon food was being passed around and everyone was talking at once.

The feeling at this table was so congenial and happy and warm—so unlike anything else that Sunny had ever experienced—that she found it difficult to even participate in the lively conversation. Fortunately, no one seemed to notice. Or so she told herself as she sat mesmerized, listening to the happy chatter of a family that appeared to have shared a multitude of moments like this. She suspected that, to them, this was just another ordinary family mealtime. Amazing.

When dinner was done, including a dessert of ice cream and berries and decaf coffee, Sunny insisted on helping Cindy clear and clean up.

"Thanks for the hand, Sunny," Cindy said as Sunny remained in the kitchen to continue helping. "But you should go join the others. I'm fine on my own. I'm used to this."

"I really want to help you," Sunny assured her. "Probably because I'm *not* used to this."

"You're not used to helping in the kitchen?" Cindy asked as she opened the dishwasher.

"No, I'm not used to being included in a big family like this. I feel like I'm an alien visiting from another planet."

Cindy laughed. "Well, you're an adorable alien, Sunny. And you are welcome on my planet anytime."

As they rinsed dinner plates, Sunny suddenly began to confess her ill-conceived invitation for Echo to come visit her in Portland. But even as she shared, she wondered over the sensibility of opening herself up like this.

"I really don't see anything wrong with that," Cindy told her as she reached for a dish towel.

"But I could tell that Cody didn't appreciate my interference," Sunny admitted. "And I can't blame him a bit. He's right. He hardly knows me, and I have no right inviting his daughter to come to a big city to visit me."

"Oh, but we *do* know you, Sunny. You're Aubrey's friend. You're staying in our home. And we all love you. I can't imagine why Cody would've reacted like that."

"I can. And I don't blame him. What if I were a kidnapper trying to make off with Echo? Things like that probably happen."

Cindy blinked. "Well, I suppose that could happen. But not with you, dear."

"Yes, but anyway, I feel badly that I made him uncomfortable like that. I honestly hadn't meant to. I was simply trying to reassure Echo that we could still be friends despite the miles. Poor Echo was trying to talk me into staying here forever." Sunny laughed. "As if I could sell my house and pull up my roots and live here indefinitely."

Cindy grew quiet now. "It could be done, you know, if you truly wanted to do it."

Sunny turned to look at Cindy, seeing that she appeared quite serious.

"Well, yes, of course. I suppose it *could* be done. I mean, perhaps someone could do it. But not someone like me."

"Someone like you?" Cindy paused to look at Sunny now. "Why not?"

Sunny held up her hands with a weak smile. "Because I've lived in the same house for more than twenty-five years? Because I've never been a person to welcome changes of any kind? Because I need to feel safe, secure, and I like my boring status quo?"

Cindy placed a warm hand on Sunny's cheek, gazing into her eyes with a surprising intensity. "That's how you've lived *up until now*, Sunny. It's not necessarily how you should continue to live. A girl like you needs something more. I can see it in your eyes. And I've seen you on a horse." Her hand slipped down as if she were suddenly uncomfortable with the familiar gesture. Cindy turned back to the sink but continued talking. "Mark my word, dear girl, you will go home, but I sincerely believe you will discover that you no longer fit into that little world anymore. You have outgrown it."

Sunny forced a laugh as she dried a large platter. "That's an interesting theory, Cindy. And, who knows? You could be right. I'll keep it in mind." But even as she said this, she felt a rush of fear. What if Cindy was right? What if Sunny really had outgrown her little house, her little life, her little comfort zone, her safe little world? What if, with or without a job, it no longer fit? What then?

Chapter Twenty-three

After finishing up in the kitchen, Sunny told Cindy that she was tired. "And we have that photoshoot in the morning. More than ever, I need my beauty sleep, so I think I'll turn in early tonight."

"Thanks again for your help." Cindy gave the granite countertop one last swipe.

"And thanks for a lovely meal…and for listening."

Sunny welcomed the quiet solitude in the bunkhouse. Not wanting to get caught in a conversation with Aubrey, she hurriedly took her shower, got ready for bed, and turned off the lights. But as she lay there in the darkness, all she could think about was Cody.

As much as she'd tried to convince herself that Cody had been uneasy about Sunny's relationship with his daughter, in the quiet of night, she wasn't so sure. The look in his eyes somehow suggested more. Or maybe that was simply her hopeful imagination trying to attribute it to more. But what if? What if Cody really did have feelings for her? What if?

Sunny knew this was a dangerous game to play. She knew the hurt she'd suffered from falling into this kind of thinking—assuming a man cared more than he really did, building a relationship into more than it was ever meant to be—and she had promised herself she would never do it again. In the same way she'd been pushing the possibility of being related to Jackson Sundown away from her—without hard evidence—she would push any thoughts of romance away too. Not without hard evidence. And so far, she had none.

* * * * *

The photoshoot in front of the rodeo grounds went fairly smoothly. Especially considering that Round-Up grounds was already buzzing with pre-rodeo activity. Marsha had to pace the shot locations so that rodeo fans were, for the most part, only in the background. The most fun was when they moved the location for the shoot up to the tipi village behind the rodeo grounds.

"This is amazing," Sunny said as they walked past row after row of authentic tipis, where Indians from all over the Northwest had been camping for several days now.

"Not only amazing," Marsha told her, "but it's a fantastic backdrop to this shoot. I can't wait to see how it turns out."

Marsha's assistants had already gone around to the back of the tipis and roped off an area to hold curious onlookers at bay while they continued to shoot the models. Fortunately, with fewer models in this particular shoot, it only took about an hour to finish up.

"I want to do one more setting," Marsha told them. "I know it wasn't planned, but I decided that a backdrop of the Indian horses would be charming as well." She pointed to Sunny. "And I'd like to have your buckskin jacket in that shot too, if you don't mind."

"I don't mind using it," Sunny told her, "as long as the woolen mill doesn't mind since it's obviously not their product."

"It's just for fun," Marsha reminded her. "And it looks great with the native print skirt I'm having you wear. I just know that one of those shots is going to be stellar, maybe even a cover photo."

Sunny put her full effort into cooperating. By now she knew that was the only way to get things done. And as they were finishing up, she felt more like a pro than ever. Not that she planned to do anything like this again. But the money she was earning would come in handy this fall. Perhaps she'd even look back on this time with fond memories someday.

"Thank you so much," Marsha told Sunny when they'd finished. She handed her a business card. "I know you keep saying you're not really a model, but in case you change your mind, I have a couple more northwest catalogs to shoot, and I'd love to include you."

"I'll keep that in mind," Sunny promised, mostly to be polite, although if she got desperate enough, she might just take her up on it. "And it's been a pleasure"—Sunny grinned—"well, *mostly* a pleasure working with you."

Marsha laughed. "Thanks. I appreciate your honesty."

After they got back into their street clothes, emerging from the tipi that Marsha had rented from a nice young couple to use as a dressing room, Aubrey asked Sunny if she wanted to grab a late lunch. "We could head over to GP. My treat."

"What's GP?"

"The Great Pacific. It's this cool little deli that my friends and I used to meet at after we graduated high school and came back to town to kick up our heels. We still go there."

Town seemed much busier today as Sunny, directed by Aubrey, drove through in search of a parking spot. Finally they found one a couple of blocks away.

"This will all be shut down by tomorrow," Aubrey told Sunny as they walked down Main Street.

"Shut down?" Sunny was confused. "You mean they close the whole town for Round-Up? Don't the business owners complain?"

Aubrey laughed. "No. I mean the street will be closed to traffic. Venders and musicians and all sorts of fun things will fill up the entire street, from one end to the other. It's like a small fair."

"That sounds like fun."

"It is." Aubrey nodded. "Here we are."

Sunny scanned the cavernous room. "This is a *small* deli?"

Aubrey chuckled. "It started out as a little deli, then grew."

They ordered their food, then went looking for an empty table, which turned out to be a challenge.

"Hey, Aubrey and Sunny," called out a male voice. "Over here!"

Sunny glanced over her shoulder to see that Mitchell, from the other night, was waving wildly from a table by the window. Seated across from him was Wesley, also waving.

"Small world," Aubrey said as they went over to their table.

"Please, join us," Mitchell offered. "We're in need of some pretty women."

"We just finished our last photoshoot." Aubrey set her deli number on the table, then sighed loudly as if the work had been exhausting.

"Then you should celebrate." Mitchell held up a glass of red wine as if to make a toast.

"Good idea!" Aubrey nodded. "But I didn't think to order—"

"I'll take care of that." Mitchell stood. "It's their house pinot noir," he told Aubrey. "But it's good."

"Sounds delightful."

Mitchell did a mock bow, then headed toward the counter.

"So are we still on for Round-Up on Wednesday?" Wesley asked hopefully.

"Yes," Aubrey said eagerly. "It turns out that Daddy bought a slug of extra tickets several years back. He knew the hundredth anniversary was a no-brainer. Anyway, if you'll give up your tickets, we can do some switching around so that we all get to sit together in the North Grandstand."

Wesley nodded with obvious approval. "Very cool, Aubrey. I hear the North Grandstand is the place to be."

"Yes. My dad always has seats there, but this year our friends and family will practically fill a whole section. It's going to be great!"

"And it's okay to switch our less-desirable tickets for the North Grandstand?" Wesley looked a little concerned.

"We'll switch with some relatives who've never been here before. Really, I doubt they'll even know the difference," Aubrey assured him. "And we will be sitting directly right over the bucking chutes."

"Great." Wesley gave a thumbs-up sign. "I really tried to get a press pass to be on the field, but it was just not happening. Above the bucking chutes is almost as good." Then he told them about the bull riding event that he and Mitchell planned to attend this evening.

"Round-Up starts tonight?" Sunny asked.

"Not officially. The bull riding is kind of a warm-up show. It runs tonight and tomorrow night."

"It's more than just a warm-up show," Mitchell told Sunny. "The PBR is a big deal. Bulls and bull riding like you've never seen before."

"He's right. The men in my family love those shows." Aubrey made a face. "Me, not so much."

"Why?" Sunny asked.

"I don't like seeing a perfectly good cowboy getting his head stomped by an angry bull."

Sunny bristled. "Seriously? Does that really happen?"

"You never know." Aubrey shook her head. "Sometimes they walk away; sometimes they get carried."

"That's terrible." Sunny frowned.

"It's a dangerous sport," Wesley said in a serious tone. "But that's just rodeo. The danger is part of the thrill."

"Maybe I'm not going to be much of a rodeo fan after all," Sunny murmured.

Wesley moved his face close to hers. "That doesn't sound like the great-granddaughter of Jackson Sundown to me."

She shrugged. "Maybe I'm not."

He shook his head. "I think you are, Sunny."

Just then Mitchell returned with not one, but two glasses of red wine. "Here you go, ladies."

Sunny didn't want to be rude, so she just watched as he placed the glasses in front of them. Perhaps the guys would want to have hers since she was certainly not going there. Then, as Wesley lifted his in a toast, simply to be polite and to avoid having to make a statement, Sunny lifted hers as well.

"Here's to the hundredth year of Round-Up," Wesley said. "And to the possibility that we are sharing this toast with a direct descendant of Jackson Sundown."

They all took a sip, and Sunny did what she hoped was a pretty good imitation before she set her glass down and turned to Wesley. "You seem awfully sure about me being related to Jackson Sundown. Have you come up with any concrete proof?"

"As a matter of fact, I've been doing some very interesting research. And while I haven't found anything concrete, I'm inclined to believe there's a definite possibility here."

"Here's to the possibilities." Aubrey held up her glass for a second toast. "May they be limitless."

With halfhearted enthusiasm, Sunny held up her glass again, clinking it against the others, but just as she was about to fake another sip, she got the distinct impression she was being watched. Glancing over toward the counter, she felt a wave of panic to see Cody staring directly at her with a perplexed expression. Standing next to him was Trina, but her attention was fixed on Cody, until she turned and followed his gaze. Then she locked eyes with Sunny in a stern disapproval that quickly transformed itself into a smirking smile. Trina made a little finger wave, then turned to Cody, holding her hand close to her mouth as she stood on tiptoe in an effort to whisper something in his ear. For no rational or explainable reason, Sunny felt like screaming.

Instead, she turned her attention back to Wesley. "I'm curious as to what exactly you've uncovered in your research," she said in a calm, controlled voice.

Aubrey was studying Sunny with interest now. Had she witnessed that little scene? And if she had, did it even matter?

Wesley, his back to Cody and Trina, seemed oblivious as he began to report his findings—all of which were not news to Sunny.

"Is that it?" she asked with disinterest.

"Isn't that enough?" He cocked his head slightly to one side.

She forced what she hoped would come off as a genuine smile. "I have to agree, it's enough to raise the question. Unfortunately, it's not enough to answer it."

Wesley laughed. "You are a hard nut to crack, Sunny Westcott. But I happen to enjoy a difficult nut on occasion."

Sunny made a slightly glib remark to that, all the while using every bit of self-control to keep from looking back at Cody and Trina. It was fine if they wanted to stare and whisper about her, but she was not going to give them the satisfaction of looking back…or of showing the slightest reaction.

As it turned out, Sunny outlasted them. With relief, she saw them leaving the deli together. Actually, it was relief mixed with angst because she would've been more pleased to have witnessed them leaving separately. But, once again, she reminded herself that it was none of her business.

She glanced at her watch, surprised to see it was after three. "I hate to break up the party," she said, "but I'd like to get back to the ranch for a ride."

"A ride?" Wesley looked curious.

"Sunny rides horses with my niece every day about this time," Aubrey explained. "Although, since school is out this week, I wouldn't be surprised if Echo already finished up her riding time today. I think I heard Mom saying they were going to do something together afterwards."

A wave of disappointment washed over Sunny.

"Not that you can't ride on your own," Aubrey said quickly.

"Don't you ride?" Mitchell asked her.

Aubrey rolled her eyes in answer.

"Hey, if you want company, why don't you let me ride with you?" Wesley suggested. "I haven't been on a horse for years, but I'll bet it's a lot like riding a bike."

"Oh, I don't know," Sunny said quickly. "They aren't even my horses, and I'm a guest and—"

"Well, one of the horses happens to belong to me," Aubrey interrupted. "I am not a guest, but a member of the family." She smiled at Wesley. "And you are both welcome to come out and ride if you like."

"Hey, I have an idea," Wesley said suddenly, turning to Mitchell. "How about if you get a shot of me on a horse, and I can use it for my author photo in this feature article?"

Mitchell nodded eagerly. "You bet. I'd love to get a photo credit for that."

"We'll have to hurry." Wesley stood, tossing a tip on the table. "To make it back to the bulls in time."

And so, before Sunny could think of a way to protest, she was behind the wheel of her car and driving out to the Lowenstein Ranch with a tan Jeep Wrangler trailing behind them. She wanted to be irritated at Aubrey for interfering but didn't really see the point. Instead, she simply drove in silence.

"I noticed Cody and Trina at GP," Aubrey said in a tone that suggested something more.

"Oh?"

"I noticed that you noticed them too."

Sunny just nodded, keeping her eyes on the road ahead.

"And, unless I'm wrong, you seemed a little upset to see them."

"I think I was a little surprised." Sunny felt her cheeks warm to the small lie. Sunny did not like dishonesty. But sometimes the truth was too hard.

"You seemed more than a little surprised to me, Sunny. I'm curious. What's up?"

"What's up?"

"Yeah. Are you into Cody?"

Sunny vigorously shook her head. "No, of course not. That's ridiculous. I barely even know him. And besides, he's involved with Trina."

"Says who?"

Sunny shrugged. "Says Trina."

"When exactly did Trina say that?"

"Oh, you know. You said it yourself, Aubrey, about her getting jealous if another woman is around Cody. And I saw it in person on Saturday."

"Really?" Aubrey's tone oozed with curiosity now. "Tell me more."

"I already told you," Sunny said quickly.

"You told me Trina ripped into your great-grandmother."

"Okay, the truth is, I think she was ripping into me just as much."

"Well, duh. I'm glad you can at least admit that."

"And your point is?" Sunny glanced at Aubrey, then back at the road.

"My point is that I think there's something between you and Cody."

"Why on earth would you say that?" Sunny let out an exasperated sigh.

"I have my reasons."

"And those would be?"

"I have eyes in my head, Sunny."

"Yes. And so do I."

"I don't think so."

Sunny wanted to squelch this conversation before it went further, but she couldn't think of a new subject.

"I noticed Cody looking at you last night."

Sunny clamped her mouth shut.

"And that's a look I haven't seen him giving a woman…for, well, a very long time."

"You mean Lenora."

"That's right. And, to be honest, it was a look he gave Lenora early on—not so much after they were married."

"What's that supposed to mean?"

"Just that their marriage had its problems."

"Really?" For some reason Sunny had imagined them as completely happy, the ideal couple, and the perfect little family of three when Echo came along.

"I wouldn't tell just anyone this." Aubrey's tone grew confidential. "But for some reason, I think you should know. I loved my sister…in fact, I still love her. But she could be difficult."

"Difficult?"

"She was used to having things her own way. And when she married Cody, she had to make some compromises."

"Compromises?"

"Not in a moral sort of way. But she had to do with less. And for a girl who was used to having it all, it wasn't easy."

"Oh."

"Like when Lenora wanted to redecorate all of Cody's house and they couldn't afford it, so Mom and her went behind Cody's back and just did it. Meaning Mom paid for it. Well, that created some fireworks."

Sunny cringed. "Oh, dear."

"Yeah. And you'd think Lenora would've learned. I know my mom started to figure things out. But Lenora would keep pushing. And sometimes she'd go out and max out her credit card, knowing full well she didn't have a means of paying it off."

Sunny wanted to point out this sounded a bit like someone else in the family, but out of consideration, she didn't. "So your perfect sister wasn't completely perfect."

Aubrey slapped her knee as if this was a fresh concept. "You're right, Sunny, she wasn't so perfect, was she? It's funny, because I always tell myself that she was perfect. Growing up, she was always five steps ahead of me, and more the kind of daughter my parents seemed to want. So it seemed she always had everything I didn't."

"But maybe that was just because she was older," Sunny suggested.

"Maybe."

"And then she got sick." Sunny waited.

"Yeah," Aubrey almost whispered, "and then she got sick."

"Unless I'm wrong," Sunny said quietly, "you probably began to idolize her even more then."

"You are spot-on right, Sunny." Aubrey let out a long sigh. "How could I possibly think anything bad about Lenora when we realized she was dying? All I could think was that I was losing a sister—a perfectly perfect sister—one I'd never even appreciated while I had her." Aubrey was crying now.

"Tissues in the glove box."

Aubrey opened it, pulled out one, and loudly blew her nose. "Wow."

"I didn't mean to make you cry," Sunny said softly as she turned into the Lowenstein Ranch. "I'm sorry, Aubrey."

Aubrey blew her nose again. "Hey, don't be. You're a good thera-pist. Maybe if you don't go back to teaching, you could—"

"Yes, yes. But are you okay, Aubrey?" Sunny glanced at her.

"I'm fine. You've actually given me something to think about—something I've probably been burying."

Sunny peered up into the rearview mirror to see the Jeep still behind them. "The wannabe cowboys are still on our trail," she said without enthusiasm as she pulled up to the bunkhouse.

"Well, they probably won't be here long." Aubrey opened her compact then and used its small mirror, retouching her makeup to conceal that she'd been crying. "You go ahead and park here. Run in and get on your riding duds while I show the boys the horse barn and help Wesley get set up."

Chapter Twenty-four

. . . .

Sunny quickly changed into riding clothes and soon they were all out at the horse barn, where both Wesley and Aubrey were struggling to figure out how to put a bridle on. Aubrey had chosen her dad's horse, Chase. And, fortunately, Chase seemed to be cooperating—a good thing since Sunny thought she'd heard Echo say that he could sometimes be a little stubborn.

"It goes like this." Sunny stepped in to show how to slide the leather over the horse's ears. Next they went to the tack room and with Aubrey's "help," it ended up taking about thirty minutes to get both horses ready to ride. But finally both Wesley and Sunny were walking the horses around the corral. Feeling like she was imitating Echo, Sunny gave Wesley a few reminders about how to hold the rein as Mitchell attempted to get some good photos.

"Hey," called Echo as she jogged across the road toward them, "I didn't know you were here, Sunny."

"Now there's the real horsewoman," Sunny told the guys. "That girl taught me everything I know about riding."

"You mean you didn't know how to ride before?" Wesley looked skeptical.

"I'd never been on a horse before Echo took me under her wing. Right, Echo?" She grinned at the girl.

"Well, so you say. But if you ask me, she's got horse sense in her blood." She winked at Sunny. "But if I knew you were riding today, I would've waited."

"And if I knew you didn't have school today, I would've come home sooner." Then, remembering her manners, Sunny introduced Echo to the guys, explaining about how Wesley was a writer here to cover the Round-Up.

"That's cool." Echo climbed up next to Aubrey to sit on the corral fence.

"And I'm trying to get a shot of him on a horse," Mitchell explained. "To use in the article."

"So you decided to saddle up old Chase?" Echo appeared concerned.

"Actually, Aubrey picked the horse," Sunny quietly told her. "Is that a problem?"

"Just take it easy," Echo told Wesley, "but not too easy. Chase needs to know who's boss. Besides Grandpa, Dad's about the only one who ever rides that horse, and he get ornery sometimes."

"I hope he's okay with strangers," Wesley said with some uncertainty.

"Oh, Grandpa won't mind. I just don't want Chase to act up with you."

"And I don't want to break a leg or anything," Wesley joked.

"Although getting thrown from a horse would make a good photo," Mitchell teased. "I'll keep the camera ready."

"Very funny."

Sunny heard a vehicle coming up the driveway. When she looked up, she saw it was Cody's truck. "Is your dad picking you up?"

"Yeah," Echo said. "I asked him to come at the regular time so I could help Grandma with some baking. I think we made about two hundred snickerdoodles. I better go get the bag she made for us to take home. See ya." Then Echo hopped off the fence and galloped toward the house. Meanwhile, Sunny tried to act oblivious to the pickup that was slowly approaching.

"Easy on that rein," she warned Wesley as the horse began to fidget and go sideways, almost as if he expected to start circling or twisting. "If Chase thinks you're pulling too tight, he won't like it. Go easy."

Cody was out of his pickup now, making his way up to the corral with a curious expression. "What's going on here?" he asked.

"Sunny's giving Wesley a riding lesson," Aubrey said in a slightly smug tone. Then Aubrey did introductions, but she did it in a way that made Sunny suspect the girl was up to something. The way she went on about Wesley and how he was doing this big article on the Round-Up—well, she made it sound as if it were going to be printed in the *New York Times* or something equally impressive.

But Sunny was too distracted to intervene. Chase was acting skittish, and she was trying to get Brownie Anne closer to help out. But when Chase started doing a little sidestep to get away, and got a certain look in his eyes, Sunny was concerned.

"And I'm getting some photos," Mitchell was saying to Cody. "Keeping the camera ready in case Wesley gets dumped."

"That could happen on that horse," Cody warned just as Chase skittered across the corral with Wesley bouncing in the saddle.

"That's my fault," Aubrey confessed. "I picked the horse."

"In that case, Wesley should be relieved." Cody spoke calmly as he slipped between the rails and into the corral, moving directly to Wesley, who looked uneasy or maybe even scared. Cody reached for Chase's bridle now, walking alongside as the nervous horse continued doing his dance. "If Sunny had picked this horse for you, you might wonder just how much the girl likes you."

Wesley gave an uncomfortable laugh.

"Easy does it," Cody said soothingly as he continued to walk alongside Chase with one hand on his bridle and one hand stroking his head. "See how Chase's ears are back," he explained. "Not a good sign."

"I was thinking the same thing." Wesley was holding to the saddle horn now. "Do you mind if I get off before this horse decides to take the matter into his own hands or, rather, hooves." He chuckled nervously.

"Not at all." Cody firmed his grip on the bridle as he attempted to slow the horse. "Easy there, boy." Cody's voice was gentle but firm, and Chase finally stopped skittering. "Easy there." Now he reached up to give Wesley a hand as he slid from the horse.

"Well, that was certainly fun." Wesley backed away from the horse. "Got my adrenalin going. I think I'm all ready for some bull riding now."

Cody frowned. "You're riding bulls tonight?"

"No, I'll be safely in the grandstand," Wesley assured him. "Thanks for the help with the horse, man, I owe you one."

Cody nodded. "Good luck with that article."

"And if you'll excuse us." Mitchell was putting the lens on his camera. "We better rock and roll if we want to get a parking spot and catch the first ride."

Echo was back now. "I'm ready when you are, Dad." She held up a bag. "And I've got cookies to take home."

"You might need to hide those from your grandpa," Sunny warned.

"Yeah, I've got a couple of secret spots."

Cody was leading Chase around the corral now, but the horse had settled down considerably. "Seems a shame to put old Chase through all the trouble of getting saddled up without giving him a real ride."

"Go ahead and ride if you want, Dad." Echo sounded eager. "I'm not in a hurry to get home."

"I think Chase would appreciate a chance to stretch his legs." Cody checked the cinch, then swung easily up into the saddle. "How about you, Sunny? Want to ride some more, or are you calling it quits now that your friend is gone?"

She sat straight in the saddle. "I'm ready to ride."

His eyes twinkled as he gave her a little half smile. "All right then."

Echo already had the gate open. "You guys ride as long as you like," she said congenially, like she was happy to get rid of them. "Take your time."

"That's right," Aubrey agreed. "Echo and I will be in the house. You guys have a good ride."

"Ladies first." Cody grinned as he waved Sunny through the gate.

"Thank you." She tipped her head as she passed him, nudging Brownie Anne into a trot and directing her toward the usual path that led to the creek.

But then she heard the thundering of hooves, and Cody and Chase whipped right past. "Don't try to keep up," he yelled over his shoulder.

Without missing a beat, Sunny gave Brownie Anne a sharp kick in the withers and, like magic, or perhaps the horse had speed envy, Brownie Anne bolted so fast that Sunny almost reached for the saddle horn. Instead she simply squeezed her knees tighter, leaned forward, and imagined she was one with the horse as Brownie Anne raced after Chase.

For one breathtaking moment, Sunny saw the ground and the fence streaking by her at astonishing speed. And then she returned her focus to the horse, the rhythm of the gait, the ride, and suddenly they were mere seconds from the creek, where Cody was just turning Chase around to look back. Sunny pulled in the reins now, slowing Brownie Anne and telling her to "Whoa." And God bless the horse, she stopped perfectly. "Good girl." Sunny reached down and patted her silky neck. "Good girl."

She thought Cody would be pleased, but instead he seemed disturbed. "I'm sorry, Sunny." His brow creased. "I shouldn't have raced Chase like that. Did Brownie Anne run away with you?"

She walked the horse closer to him, stopping a couple of feet away. "No, not at all. I urged Brownie Anne to run. I didn't think the old girl would have it in her. But it was like she wanted to run."

Cody looked slightly relieved, but still a bit troubled.

"And it was a great ride." Sunny smiled. "Really exhilarating."

"You were going so fast, I figured the horse had taken the rein."

"No." Sunny patted her neck again. "Brownie Anne is a good horse. She only did as directed."

"Then you should've known better."

"What do you mean?"

"You're not an experienced rider, Sunny. You need to be more careful."

She held her chin up and stared at him. She wasn't sure whether she was angry or hurt, but she did not like being treated as a child.

He looked like he was about to laugh. "You should see your face, Sunny."

She held her head even higher, narrowing her eyes. Was he making fun of her?

Cody grew somber again. "Anyway, until you're a little more seasoned in the saddle, I'd recommend you take it easy."

She glared at him. "Take it easy?"

"Yes, so you don't break your neck."

"And what, may I ask, makes you the expert on my horseman skills or lack of?"

He shrugged. "Don't get mad just because I don't want to see you get hurt, Sunny."

"I assume you mean *physically* hurt." Now that the words were hanging out there between them, she wished she could pull out a lasso and, like a real cowgirl, yank them back. Why had she said *that*?

He looked perplexed. "What do you mean?"

"I'll tell you what I mean," she sputtered. "I mean you don't need to worry about me, Cody Barrett. If I get hurt, I get hurt. And it'll be my own dumb fault." Totally frustrated, she turned the horse around and, although she was tempted to run her back, she simply started the horse walking.

The next thing she knew, Chase was riding right next to her. "Sunny," he said slowly, "I didn't mean to step over the line. I do realize you're an adult and that you're a very good rider. But when I saw you barreling across the pasture, I got worried."

"So you've mentioned." With her head still high, she kept her gaze forward.

"The horse could've tripped on a gopher hole, and you could've been thrown and—"

"And the same thing could've happened to you," she challenged.

He nodded. "That's true. But when I saw you racing toward me, I got really worried about you, Sunny. I didn't want to see you get hurt."

She reined Brownie Anne to a halt, then turned boldly toward him. "That's the second time you said you didn't want to see me get hurt, Cody. Do you have any reason to believe that I'm going to get hurt?"

He was slightly flustered now. "No, probably not."

"Because if this is some kind of camouflaged warning about something besides horses and riding, I wish you'd just come right out and say so. I realize you don't know me that well, Cody, so I'll tell you up front. I'm not much into game playing."

"I'm not either."

She nodded. "Okay then. As long as we understand each other."

"Sunny." He gazed into her eyes with what almost seemed like longing.

"Yes?" She felt an unexpected flutter inside her chest. Was Cody about to tell her that he really cared for her?

"I've never known anyone quite like you, Sunny."

She took in a slow breath to steady herself. It seemed the world around her was whirling too fast, like she might lose her balance and tumble from the standing horse.

"And I would like to get to know you better." He smiled.

She smiled back. "I'd like to know you better too, Cody."

He looked genuinely surprised. "Really?"

"Remember, I'm not into playing games. I usually say what I mean."

"Right. So am I." He focused his eyes on the west, almost as if he were trying to think or get his bearings. "But I have to admit I'm not used to this kind of thing."

"What kind of thing?"

He gave a partial shrug and smiled as if uncomfortable. "You know, getting involved with someone. It's been a long time for me."

She cocked her head slightly to one side. "I'm feeling confused."

"Confused?" He seemed even more uneasy now. Perhaps he wanted to retract his words. Or perhaps he was concerned that she was misreading him. And maybe she was.

"I don't understand what you said about not being involved with anyone for a long time. That's what you said, right?"

He nodded. "That's right. It has been a really long time, and I feel like I'm a little over my head."

"But that doesn't make sense to me."

"Why?"

"Aren't you sort of involved with someone right now?"

"Right now?"

"I was under the impression that you and Trina were involved."

His shoulders slumped in relief. "No, no, not anything like that. We're not involved. Not like that."

"Are you sure?"

"I'm positive." He nodded eagerly. "We are only friends, Sunny. Nothing more."

She slowly shook her head. "I'm sorry, but I'm not convinced."

"I wouldn't lie about something like this, Sunny. Trina and I are only friends." Cody's brow creased again. "In fact, while we're on the subject of being involved, how about you and Cowboy Wes?"

Sunny actually laughed.

But Cody's expression remained serious. "I saw you with Wesley at GP this afternoon."

"And I saw you with Trina."

He waved his hand. "Yes, but it's not what you think. Trina simply invited me to meet her for coffee. She was supposed to have brought a friend along, a mother with a teenage son who's been having some problems. Trina thought if I could talk to the woman, it might help the situation."

"But I only saw you and Trina. You sat alone."

"The woman didn't show."

"Oh, really?"

"I know that probably sounds lame, as my daughter would say, but I swear it's the truth."

Sunny nodded. "I believe you, Cody."

He sighed in relief. "Thank you."

"I believe you're telling the truth from your perspective, but I also believe there's another kind of truth that you're avoiding."

"What's that supposed to mean?"

"I'm talking about the truth from Trina's point of view."

"Are you suggesting that I've been dishonest? That I've lied to Trina or deceived her somehow?"

"No, not at all, Cody. If anything, I suspect it could be the other way around."

"That Trina lied to me?" He cocked his head to one side like this was inconceivable. "You think Trina concocted the story about her friend just to meet with me?"

"That's not what—"

"Because I happen to know the woman and boy in question and they really are in need of some serious counseling. If Trina can help them recognize this, I would be extremely grateful. I'd rather take preventative measures than pick up the pieces later. And that's how it usually goes. Trina was simply trying to help me."

Sunny looked off toward the horizon, where the sun was about to slip below a bank of clouds. "Yes, I can see your point, but you misunderstood me. I wasn't suggesting that Trina had misled you today."

"What then?" He leaned forward—sincere but confused.

"I wish I were wrong, Cody, but I'm pretty sure that Trina is in love with you. And that's why I question you saying that your relationship with her is only *friendship*. I suspect if you talked openly with her, and if you got her to tell you the truth, you would find out that I'm right."

"I really don't think so." He shook his head.

"You say you don't *think* so, but you'll never know for sure if you don't ask the question. And Trina deserves that." She looked into his eyes. "And you deserve it…and so do I."

Cody frowned, as if he'd been blindsided, or she'd just pulled the ground out from under him. She felt seriously irked at herself too. Why had she gone there? Why had she ruined what could've been a wonderful moment?

Just like that Sunny knew the answer. It was because she was a realist, and because she refused to settle for a secondhand love. Feeling on the verge of tears, Sunny nudged her boot heels into Brownie Anne's sides again, clicking her tongue until the horse broke into a fast trot, then a canter. Sunny was tempted to push her into a full-out run, but decided that might simply convince Cody that he'd been right about her sensibilities, or lack of them.

As the horse cantered, Sunny expected Cody to follow and then join her, perhaps to even discuss this further. But he did not seem to be coming. And when she looked back, all she could see was the remnant trail of dust from where he and Chase had gone in the opposite direction. She took in a deep breath and told herself to be mature. It wasn't like she was seventeen and suffering her first broken heart. She would get over this. And perhaps it wasn't really as over as it felt at the moment. Sure, it might not be a very pretty hand, but at least her cards were on the table now. As far as she was concerned, the next move was up to Cody.

Chapter Twenty-five

Sunny had expected to hear from Cody. But Monday evening came and went...and nothing. Then Tuesday morning...more nothing. By Tuesday afternoon, she felt fairly certain he had no intention of continuing that conversation with her. Maybe he'd simply been toying with the idea of getting involved with her, but when she'd confronted him like that, he might've realized that she wasn't the kind of woman he'd imagined her to be. Maybe she'd scared him away. If that was the case, it was probably for the best.

Sunny had no idea what Cody's true feelings toward Trina were, and she suspected that Cody wasn't too sure himself. Sunny even wondered if he might be somewhat trapped—perhaps a trap he had unwittingly created himself. And maybe he was comfortable in it. Sunny suspected that Cody's promise to look after Larry's survivors had proved more binding than expected, yet Cody couldn't back out of it—she wouldn't even want him to. Knowing this only made her decision to step aside easier.

Sunny rationalized that she was merely a catalyst: the means to bring two people together and to show them that they needed each other. Considering the evidence, it made sense. For starters, both Cody and Trina had suffered the loss of a spouse. Both had teenage children. Both lived and worked on the reservation, understood the reservation, had friends in common. Plus, they had known each other for years. Even though Sunny had no surplus of fondness for

Trina, she figured that if she and Cody loved each other, it would all be for the best.

In light of this revelation, Sunny had decided to attend the opening of Round-Up on Wednesday, as promised, and to depart Pendleton directly afterward. It wouldn't be easy, but she would call Hank and make up some believable excuse for missing his barbecue. Because the sooner she put miles between herself and this town, the happier she would be. After witnessing the caravans of motor homes, trailers, and tents suddenly taking up residence at the Lowenstein Ranch, she realized the timing to get out of Dodge was good. Plus, she wasn't looking forward to sharing a bedroom with Aubrey. As much as she liked Aubrey, she wasn't impressed with her housekeeping skills. When Sunny had peeked in Aubrey's room this morning, it looked as if the closet in there had erupted, spewing every item of Aubrey's clothing onto the bed, floor, dresser, and chairs. Sunny figured she'd need a shovel just to plow a path to the bed tonight.

Now that she knew she was leaving, Sunny wanted to make the most of her time left. And to that goal she had spent the bulk of the day driving around on the reservation, taking it all in and trying to gather whatever information she could to take back to Portland with her. Her plan was to continue to research her ancestors and tribal heritage—to pull together as many pieces as possible and hopefully reach a peaceful place, then move on.

The final item on her agenda today was to visit the Tamástslikt Cultural Institute. She'd already driven past the museum several times, unable to work up the nerve to go inside. She knew Trina worked there, and the last thing she wanted was to see her.

"Don't let that woman stop you," Aubrey had told Sunny this morning after she'd confessed her concerns. "Tamástslikt is really worth seeing, and it's a big place, so chances are you won't even see Trina."

As Sunny parked her car, she told herself that Aubrey was probably right, and with only an hour until closing, it was now or never. Bracing herself, Sunny entered the building, and to her relief, there was no sign of Trina. With numerous rooms and offices, a shop, and even a small café, it really did seem unlikely that Sunny would run into her. Sunny went directly into the museum, taking her time to go through it. When she saw the incredible cultural treasures, she wished she'd come sooner.

Before leaving, she decided to stop by the gift shop to search out a book on the Cayuse tribe. Wesley had mentioned it, saying it might be helpful to her. After some quick perusing of the well-stocked bookshelf, she carried a load of books to the counter, where she was a little taken aback by the total. Still, it was worth it. These books were an investment that would link to her ancestors—if not in real life, at least on paper. Then, feeling victorious that she was about to make a clean getaway, she hurried toward the exit and nearly ran smack into Trina Strong Horse.

"*Excuse* me," Trina said with sarcasm. "I guess we need to install traffic lights in here now."

"I'm sorry." Sunny forced the words. "I was in a hurry. I realize the place is about to close."

"Yes. I was on my way out too." Now Trina gave Sunny a curious look. "In fact, I think I'll walk with you."

Sunny couldn't think of a polite way to decline this unexpected offer.

"I wanted to talk to you anyway." Trina's tone grew a degree or two warmer, teasing Sunny's curiosity.

"Really?" Sunny waited as Trina held the door open for her.

"I really should thank you."

"Thank *me*?" Sunny blinked in the bright sunlight as she continued toward the parking lot.

"Yes. Cody told me about your little chat."

"Oh."

"And I have to say I appreciate the way you made him understand some things."

"You mean about you and him?" Sunny stopped walking and turned to study Trina. This woman really was strikingly pretty. And her pale yellow dress and accents of amber jewelry were truly eye-catching.

Trina smiled brightly. "Yes. I suppose you saw what only a woman could see. And you helped to open Cody's eyes to the truth. *Thank you*."

"So Cody was able to admit that your relationship was really more than just friends?"

Trina's smile faded slightly. "Is *that* what he told you?"

"What?" Now Sunny was confused.

"That we were only *just friends*?"

"I'm not sure what his exact words were, Trina. But that's the impression I got."

Trina folded her arms across her front and frowned.

"I know he takes his promise to Larry quite seriously," Sunny continued. "And he is fully committed to your friendship."

"He told you that too?"

Now Sunny didn't know what to say. What did Trina want from her?

"So, you think that Cody is only with me because of an old promise to Larry? You actually believe that?"

"I, uh, I didn't mean to make it sound like that. I'm sure there's more—"

"Yes. There is a lot more. Cody and I are much more than *just friends.*" Trina's dark eyes flashed, boring into Sunny as she continued. "And I'm sure you've already noticed that I'm a woman who's not afraid to speak her mind. I call it as I see it, and if you can't take it, you should just stay out. Be assured, I'm not afraid to fight for what belongs to me."

Sunny nodded. "Yes. I can see that."

Trina's smile returned now. "I wanted to make sure we understood each other, Sunny. So we're all on the same page."

"Meaning the page where you and Cody are a couple?" Sunny suggested. "And that your relationship is more than a friendship and quite serious?"

"Exactly. So you really do understand?"

"Sure." She was eager to get away from this slightly obsessed woman. "I get that, Trina."

"Good."

"Now, if you'll excuse me, these books are getting heavy." Sunny tipped her head as a good-bye, then hurried toward her car. But Trina, like a small dog on the heels of a larger one, kept following Sunny. The sound of her high heels clicked quickly on the pavement until she caught up.

"So when are you leaving Pendleton?" she asked Sunny in a cheerful tone.

"I promised Aubrey to go to opening day of Round-Up with her."

Sunny set the bag of books on the hood of her car. "And then I think I'll just head out—probably tomorrow evening."

Trina looked relieved. "That sounds like a sensible plan. The traffic should be minimal by then. Everyone will either be here or coming this way."

"That's a good point." Sunny forced what she hoped would be the last smile she would ever have to fake for this woman. "And good luck."

"Good luck to you too."

Conflicted with relief and regret, Sunny got into her car and, without looking back, drove until she came to Saint Andrew's Mission. The next thing she knew she was standing in front of Polly Wikiapi's grave, crying. The cemetery seemed an appropriate place for grief, and with no one around to witness her spectacle, Sunny allowed the tears to flow freely.

Finally, all cried out, Sunny sat down beside her great-grandmother's grave. "Tell me your story," she said quietly. "What really happened with you?" She looked at the dates on the stone. "You were so young when you died—younger than I am now. And you were so young when you had your baby, still in your teens. Were you really crazy, like some people say? Or was that just a label you were given, something you wore because you had no choice? I know you were beautiful. Was it your beauty that brought your heartache?"

"Probably so."

Sunny leaped up at the voice. There, behind her, was a very elderly woman. At first Sunny thought it might be her great-grandmother's ghost. But the woman was far too old, and the purple polyester blouse and Hawaiian print skirt seemed all wrong.

"I am sorry," the woman said. "I didn't mean to startle you."

"It's okay." Sunny nodded. "I didn't hear you walk up."

The woman pointed to her moccasins. "Quiet shoes."

Sunny smiled, then introduced herself.

"And I am Wayla, although my friends call me White Dove."

"This is my great-grandmother." Sunny waved to the grave. "Polly Wikiapi."

"Yes, I know."

Sunny was startled. "Do you mean you know who she is? Did you know her?"

White Dove pointed to the grave next to Polly Wikiapi's. "That is my mother's grave. She was your great-grandmother's friend."

"Really?" Sunny could hardly believe her luck. "You know that for sure?"

"Oh, yes. When I was a little girl, my mother and I would put flowers and things on Polly's grave. My mother told me stories about her."

"You know stories about Polly Wikiapi? True stories?"

"Yes." The old woman sighed as if she were weary.

"Is it too hot out here for you?" Sunny said suddenly. "Would you like to find a cool place to sit down—and talk?"

White Dove nodded, then pointed to the church. "We can talk in there."

Soon they were seated in the back of the church.

"How old are you?" Sunny asked.

"I am nearly eighty."

Sunny did the math. "So you probably didn't actually know my grandmother."

"My mother knew her. She told me about her."

"Can you please tell me what you know?" Sunny pulled out her little notebook, where she'd been recording all the information she could gather.

"My mother was younger than your great-grandmother. And, like Polly Wikiapi"—she studied Sunny—"and, like you, my mother was a beautiful woman too. Like you said out there: *beauty came with heartache.*"

"Yes, I've heard that."

"Men—sometimes uncles or cousins or neighbors—they get drunk. They take advantage of beautiful young girls. So it was with your great-grandmother. So it was with my mother."

Sunny wrote quickly. "Do you mean they were sexually abused as girls?"

White Dove simply nodded. "My mother's family was no good. My grandmother did not protect my mother. Men used my mother, they hurt her. And she found refuge with Polly Wikiapi."

"Really?"

"Polly understood my mother's pain. She took her in. Polly had left the reservation—left her child with the grandmother and aunts. And she lived in town to escape the shame that her people heaped on her. My mother lived with her. But it was not easy to live. My mother and Polly were very beautiful, and they did things that provided them with food and clothes…things that brought more shame."

Sunny suspected that White Dove was talking about prostitution now. "Did they exchange their bodies for money?"

Another slow nod. "And then my mother became sick—very sick with influenza. Polly took her to the doctor and paid for my mother's medicine. She took care of her. But my mother was very sick. So Polly brought my mother out here—to Saint Andrew's Mission— to get more help. Polly Wikiapi saved my mother's life."

"How old were they then? When they came out here to the mission?"

"My mother was twenty-two. Polly was almost thirty."

"Polly died when she was thirty."

White Dove nodded again. "Yes. Polly became ill with influenza too. She had lived a very rough life. She did not get well. And she died here."

"Oh." Sunny felt a strange sense of sadness and peace. "Thank you for telling me about this."

"My mother loved Polly Wikiapi like a sister. She always remembered to visit her grave…always honored her memory."

"You say your mother told you about my grandmother, Mary Sunrise. Do you remember much about her?"

"She was sent to white school."

"To learn white man's ways?"

"Yes. I think it was bad, very bad. I think it hurt Mary Sunrise."

"That makes sense."

"White school is like breaking a horse badly. When you break a good horse, you do not beat it. You do not hurt it. Or else you have a bad horse. White school stole her spirit. Mary Sunrise was broken."

Compassion swept through Sunny now. "Poor Grandmother. I guess she did the best she could with the life she had left. She was a good woman. But, yes, I think you're right. I think they broke her spirit."

"There are many stories like that." White Dove sighed as if she were tired.

"Can I ask you one more question?"

"About Jackson Sundown?"

"Yes!" Sunny nodded eagerly. "Do you know about him?"

White Dove smiled. "Only that it's a mystery."

"What did your mother tell you?"

"She said that Polly loved Jackson."

"Was he the father of her baby?"

White Dove shrugged. "Maybe."

"But you don't know for sure?"

Now White Dove looked into Sunny's eyes, as if searching for something buried deep within. "What do you think?"

Sunny slowly shook her head. "I don't know."

"I think the answer is inside you."

"Mother," called a woman's voice.

"In here," White Dove called back. "That's Coral, my daughter."

A heavyset woman came into the sanctuary. "Oh, there you are, Mom. Sorry I'm so late, but we need to go now."

Sunny helped White Dove to her feet. "Is there a way I can contact you? I'd like to keep in touch, if you don't mind."

White Dove smiled. "I live with Coral. She can write it down for you."

Sunny offered Coral her notebook and pen. "I appreciate it."

But Coral just stood there, staring at Sunny as if she thought she was trying to swindle them somehow.

"This is my friend Sunny," White Dove explained. "Her great-grandmother was my mother's best friend…Polly Wikiapi."

Now Coral smiled as if she recognized the name. She eagerly took the notebook and began writing. Then the three of them slowly made their way outside.

"Thank you so much for talking to me!" Sunny hugged White Dove. "You have no idea how much it means to me—what a gift you are."

"God is the one who led you here." White Dove's dark eyes sparkled as she looked up into the clear sky. "And my mother and your great-grandmother are up there, laughing and smiling. We have made them very happy today."

Chapter Twenty-six

Sunny was barely in her car when her cell phone rang.

"Where are you?" Aubrey asked from the other end.

"At Saint Andrew's Mission."

"Why?"

"It's a long story. But—"

"Yeah, yeah, tell it to me later. Right now I want to know if you spaced our dinner date tonight."

"Dinner date?"

"With Wesley and Mitchell. Remember I told you this morning that they wanted to take us to dinner as a thank you for swapping out the tickets?"

Sunny slapped her forehead. "Oh, I did forget about it. I'm sorry. Is it still on?"

"It is. Mitchell just called and asked us to meet them at Hamley's at seven. They got reservations. Are you going to be able to make it?"

Sunny squinted toward her dashboard clock and was shocked to see it was already 6:15. How long had she been in the cemetery before White Dove showed up? "Sure, of course. I'm on my way right now. I should be there around six thirty."

"Which doesn't give you much time to look stunning. And you have to look stunning, Sunny, because I plan to really dress up. I like

Mitchell a lot, and I think he likes me too. In fact, I'll go ahead and get an outfit ready for you so all you'll have to do is clean up and jump into it."

Sunny didn't know whether to thank her or beg her not to go to the trouble, so she simply said "Good-bye." Although she wasn't looking forward to this dinner date, she felt so encouraged from her surprising conversation with White Dove that she decided to make the best of her last night in Pendleton. Really, it was a night to celebrate, even if her heart did feel a bit heavy. But the best way to get over a heartache was to go out and have a good time. Right? At least that's what she was telling herself. Not that her heart was convinced. She couldn't help but think of Cody...and his sweet old father—as well as the barbecue she'd be ditching. But, really, it was for the best...for everyone.

When Sunny pulled into the ranch, the place was hopping. People seemed to be everywhere, and the decibel level had increased considerably. With dogs, kids, people of all ages, it was like a seven-ringed circus. More than ever, she was determined to leave town after the rodeo tomorrow. She found a place to park near the barn and went into the bunkhouse to discover it was full of people too. She'd already cleaned her room and packed up her things, setting them temporarily in the hall closet. And already her old bedroom was occupied.

"There you are!" Aubrey exclaimed when she spotted Sunny standing in the living room. "It's time to get you dressed, cowgirl."

"Wow." Sunny took in Aubrey's outfit. "You look fantastic. Where did you get all that beautiful jewelry?"

"I raided Mom's closet and jewelry chest. I swear that woman is a poster girl for *Cowboys and Indians*." Aubrey picked up the glossy magazine and pointed to an ad where a pretty woman was literally dripping in Native American jewelry. "This is my inspiration."

"Right." Sunny nodded.

"And here's what you're wearing." Aubrey held up a long, full denim skirt. "I know it doesn't look like much, but trust me."

Sunny frowned at the elastic waist. "Seriously?"

"Yeah, yeah. It's my mom's, and it'll be a little too big, but…" She held up a wide leather belt with silver medallions all around it.

"That's really pretty," Sunny admitted.

"It's a concho belt and, believe me, with that belt, no one will even notice the skirt. It's more like a backdrop." Aubrey handed Sunny a plain white shirt next. "Again, this is a backdrop." She held up a bunch of gorgeous necklaces made with turquoise, coral, and silver. "Because everyone will be looking at these babies."

Before long, Sunny was dressed and Aubrey was nodding in approval. "Now you need your Old Gringo boots and your buckskin jacket, in case it gets cold, and we're ready to roll."

Sunny took one last glimpse in the mirror. "This jewelry must be really valuable," she said to Aubrey. "Are you sure your mom is okay with us wearing it?"

"Not only is she okay, she insisted we come into the house before we go so she can take some photos. We need to hurry."

From the bunkhouse to the main house, the girls picked up compliments, hoots, and whistles from the friends and relatives roaming the grounds. And when they got to the kitchen, where Cindy appeared to be holding court with a bunch of middle-aged women, the praises just kept on coming.

"You girls must be having some hot-hot date tonight." An older woman winked at Aubrey. "Maybe you'll tell us all about it later."

"Stand over there," Cindy commanded as she picked up her camera. "And strike some poses for me."

Much to the amusement of the women, they cooperated. Comments were made about how they really were professional models and would soon be appearing in the Pendleton catalog. "You'll have to sign my catalog for me," one woman said. "How fun having a celebrity niece," another one said to Aubrey. "When does the catalog come out?"

As Aubrey was explaining, Cindy took Sunny aside. "Cody has been trying to reach you," she quietly told her.

"Oh?"

"I promised to have you call him."

Sunny nodded. "Sure. I'll do that as soon as I can."

Cindy peered into Sunny's eyes. "Is everything okay between you two?"

Sunny shrugged. "As far as I know."

Cindy frowned. "Well, Echo sounded concerned."

"Come on." Aubrey pulled on Sunny's arm. "We're already late."

"I'll talk to you later," Sunny promised Cindy.

"What did Mom want?" Aubrey asked as Sunny drove to town.

"Just to tell me Cody had called and that I should call him."

"Oh?"

"It's probably nothing." Then Sunny told Aubrey about her little run-in with Trina today. "That's probably why Cody called. He might not appreciate that I talked to her. Not that I wanted to. Mostly it was unavoidable."

"And she actually *thanked you*?" Aubrey sounded incredulous. "That's a little weird. Was it like she thought you'd handed Cody over to her or something?"

"Not exactly. Although I think she appreciated that I told Cody to talk to her. He was obviously in denial about their relationship. At least they should know where they stand now."

"And that is where exactly?"

Sunny exhaled. "I don't know for sure. But, according to Trina, he's her man, and she will fight for him if necessary."

"She told you that?"

"Pretty much."

"Wow, that woman is bold."

"I guess you can't blame her. I mean, if you loved someone that fiercely, well, wouldn't you fight for him too?"

"I don't know. Would you?"

Sunny thought about it. "I don't think so. I'd rather have the guy doing the fighting for me."

Aubrey laughed. "Yeah. Me too."

* * * * *

Hamley's was busy, but the dinner was delicious, and the service excellent—almost as if the waiter thought he was waiting on celebrities. The general feeling was happy and celebratory and the conversation lively. Sunny hadn't missed that she and Aubrey had turned some heads when they'd entered the restaurant. And even though Sunny wasn't usually into that kind of thing, she had to admit it was amusing. Despite the heaviness in her heart, Sunny was feeling more hopeful. She could survive this.

"Now we have to do Main Street," Aubrey announced as they were leaving the restaurant.

"Great idea," Wesley said. "We barely saw it on our way here, but it looked like fun."

"There's a good band at eight thirty," Aubrey told them. "And I don't know about anyone else, but I plan to do me some boot scooting boogy tonight. I'm gonna let 'er buck."

They walked up and down the blocked-off street, stopping to check out the various vendors and to see the performers and musicians before they returned to the main bandstand where the country group was beginning to play.

"Come on!" Aubrey grabbed Mitchell's hand. "Let's dance." And suddenly they were out there with several couples who were literally dancing in the street.

"I'm not much of a dancer," Wesley told Sunny.

"I'm not either," she admitted.

"But it looks like fun." He smiled hopefully. "Are you game?"

"Come on," Aubrey yelled at Sunny as Mitchell whipped her around in a fast turn. "What are you waiting for?"

"Dance lessons!" Sunny yelled back.

"Get out here then." Aubrey pointed next to her. "We'll teach you."

"Ready for this?" Wesley asked as he took her hand and led her over to where Aubrey and Mitchell were dipping and spinning like they'd been doing this all their lives. "Really, what do we have to lose?"

"Our dignity?"

He laughed. But before long, and with some help, Sunny and Wesley were starting to get the hang of it. And Aubrey was right—it was fun!

"See," Aubrey told her, "I might not be any good on a horse, but I do know how to cowboy dance."

"And how to have fun," Sunny said as Wesley spun her around.

"Hey, there's Hank." Aubrey pointed across the crowd. "And Cody too."

Sunny felt a jolt run through her at the sound of that name. But instead of looking his direction, she attempted to calm herself as she focused on her footwork. Then, a few seconds later, she casually glanced over to see that it wasn't just Hank and Cody, but Echo and Trina as well. And, really, what was the harm in that? Except that their faces were a little hard to read. While Trina seemed fairly happy—unless it was a pseudo smile—both Cody and Hank appeared downright mad. And poor Echo just looked plain miserable, like she'd lost her best friend, which wasn't far from the truth. She was probably wishing she had someone her own age to hang with instead of the old folks.

Sunny was relieved when the band took a break. But suddenly the two foursomes were all standing together in the middle of the street while Aubrey did a quick introduction for Trina and Hank's sake.

"What I want to know is, why aren't you out there dancing too?" Aubrey tapped Cody on the chest with a teasing smile.

He shrugged, then glanced away.

"You and Lenora used to tear up the dance floor," Aubrey continued. "Did you forget how?"

"It's my fault," Trina said. "I'm not much of a dancer."

"I wasn't either," Sunny admitted. "But Aubrey and Mitchell are really good teachers."

"Can you teach me too?" Echo asked her aunt.

"Of course I can, Baby Doll." Aubrey took Echo's hands now and immediately started to explain the two-step.

"How's your magazine article going?" Cody asked Wesley in a slightly formal tone.

"It's coming along." Then he told Cody a bit about the bull riding last night.

"Are you still coming to our barbecue tomorrow night?" Hank quietly asked Sunny.

She winced to remember her plan to evacuate town. She would probably be long gone by then. "Uh, I'm not sure I can make it."

He frowned. "You promised you'd come, Sunny."

She glanced at Trina now. "I know, but maybe it's not such a good idea."

"You're backing out on your word?" Hank challenged.

Sunny didn't know what to say, so she changed the subject, talking to him in a quiet, confidential tone. "You know, Hank, I met this woman at Saint Andrew's Mission today, and she told me about my great-grandmother."

His brows lifted with interest. "Really?"

She stepped aside now, pulling him along with her as she poured out the story.

"That's real nice, Sunny. I'm happy to hear about that."

"And Hank?" She stepped even further away from the others now. "I would love to come to your barbecue, but I'm not sure Trina would appreciate it."

His frown deepened. "It's not *her* barbecue."

Sunny took Hank's hand in hers and squeezed it. "Not yet."

"What do you mean?"

She glanced back over at Cody. Trina was so close to him that Sunny wondered if she'd applied superglue to their elbows. "Don't say you heard it from me, but I think Trina and Cody might have some kind of an announcement to make before long."

He scratched his chin. "Don't know where you get ideas like that in your head, Sunny, but I'm pretty sure you're wrong."

"Then maybe you should talk to Trina. I ran into her at the museum, and she seemed fairly sure of herself."

His eyes narrowed. "Well, maybe you ought to be talking to Cody instead of Trina."

"But look at them, Hank. They're here together."

"And you're here with someone too, Sunny. Mind explaining that to me?"

She couldn't help but chuckle at what almost seemed like jealousy. "Aubrey set this up. Honestly, Wesley is just a friend."

He nodded, but she could see suspicion in his eyes. "It's not my place to say this to you, Sunny, but you seem to have hooked my boy. Hooked him good. And now, unless I'm wrong, it looks to me like you plan to throw him back."

Sunny was too stunned to speak.

"I can understand you being a city girl and coming out here to have your fun, then go on home. And I know your main purpose was to learn about your roots and all. But what about your future? Did you think about that? Do you honestly think you can be happier back in the city than you can be out here?"

She frowned. "Who told you that?"

"I got my sources." He stuck his chin out. "And furthermore, I've noticed you watching Cody as much as I've seen him gawking at you. It's as plain as the nose on my face that you two are in love with each other. Why you don't just come out and say it beats the hooey outta me."

The music was starting to play again. Sunny glanced over in time to see Echo grabbing her dad and miraculously peeling him away from superglue woman. "Come on, Dad," Echo told him. "Aubrey said you're really a good dancer. I want to see if it's true."

"How about you, Hank?" Sunny asked. "Are you a good dancer too?"

He chuckled. "Why don't you take me for a spin and find out?"

Wesley nodded at Sunny as she and Hank joined the others on the dance floor. He was obviously not bothered by her switching partners. And, really, how could anyone resent an old guy like Hank? To her surprise, after he loosened up a bit, Hank turned out to be an excellent dancer. Much better than Sunny. "I'm impressed," she told him as he guided her through a graceful turn.

"Now, for your information," he quietly said as the music stopped, "Trina did *not* come here with us tonight. We just happened to run into her—or so she made it seem."

"Oh." She nodded as the music started up. "Care to go again, or did I wear you out already?"

"It's all that stepping on my toes that's wearing me out," he teased back as he led her out.

"I never stepped on your toes once," she argued as they started dancing. "Not that I won't now."

Hank seemed to be guiding them over to where Cody and Echo were just coming back out to the dance floor again. Then, in a very smooth motion, Hank managed to grab Echo's hand, pull her to him, and at the same time, practically shoved Sunny straight into his son's arms.

"You better give that girl some real dancing lessons," he called out to Cody. "And watch out that she don't stomp on your toes."

Cody looked both surprised and amused, but without missing a beat, he continued to dance with her. "I see you're with Cowboy Wes again tonight."

"And I see you're with Trina."

He scowled.

"Cindy told me you called."

"I did."

"Did you still want me to call you back?" she asked. "Or can you just talk to me face-to-face?"

He didn't answer. For a few moments, they both seemed to focus on the dancing. Sunny wished that was all they had to focus on—that, and each other. But, of course, things were never that simple.

"Did Trina tell you about our conversation today?" she asked.

"No." His eyes flickered with interest.

"Oh."

"What did Trina say to you?"

Sunny stepped soundly on his toe just then. "Sorry." She jumped back.

"Barely felt it," he told her. But now they had lost the beat and stopped dancing. They were merely standing in the midst of the other dancers. It reminded Sunny of a snag in a roaring river.

"Is there a place where we can speak privately?" she asked.

He grinned. "Now there's an idea."

"It's hard enough learning to dance—without trying to have a meaningful conversation as well."

Cody glanced over her shoulder. "Are you sure Cowboy Wes won't mind me stealing you away?"

Sunny cringed to spot Wesley standing alone on the sidelines. She'd forgotten all about him. "Oh, dear." She frowned. "I guess I should go talk to him." Then she noticed Trina, arms folded across her chest and fire in her eyes. Sunny felt uneasy. "I think Trina is on the warpath—and I suspect the path leads straight to my door."

"Don't worry. I'll take care of her."

"Then I'll take care of Wesley."

"Meet me right back here."

"It's a deal," she said, and they turned away from each other.

Feeling both hopeful and apprehensive, Sunny went over to Wesley. "I'm sorry for ditching you like that," she began. "It's just that, well—"

"Look, Sunny, I know this wasn't a *real* date. It's not like I asked you out. And I realize that Mitchell and Aubrey set things up, and you girls drove to meet us. So it's not like I should've had great expectations. But I suppose I had hoped for a little bit more than this."

"I really am sorry," she said again. "But Cody and I—well, it's complicated."

He nodded. "Yeah, I could tell there was something between you two the day I met him."

"Really?"

"Oh, yeah." He shoved his hands in his pockets. "That whole deal with the horse—and the way he looked at you, how you acted—I actually wondered if he was your ex."

"My ex?"

"Or something with some strong emotions attached."

She sighed. "I can tell you're a great guy, Wesley—"

"But…"

She nodded. "But I need to figure this thing out with Cody."

"What if it doesn't work out?"

She shrugged. "I don't know."

"Okay. I understand. And I apologize for being so pushy. I'm not usually the aggressive type. But you're the kind of woman a guy could get pushy for." He grinned.

"Thanks, Wesley."

"Would you mind telling Mitchell that I'm calling it a night and that I'll just walk back to the house?"

"Sure." And just like that, Wesley was on his way. She wondered if things had gone that smoothly for Cody. Probably not. She moved through the dancers and to the other side of the street, where she found Aubrey and Mitchell. She quickly explained Wesley's departure, and although they seemed momentarily concerned, it was obvious they were having way too much fun to give any of it much thought.

"Do you think Mitchell can give you a ride back to the house?" Sunny asked Aubrey hopefully. "In case I leave early too?"

"No problem," Mitchell assured her.

Sunny made it back to where she and Cody had agreed to meet, but he wasn't there. She looked over to where Trina had been glowering just minutes ago. She too was nowhere to be seen. Finally, spotting Hank and Echo, Sunny went over to find out if they knew what was up.

"Trina got really, really mad." Echo's eyes were worried. "She started acting totally bonkers."

"Bonkers?" Sunny turned to Hank and he nodded grimly.

"Didn't you hear her yelling?" Echo actually looked a little scared.

"Not really, but I was on the other side of the street, and the music was loud."

"Trina started screaming at Dad—yelling all kinds of horrible stuff about him—and stuff about you too, Sunny."

Hank just shook his head. "Cody, well, he sort of removed Trina from the scene."

Sunny could only imagine what that must've been like. Trina might be petite, but she was ferocious. And the name *Spitfire* was probably more than appropriate tonight.

"It was really terrible." Echo twisted a button on her denim jacket.

"Is this my fault?" Sunny glanced from Hank to Echo, then back to Hank again.

He pushed his cowboy hat up on his brow. "Don't rightly see how you can blame yourself for someone else behaving badly."

"Are you and my dad in love?" Echo said suddenly, studying Sunny with wide, curious eyes.

"Oh, Echo." Sunny put a hand on her shoulder. "I don't even know how to answer a question like that. The truth is, your dad and I just wanted to sit down and have a good long talk." She held up her hands in a helpless gesture. "But I guess that talk will have to wait."

"But do you *love* him?" Echo persisted.

Sunny thought. "How would you feel about it if I *did* love him?"

Echo's serious expression melted into a smile. "That'd be cool with me."

Sunny blinked. "Really?"

"Sure."

Hank was grinning. "So, do you?" he asked.

She was determined not to reveal her true feelings…not yet. "Don't you guys think that's something I should talk to Cody about?"

"So when are you going to talk?"

"We were going to talk tonight, but that's obviously not happening."

"But he'll probably come back," Echo said eagerly.

"Or else he'll call you," Hank offered.

"Are you going to wait here for him?" Echo asked.

"I told him I would."

Echo opened her cell phone, pushed a button, waited, then frowned. "He's still not answering his phone."

"I expect he's got his hands full with Trina." Hank checked the time on his watch. "And I'm pretty tuckered out myself. Think maybe we should be heading for home, Echo. Cody's got his own truck in town, so he'll be fine."

Sunny was worried now. "Trina wouldn't do anything really crazy, would she?"

"If you ask me, she was already acting crazy," he said sadly. "Anyway, Cody's trained in these kinds of things. He'll handle it. Don't you worry, Sunny. And I'm guessing he'll be back any minute now. Let him know we went home, okay?"

Echo hugged Sunny. "And I'll call you if I hear from Dad."

Sunny watched as Hank and Echo walked away. Then she went back to the spot where Cody had asked her to wait, and there she waited.

Chapter Twenty-seven

An hour passed and Sunny was feeling both frustrated and worried. Frustrated that Trina, once again, had called the shots and controlled the situation. At the same time she was worried that Trina might be so crazed with jealousy that she could actually hurt Cody. Or, for all Sunny knew, Trina might be planning a way to take her vengeance out on Sunny. Maybe right this moment Sunny was in real danger but didn't even know it. Yet that seemed a bit dramatic. Besides, with all these people around, what could Trina do?

Sunny was glad that Aubrey had told her to bring her buckskin jacket because the night air was getting chilly. Even so, maybe she was a fool to stay here, waiting. If she was really being stood up— for whatever reason—she should just go home. The sounds of sirens reminded her of the situation, so, once again, she prayed for Cody to be safe…and for Trina to be sane. The band had quit and the dancers, including Aubrey and Mitchell, were gone. Sunny was starting to feel like she should go too. Really, what were the chances that Cody was coming back?

Just then her phone rang. To her relief, it was Echo. "Is everything okay?" Sunny asked eagerly.

"Not exactly."

"What do you mean?"

"Dad just called. He had to take Trina to the hospital."

"What happened?"

"Trina was threatening to kill herself."

"Oh, dear."

"Yeah. Grandpa went and got Jackson. He's staying with us."

"That's good."

"And Dad is staying with Trina."

"Oh, that's good too."

"Yeah. I wanted you to know. You're not still in town, are you?"

Sunny sighed. "I was just leaving."

"I'm sorry, Sunny."

"Why are you sorry, Echo?"

"Because our family's kind of messed up. I guess I can see Dad's point now."

"Dad's point?"

"Oh, about you not wanting to leave your life in the big city behind…you know, for us."

Sunny laughed. "Okay, your dad is a smart guy, Echo, but does he always jump to conclusions like that?"

Echo let out a meek laugh. "Not always. I think he's just not used to dealing with stuff like this."

"Well, if you see him, tell him I'm fine. Hopefully we can talk tomorrow."

"Are you going to Round-Up with Aunt Aubrey tomorrow?"

"That was the plan, but maybe—"

"Dad and Grandpa and I were supposed to go tomorrow too," Echo told her. "Opening day is the best."

"So, I guess I'll see you tomorrow."

"Yeah. We all sit in the same section. It'll be fun." But even as she said this, Echo's voice sounded unsure.

They said good-bye, but as Sunny closed her phone, she wondered just how fun it would be for any of them tomorrow. And what about Trina? What if she'd really done something serious? Sunny was tempted to stop by the hospital to see how both Trina and Cody were doing. But images of a crazed Trina flipping out when she saw Sunny stopped her cold. No, her presence would not be helpful.

She had just started her car when her phone rang again. "This is Cody," his voice said quietly.

"Cody," she exclaimed. "Are you okay?"

"Yes. I'm fine." He sounded bone-tired.

"How about Trina?"

"Not so fine."

"What happened?"

"Well, you probably heard about how she lost it on Main Street."

"Echo and Hank kind of filled me in."

"It was a mess. In fact, she was screaming and carrying on so badly that someone actually called the police, thinking that I was abusing her."

"Oh no."

"I didn't tell Dad or Echo that part, and I'd appreciate it if you didn't, either."

"No, of course not."

"My plan was to just drive her home because I was worried that, in her state of mind, she might get in a wreck. But we were almost to my truck when she flipped out and tried to run in front of a car. I grabbed her in time, but in the driver's attempt to miss her, there was a little wreck."

"Oh my."

"Yes. So I called 9-1-1 and explained that we had both a wreck and a suicidal woman and after what seemed like hours, I finally got her checked into the hospital. Now she's sedated and being restrained." He let out a big sigh. "I feel like it's my fault, Sunny."

"I was just feeling like it was my fault."

"No, it's definitely not your fault, Sunny. Don't think that. But what you said the other day, about how I needed to be honest with Trina. Well, you were right. I should've told her a long time ago that I would never feel that way about her. But I guess I was just fooling myself, pretending it really was just a friendship."

"And you're sure that's true? You're sure you only care for her as a friend?"

"Absolutely."

"Is there anything I can do to help?" she asked. "I mean, short of leaving town."

"Please, don't leave town, Sunny."

"I won't."

"I feel like I need to stick around here for a while. And it's late. Do you think we could reschedule our talk for the morning?"

"Of course."

"But there's one thing I want to say before then."

"What?"

There was a long pause. "I want to say…well, I love you."

Sunny felt slightly dizzy and tingly as she wondered if this was really real.

"And don't feel you have to say the same thing back to me. I know it's been a rough ride with me so far. And for all I know, it could get even rougher. But for what it's worth, Sunny, I really do love you. I think I loved you the instant we met on the back deck at Cindy and Doug's. I saw you there with Echo and you had on your buckskin jacket. You held your chin high, and something inside me just seemed to click. It probably sounds crazy, but it was like I knew we'd be a perfect fit, like there was this missing part of me, and that was you. Does that make any sense?"

"I know exactly what you mean."

"Really?"

"That's exactly how I felt too. But I tried to suppress it. I told myself it couldn't be for real." Her heart was beating fast.

"We have so much to talk about, Sunny."

"I know." Feeling slightly lightheaded, she took in a breath.

"I have so much to tell you, so much to explain, so much you need to know."

Sunny chuckled. "You might be surprised at how much I already do know."

"What do you mean?"

"I mean, there have been a lot of little birds chirping in my ear."

"Huh?"

"Your dad, for starters. Then there's Echo. And, of course, Cindy. Even Aubrey filled me in on some details of your life. Honestly, Cody, I think I may know you even better than you know yourself by now."

"Hopefully there'll still be a few things left for me to tell you."

"I'm sure you'll think of something."

"And there are a lot of things I still want to know about you."

They talked awhile longer, but she could hear the tiredness in his voice. "I'll see you tomorrow," she finally said. "And, though it might not mean much to her, I'm praying for Trina." He thanked her and then she shut her phone.

As she drove back to the ranch, she wondered if she'd even be able to sleep.

Fortunately, she did sleep. She barely woke up when Aubrey stumbled in at two in the morning. Then she got up at seven, grabbed the first shower while the rest of the house was sleeping, got dressed, and went outside.

It was a gorgeous clear day. The air was fresh and clean. The birds were singing. And the Lowenstein Ranch looked like an RV park. She tiptoed over to the garden, where she inspected the plants and picked enough ripe tomatoes and cucumbers to fill the garden basket. Suspecting everyone would be sleeping, she tiptoed up to the deck to set the basket on the table by the back door.

"You're up early."

Sunny looked over to see Cindy sitting in her bathrobe, a cup of steaming coffee in hand. "So are you." She held up the basket of produce. "Thought you might like these."

"My garden angel." Cindy smiled and held up her cup. "Why don't you go get yourself some coffee, then get back out here and tell me what's going on between you and my son-in-law?"

Sunny did as she was told. Soon she was pouring out the whole story, including Trina's suicidal attempt to run in front of a vehicle.

"Goodness gracious." Cindy shook her head. "I always wondered about that girl. She's cute as a bug and smart as can be, but she's always seemed a little tightly wound to me."

Sunny couldn't disagree.

"So, are you and Cody going to get married?"

Sunny almost choked on her coffee. "What?"

"It seems an obvious question."

"But we're not really to that place yet."

Cindy patted Sunny's hand. "Oh, you'll get there. And when you do, no one will be happier than me. Well, unless it's Echo. Does she know yet?"

Sunny felt she was swimming in fast water now. "Actually, there's not that much to know. Cody and I are going to talk this morning and—"

"Don't mind me, Sunny. I'm just eager, that's all." She pointed to a blue pickup that was turning up the driveway. "Apparently I'm not the only one either."

"Maybe I should go out and meet him," Sunny suggested. "So his truck doesn't wake the campers up."

"Good idea." Cindy grinned. "Give him my best."

Sunny hurried over to the front of the house, heading Cody off before he had a chance to go back to where the camping circus lay. "Good morning, Sunrise," he said as he opened the passenger door of his pickup. "Care to take a ride?"

"Thanks, I would." She slid in and looked at him, amazed at the way her heart fluttered as he returned her look.

He gently touched his hand to the side of her cheek. "There's something I've been dying to do."

She smiled. "Me too."

And then he leaned over and kissed her, gently at first, and then with more passion—so much so that she felt wonderfully dizzy when he finally moved back. "Even better than I'd imagined," he said as he turned his pickup around.

"Much better." She sighed.

He only went a short ways from the ranch, parking on a road stub that looked out over miles and miles of wheat fields. Then he turned to face her. "You are so beautiful," he slowly said. "But I want you to know that's not what attracted me to you."

"It's not?" She smiled.

"Okay, I'm sure it helped. But what really got my attention was your spirit, Sunny. Something about you was unlike anyone I've ever known. I think Echo figured it out even before I did. Do you know how much that girl loves you?"

Sunny felt tears coming now. Tears of joy. "I love her too, Cody. I can't even believe how much I love her."

"And my dad." Cody shook his head. "Good grief, I'm pretty sure he'd quit speaking to me if I let you get away."

"So that's why you're—"

"No. Even if my dad didn't like you, which is unimaginable, I wouldn't let you go, Sunny. Not if I could help it." Now he leaned over and kissed her again...several times. Then he stopped. "Can't keep doing that, or we won't get to talk."

She laughed and sat back. "Hopefully we'll get to do lots of both."

He nodded. "But there is one serious subject I need to bring up right now."

"Trina?"

"Yes. The thing is, I promised Larry to look after her. Now, understand me, I never promised to marry her. I would never want to marry her. She is so not my type, Sunny. But it seems I was too nice to her, too helpful, too good to Jackson, so she really believed I was going to marry her. At least that's what she says." He let out a frustrated sigh. "Although I can't help but think she's trying to do to me what she did to Larry."

"What she did to Larry?"

"Surely you've heard about it. Aubrey probably told you about how Trina got pregnant so Larry had to marry her."

Sunny was startled. "No, she never mentioned it. Do you mean Trina was trying to get pregnant—"

"No, no." He held up his hands and chuckled. "Nothing like that. But I do get the impression she's been trying to trap me somehow. I don't like saying it, but Trina can be a little manipulative."

Sunny controlled herself from laughing at the understatement.

"The trouble is, I can't just tell her to get lost. But I'm doing everything I can to make her understand that I never loved her, never intended to marry her, and never will." He shook his head. "Although it might not be sinking in."

Sunny just waited, wondering where this was going.

"And then, of course, there's Jackson. He's a good kid, and I can't just tell him to take a hike."

"No, of course not."

"So, I guess what I'm saying is that I come with some baggage." He grinned sheepishly. "Man, I never thought I'd have to say that about myself."

She smiled. "Everyone comes with some baggage."

"But how are you with that? I mean, getting involved with me while there's a crazed woman to deal with. As well as a couple of teenagers who are okay right now, but in my line of work, I know that can change overnight." He sighed. "That's a lot of baggage."

She reached over and took his hand. "I'm a strong woman, Cody. And I'm good with baggage."

He took her hand in both of his and squeezed it. "I kind of thought you would be."

As they talked more, she told him a bit about growing up with her grandmother and the conversation with White Dove yesterday—and the different version of the story of Polly Wikiapi.

"You know, Sunrise—is it okay if I call you that sometimes?"

She nodded.

"I can honestly believe you're Jackson Sundown's great-grand-daughter. It makes total sense to me. But I know you want proof."

"I *need* proof."

"To me the proof is in your character, Sunrise, in your strength, your wisdom, your heart. That's all the proof I need."

"Thank you."

"But you've made me do some thinking about things like heritage. And I got to thinking that maybe it doesn't really matter."

"Our heritage doesn't matter?"

"I'm thinking that maybe heritage is like home: it's where the heart is."

She considered this. "You could be right."

"And family is the same way. When you take people into your heart, they become your family—your heritages mix, and then you create your own story."

"Yes! I think you're absolutely right."

"I wish we could sit here and talk like this forever," he told her.

"But I promised to take Jackson to see his mom this morning."

"Oh, that's good. I was worried about him and how this would affect him."

"Jackson is an amazing kid. Really resilient and mature."

"I'm sure that means a lot to Trina." Sunny paused. "Last night, when I was praying for her, I got to thinking about *Tamástslikt*…the meaning of the word."

"Doesn't it mean to turn around?"

"Yes. To change direction, or turn around, or go a different way. I was praying that Trina would have a Tamástslikt experience that would turn her around."

"That's a great prayer. I think I'll pray that way too."

"I think I've already had my own Tamástslikt," Sunny admitted. "If anyone would've told me my life could've turned around this much, in such a short time, I wouldn't have believed it."

"I hope I'm not being premature, Sunny, but I happen to know the reservation council is looking to hire someone with a background in anthropology and archaeology to do some research. They'd expected to hire a white person, but someone with Native roots would have a definite advantage."

"Really?" She stared at him. "You think I'd have a chance?"

"Oh yeah." He nodded as he started the pickup.

"That would be so amazing." Was she dreaming this whole thing? she wondered. But no, she felt fully awake—and incredibly happy.

"Anyway, we were all going to the rodeo today—Hank and Echo and me. And now we'll bring Jackson along too."

"Good. That might help to keep him from worrying about his mom."

"And Echo has assured me you were planning to come today as well." He looked hopefully at her.

"Yes. Opening day, Echo said it's the best day of Round-Up."

"Maybe we can do some seat swapping so we can sit together."

"Yes. I'd love that." Then she explained about how Aubrey had traded tickets for Wesley and Mitchell, but that it no longer mattered.

Cody made a stern face, then chuckled. "Poor Wesley, it's not that I want to hurt him exactly, but I sure don't want to see him sitting next to *my* girl at Round-Up."

* * * * *

A few hours later, Sunny was happily seated between Cody and Hank at Round-Up. Echo and Jackson were directly behind them, and high anticipation was in the air. Sunny jumped when the cannon was shot—the signal that the rodeo was officially begun. And her eyes got misty during "The Star-Spangled Banner" and when the Round-Up court raced their horses into the rodeo grounds, the queen leaping the fence with arms spread wide. Sunny felt some concern for the safety of the bull riders, although no serious injuries occurred. She also felt concern for the welfare of the horses in the bucking contest. And she was deeply moved by the Native American parade during intermission. But at the same time she was a bit dismayed that the grandstands had partially emptied during the circle dance. She wondered why everyone didn't enjoy seeing the dancers in their native costumes. Or maybe the heat of the day simply made them all excessively thirsty.

And that's about when she noticed that Cody had left his spot on the bleachers too. She hadn't even seen him go, and it seemed a bit odd he hadn't said anything. Then, worried that there might be a problem, perhaps something to do with Trina, she turned to Hank. But he seemed oblivious as he studied the Round-Up program. And both Jackson and Echo didn't seem the least bit troubled, chatting amicably to some friends about their age. So, assuring herself that everything was fine, Sunny went back to enjoying the dancing and the costumes and the beat of the drumming and chanting.

As the Native Americans paraded out, the grandstands began filling up again, but there was still no sign of Cody. Sunny chided herself for being so fretful. Here they had barely begun their relationship, and she was already keeping tabs on him.

"I think I'll go get a soda," she told Hank.

"No." He firmly placed his hand on her knee. "Not now."

"Why?"

"Uh, because you might miss something good."

She looked down at the field where not much was happening. Although the announcer and the clown were doing some chatting and joking, for the most part there didn't seem to be anything to miss. But seeing that Hank was intently listening to the announcer, she tuned her ears in as well.

"As you all know, it takes a lot of good, hardworking folks to make a rodeo a success," he was saying, "and a lot of families have been volunteering their time and energy for generations. In fact, we have a man here who represents a whole lot of years of rodeo volunteering. Tell me, Cody Barrett, how long have you been helping with Round-Up?"

Sunny eyed Hank, who was smiling from ear to ear like this was no surprise to him. Then she looked back at Jackson and Echo, who were grinning just as big.

"I used to help my dad when I was a kid," Cody said over the loudspeaker. "My dad, Hank Barrett, put in twenty-five years as a Round-Up volunteer and board member. Then I actually competed for a couple of years, before I figured out that I'd end up broke and broken if I continued. My hat is off to the cowboys who do this for a living. Anyway, this is only my eighteenth year to help with Round-Up, but I'm hoping to get a bunch more."

"Impressive. And I know you married a rodeo princess from a family with generations of Round-Up board members and volunteers, right?"

"Yes, sir. The Lowenstein family goes way back in Round-Up history. Maybe close to a hundred years. And Doug and Cindy Lowenstein's daughter Lenora was a princess back in the eighties. A lot of history there."

"We all know the lovely Lenora lost her fight to breast cancer several years ago, which is one of the reasons we have Tough Enough to Wear Pink Day here at Round-Up every year, so all you folks out there don't forget to put on your pink duds for tomorrow's rodeo."

"That's right," Cody said. "Wearing pink is our way to support breast cancer awareness month, and we hope everyone does their part."

"But I understand you're talking to me for another reason today. I don't want to rush you, Cody, but you've got about thirty seconds left, so you better cut to the chase."

"Well, folks…" Cody cleared his throat. "I'm talking into this mike right now because I happen to be a cowboy in love."

The crowd let out a ripple of approval and chuckles. The next thing Sunny knew, Hank and Echo were escorting her down the bleachers to where Cody was standing with a microphone. He took her hand and looked into her eyes. "And in front of all these good witnesses, I want to ask Miss Sunrise Westcott to be my wife."

Now the crowd roared with clapping and cheering, and Sunny's heart was pounding so hard she felt slightly faint.

"What do you say, Sunny, darling, *will you marry me*?"

The crowd was stomping on the bleachers now and some were chanting, "Say yes! Say yes! *Say yes!*"

"*Yes!*" she said loudly into the mike, and the crowd went wild.

"You heard the woman, rodeo fans. Cody is getting himself a new wife. Congratulations, you two. Now, let's remember why we're really here today—repeat it with me, cowboys and cowgirls—*LET 'ER BUCK!*"

Cody leaned over and kissed Sunny. Then, all at once, people were clustered about them, slapping their backs and congratulating them. As they returned to their seats, it seemed that everyone in the grandstand knew Cody personally. And the way they were acting, it felt like they knew her too, like she was one of them. At last, she'd really come home...she belonged here. She was among friends and family. As they sat back down, she wondered if this was a bit how Jackson Sundown had felt on that day, so long ago, when he'd won the bucking horse contest.

No, she decided, this had to be better. Much, much better!

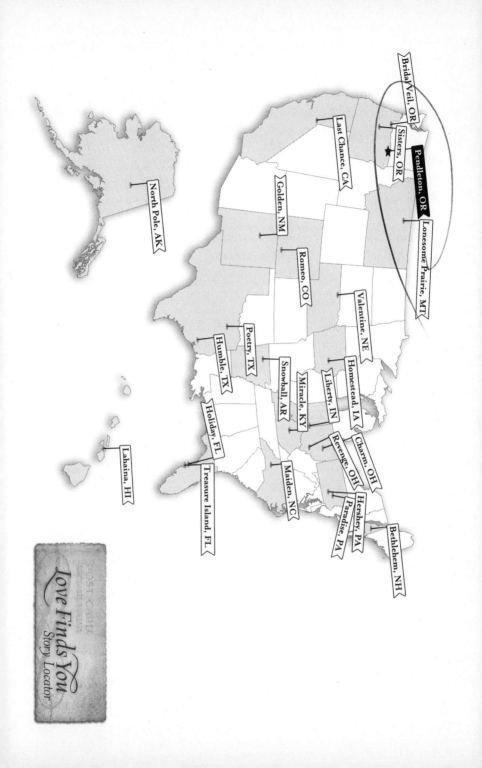

Love Finds You
POST CARD
Story Locator

BridalVeil, OR
Sisters, OR
Pendleton, OR
Lonesome Prairie, MT
Last Chance, CA
North Pole, AK
Golden, NM
Romeo, CO
Valentine, NE
Poetry, TX
Humble, TX
Snowball, AR
Miracle, KY
Liberty, IN
Homestead, IA
Charm, OH
Revenge, OH
Hershey, PA
Paradise, PA
Bethlehem, NH
Holiday, FL
Treasure Island, FL
Maiden, NC
Lahaina, HI